I0780687

JUST MY DUCKING LUCK

LOVE GONE WILD
BOOK 1

LC TAYLOR

Shelf Love
THE ROMANCE ATLANTA BOOKSHOP

Just My Ducking Luck
Copyright © 2025

All rights reserved under the International and Pan-American Copyright Conventions. No part of this book may be reproduced or transmitted in any form or by any means, electronic or mechanical, including photocopying, recording, or by any information storage and retrieval system, without permission in writing from the publisher. This is a work of fiction.

Names, places, characters, and incidents are either the product of the author's imagination or are used fictitiously, and any resemblance to any actual persons, living or dead, organizations, events, or locales is entirely coincidental.

Warning: the unauthorized reproduction or distribution of this copyrighted work is illegal. Criminal copyright infringement, including infringement without monetary gain, is a serious offense. It is investigated by the FBI and is punishable by up to 5 years in prison and a fine of $250,000.

Editor: Rejeana Reads Editing Services
Ebook Cover Model: Andrew Flanagan
Photographer: JW Photography & Covers
Cover Design: Shelf Love Formating Services
Cover Model: Andrew Flanagan

Print ISBN: 978-1-961380-70-7
EBook ISBN: 978-1-961380-69-1

Author LC Taylor
www.AuthorLCTaylor.com

For the smut readers: may your batteries stay charged, your pages stay sticky (from snacks, obviously), and your one-handed Kindle grip stay strong.

LC

PLAYLIST

Every story has a soundtrack. *Just My Ducking Luck* just happens to sound like glitter, grump, and a duck with zero respect for personal boundaries.

Frankie runs on girl-power anthems turned up so loud the neighbors consider calling in noise complaints. Beckett is more of a broody ballad type—think whiskey, woodsmoke, and a man emotionally allergic to small talk. And Bob? Bob's playlist is pure chaos. If you hear *Yakety Sax* in your head during the underwear theft scene, that's intentional.

So before you dive in, here's the vibe: hit play on whatever makes you feel messy, loud, and a little unhinged… then turn the page.

PLAYLIST

Truth Hurts – Lizzo

Good as Hell – Lizzo

Shake It Off – Taylor Swift

Good Luck, Babe! – Chappell Roan

Espresso – Sabrina Carpenter

Flowers – Miley Cyrus

Padam Padam – Kylie Minogue

Like a Stone – Audioslave

Something in the Orange – Zach Bryan

Heart Like a Truck – Lainey Wilson

Last Night – Morgan Wallen

Yakety Sax — Boots Randolph

Bad to the Bone – George Thorogood & The Destroyers

Another One Bites the Dust – Queen

Industry Baby – Lil Nas X & Jack Harlow

Earned It – The Weeknd

Take Me to Church – Hozier

Wildest Dreams – Taylor Swift

Animals – Maroon 5

Die for You – The Weeknd

Simple Man – Lynyrd Skynyrd

Bang Bang – Jessie J, Ariana Grande & Nicki Minaj

LISTEN ON SPOTIFY or LISTEN ON APPLE MUSIC

SPOTIFY

APPLE

Hope shows up in strange ways—sometimes feathered, sometimes furious, always when you least expect it.

LC TAYLOR

CHAPTER 1
WELCOME TO THE QUACKSIDE

FRANKIE

I'D SURVIVED two years of therapy, a nasty divorce, and one particularly judgmental houseplant. Moving day should've been easy.

It wasn't.

But at least this time, the chaos was mine.

I'd spent the past six months rebuilding my life—one brutally honest therapy session and one impulsive decision at a time. My most recent impulsive decision? Buying a rundown house sight unseen except for a few pictures e-mailed to me by Mabel Simmons, its elderly owner.

The house was three hours from Atlanta, the city where I was born and raised. Everyone thought I was nuts—my mother, some of my friends, even my ex, though thankfully I was at the point where I didn't give two shits what he thought. The only people who were excited for me were my two best friends—Tess and Oz. Tess and I had grown up together, and I'd met Oz in college. After Tess met Oz on one of her many trips to visit me at school, the three of us became inseparable.

Moving meant leaving Tess back in Atlanta, and that was hard. But my new, quirky hometown of Peachtree Bluff was where Oz lived, so now I'd have him close by. Or I would as soon as he got back from his vacation.

In a roundabout way, I had Oz to thank for this new start. He'd sent me a link to the town's newsletter because it featured an article on his work at the library. As I browsed the rest of the newsletter, I saw Mabel's listing for her house—and, hello! It was right. On. Main. Street. A corner lot. Three e-mails to Mabel, two e-mails to my attorney, and one wire transfer later, and the house was mine. Impulsive? You're damn right.

Sweet Mabel had said she'd leave the furnishings in it—a godsend for this newly single woman. She also said her grandson Kyle and his college friends painted houses during the summer. If I picked out a color, she'd have them slap it on. That turned out to be an easy decision, Sherwin Williams Rosy Outlook. The pale pink reminded me of peonies and the name seemed to be a good omen.

Tess and I had visited Oz here several times, so I had an idea of what to expect—the town was full of indie shops, and mine would fit right in. As I followed the U-Haul carrying my future down Main Street, I could barely contain my excitement. Even Oz's warning about nosy neighbors didn't diminish my enthusiasm. I felt like I could finally breathe. Open the bookstore I'd envisioned for so long. Build something that belonged to me alone.

Our two-vehicle caravan finally arrived at my new home. I got out of my trusty-but-rusty Chevy pickup and stood for a moment, trying to take in everything. The crooked fence. The front yard, which was bigger than I expected for a town lot. The house would need attention. Its old clapboards were now a pretty pink, but some were buckled or warped and others had gone cattywampus. The faded blue shutters were barely hanging on. The wrap-around porch sagged in places and the porch swing looked fragile. It suddenly gave a squeak as if protesting the mere thought of being sat on.

As I breathed in the sweet, heavy scent of honeysuckle that curled through the humid summer air—all I saw and smelled was freedom. This fence, this yard, this house—it was all mine. Every square inch.

There'd be no perfect suburban kitchen in this house. No controlling ex who called me "too much" when he thought I laughed too loud or was too heavy-handed with the black eyeliner. No more shrinking myself to fit someone else's idea of "wife material."

And the front half of the house? About to become the bookstore of my damn dreams.

I shook myself out of my reverie, ready now for anything. And if moving day wanted to throw a few curveballs? Bring them the fuck on.

Kyle had already started unloading the U-Haul and carrying boxes into the house. I hated that I had to rely on anyone to help, but even *I* wasn't stubborn enough to try moving what was left of my life solo. When Mabel mentioned that Kyle was available to assist… yeah, I'd jumped at the offer. I made a mental note to change the locks, though, because he'd obviously known how to get into his grandmother's house—*former* house.

"Careful with that box! It's got my entire signed Amy Daws collection in it!" The poor guy blinked, adjusted his grip, and shuffled faster. Or as fast as a person could go while carrying a box filled with books.

As I walked toward the house, I tipped my head, eyeing the wide picture window I would clean tomorrow and the hand-painted SHELF LOVE sign that Kyle had leaned against the side of the house. I envisioned the bell I'd bought to hang over the door, ready to give its first tinkle. The shelves inside? They'd be lined with indie romance books no big box chain would dare to carry.

I wasn't just opening a store. I was building a haven. For readers. For women who loved stories with spice and heart, women who had been told to lower their voices, close their legs, and stop dreaming so damn big.

Because I knew exactly what it felt like to have been told those things.

By parents who'd wanted a daughter who looked good in pearls and never said *fuck* in public. By a husband—ex-husband, now—who'd seen my ambition as a hobby and my love of romance novels as a joke. Christopher Monroe was the typical investment broker. A man who valued his pretentious appearance more than his marriage to me.

The real Francesca Bellamy Monroe had been a disappointment to a lot of people. Overlooked. Underestimated. Pushed to the edges of their lives. And I'd endured more than any twenty-six-year-old should've had to.

But here—on this porch, looking through that soon-to-be shop window—I had finally become the main character of my own story.

Filing for divorce? Pfft. That had been the easy part—terrifying as hell, but easy.

Building this life? That was the part I refused to screw up.

Fresh start, I reminded myself. Bookstore in progress. No ex-husband. No catering to anyone's fragile ego. And maybe, if the universe wasn't feeling particularly cruel, no more drama.

I inhaled deeply, trying to soak it all in—the quiet, the promise of something new, the not-a-suburb air. No curated life. No Stepford parties. No perfectly frosted cupcakes to impress people I didn't even like.

Just a well-loved old house that had seen years of real life, stacks of boxes filled with books, and a second chance.

Kyle and I worked a while longer until everything was out of the U-Haul. I wandered back out on the porch, looking for a breeze. Exhaling, I wiped my brow with the hem of my band tee, knowing—but not caring, that the movement would lift the tee's faded Metallica logo enough to expose a strip of my inked skin. Releasing the fabric, I braced my hands on my hips, smiling as I again surveyed my new front yard and my new place.

Then I heard it. A sharp—quack. Followed by about twenty more.

I blinked. What the hell…?

Frowning, I glanced toward the weathered, three-foot-high wooden fence separating my yard from the property next door. The fence my rented moving truck was currently… kissing. Why in the fuck had Kyle moved the damn truck?

Awesome. Three hours in Peachtree Bluff and I'm already responsible for property damage.

"Shit." I jogged over to assess the situation. The U-Haul's bumper had crunched one wide slat, splintering it just enough to create a jagged opening. Through which a parade of indignant ducks was now escaping.

Feathers flew. Quacks, like sharp bursts of outrage, echoed off the house's siding.

The ducks brought with them the scents of sun-warmed grass and pond water. A flurry of down spiraled past my face, some pieces catching in my hair.

"I'm sorry, Ms. Bellamy." Kyle stared, wide-eyed, at the damage.

"Just get me something to fix this." I waved him off and surveyed the flock of jail breakers now clustering at my feet.

One large white duck waddled past with deliberate slowness, webbed feet slapping against the still-damp grass. It shot me a long, beady glare—head cocked as if it was personally offended by my existence.

I stared. "You and me both, buddy."

What kind of neighbor did I have? I'd been promised quirky by the sweet Mabel. I hadn't, however, planned on poultry warfare.

Another duck—this one completely black—darted through the opening.

"Oh, no you don't."

I lunged, arms flailing in what could only be described as duck-wrangling desperation. Elegant, it was not. And it wasn't one or two ducks. Nope. Closer to seven so far. Who in the hell kept pet ducks in a town?

The ducks suddenly scattered like feathered anarchists staging a prison break—flapping, quacking, kicking up whirlwinds of grass and pure indignation.

I slid my phone out of my shorts pocket and snapped proof of this ludicrous event. No one would believe me without evidence.

One of the damn ducks darted between my feet, causing me to stumble back and my heart to start hammering. Some welcome to my new home this was turning out to be.

"Move."

The voice hit me from behind—low, rough, a warning wrapped in coarse sandpaper. He spoke slowly, like thunder rolling over a pond.

I spun—ready to let my sharp tongue fly—only to find my mouth forgetting how to work.

A man stood behind the broken fence slat.

Tall. Broad shoulders. Worn black Henley stretched over a chest that had to have been built by real work, not gym vanity. Tattoos peeked from behind its cuffs. Storm-gray eyes locked onto mine from beneath a severe scowl. Every inch of him radiated restrained intensity.

And the voice? Pure, unfiltered bedroom gravel.

My heart did an unhelpful little lurch. Of course the duck over-lord would look like a damn romance cover model, albeit a mafia romance, unless you ignored his murderous glare. Because that was my life now.

"You hit my fence," he said, voice flat but still rough.

I blinked, scrambling for composure. "Technically, the truck hit your fence." Smooth, Frankie. Real smooth.

A muscle ticked in his jaw. His stare pressed against my skin—not leering, just… assessing. Probably as I'd just assessed him. Like he was cataloging every inch of me: the pink, glittery high-top Converse still littered with feathers, the tattooed arms crossed defiantly, the loose strand of hot pink, tinsel-threaded hair blowing across my eyes.

His gaze flicked toward the pale pink house behind me. "You gonna live there?"

I tilted my head, letting a dry smile curve my mouth. "Nope. I just break fences in random neighborhoods for fun. Keeps me young."

A beat passed—thick, charged—my words hanging in the humid air between us like a dare.

His mouth twitched. Not quite a smile. Not quite a grimace. Just… something.

Until a loud quack cut through the air and we both looked down to see a small, bright yellow duck tugging enthusiastically at my shoelace.

The man exhaled sharply, raking one hand through already-mussed dark hair. "Dammit, Bob."

I snorted. "Your duck's name is Bob?"

"That duck is a menace." He stepped over the fence and came close, towering over me. I caught a faint whiff of cedarwood, soap, and pond air. Unfairly intoxicating. "Out of my way."

"I was trying to help," I said, tossing my hands up and moving aside. No sense getting flattened by six-plus feet of duck-wrangling testosterone.

He crouched, his broad frame folding easily, and expertly gathered a couple of quacking escapees. "Let's go, Norris. You too, Eggsy."

And then he spoke again. His voice smoother, softer… the low, quiet words meant only for the ducks. The ducks stilled instantly, huddling close to him like wayward toddlers.

I stared. The grumpy, duck-whispering mountain of a man next door was… weirdly hot. Of course he was.

"Name's Beckett Ford," he said without looking up. "Don't hit my fence again."

"Oh look, it glares and owns ducks. How quaint," I shot back. "Frankie Bellamy—not that you asked."

Beckett stood, ducks tucked under each arm like a barnyard bouncer. "Great." He turned, muttering something about "town newbies" and "chaos magnets" as he herded ducks back through the gap.

I watched him go, heart thumping an inconvenient rhythm beneath my ribs. Goddamn my shit luck.

Well. That was a hell of a way to meet my new neighbor.

I blew out a breath and looked down. Bob was still at my feet, beady eyes gleaming like he'd judged me and found me amusing at best.

"I'm ninety-nine percent sure you're better behaved than your owner," I told him.

Bob quacked once—short and smug—and waddled after Beckett.

I turned back toward the house just in time to catch my helper setting my Read Romance, Not Red Flags mug precariously on a stack of boxes.

"Watch it, kid!" I called.

He gave me a sheepish thumbs-up and set it on the porch swing. I wasn't sure that was any better.

I exhaled, hands on hips. First day in the new place and I'd already crashed into a fence, unleashed a duck parade, and been verbally eviscerated by the hottest man I'd seen in years.

Off to a strong start, Frankie.

I glanced one more time toward the fence where Beckett's tall frame had been. My cheeks were still oddly warm.

Yup. Definitely not boring.

I dusted off my hands and headed toward the house, picking up my mug on the way in. Tomorrow, I'd unpack, charm the town, and start building my new life one book at a time.

But tonight?

Tonight I was going to pour myself a drink, Google "grumpy hot neighbor with ducks," and try very hard not to imagine Beckett Ford's mouth when it wasn't scolding me.

The first rule of starting over—Don't immediately develop a fixation on your neighbor's mouth.

Later, after Kyle went home, taking the U-Haul to return it, and I'd sorted through some of the furnishings Mabel had left, I poured myself a whiskey. Neat—because ice felt too civilized for the day I'd had. Then I glared at my laptop screen. The search results were… unhelpful.

"Grumpy hot neighbor with ducks" yielded exactly what you'd expect—a bunch of memes, a clickbait article titled "Ten Signs You're Dating a Duck Dad" (I wasn't, thank you very much), and several deeply alarming photos of men in inflatable mallard costumes. Not exactly the wisdom I was hoping for.

I scrubbed the last photo out of my brain, because I did *not* need to envision Beckett Ford in suspenders.

I slammed the laptop shut with a sigh and leaned back against the old velvet couch I'd dragged into the living room. Boxes loomed like judgmental sentries around me. The air smelled faintly of dust, flowers, and the lingering sharp tang of adrenaline.

Beckett Ford.

Neighbor. Duck wrangler. Scowl connoisseur.

And, if the traitorous thump under my ribs was any indication, a very inconvenient problem.

I blew out a breath and let my head drop back against the couch.

"Come on, Frankie," I muttered to myself. "You moved here for peace. Bookstore. Fresh start. No men. Definitely no duck-owning, grumpy, six-foot-plus heart hazards."

The ceiling fan above me creaked once, like it was laughing in agreement.

Somewhere outside, an already-familiar quack echoed faintly across the night air.

I groaned. "Damn ducks."

And just like that, my second chance was officially off to a flying (pun intended) start.

CHAPTER 2
THE PEONY PINK PROBLEM

BECKETT

I HADN'T ASKED for a neighbor.

Even if I had, I sure as hell wouldn't have asked for *her*—a loud, tattooed, chaos agent who crash-landed into my afternoon like a jolt of caffeine wrapped in pink—electric and impossible to ignore—from the hot pink Converse on her feet to the faint shimmer of pink glitter catching in her hair like stray flecks of stardust.

It hadn't phased the ducks one bit when the kids arrived last week with their ladders and paint brushes, their laughing and shouting and loud music. But after this afternoon? The ducks were still unsettled. I could feel it in the jitter of their waddles, the brittle edge sharpening their quacks. I squatted at the edge of the pond and they huddled close, scanning my new neighbor's now-quiet yard with quick, dark eyes.

Willow—my quiet one—hovered at my feet, her small body tense, feathers ruffled, like she needed me to assure her this strange storm would pass.

I understood the feeling.

I straightened and stepped onto the dock, its rough wood creaking beneath my boots as if it was in on this afternoon's joke. Bob floated nearby, paddling in lazy circles, one eye fixed on me with the flat, unblinking confidence of a duck who knew exactly how this worked.

"You," I muttered, tossing a handful of cracked corn into the water, "are not helping, you little shit."

Bob let out a quack that landed somewhere between a scoff and a snort—typical. Then, with deliberate slowness, he paddled through the water like a king surveying tribute, snapping up the corn one piece at a time with exaggerated flair.

I narrowed my eyes. "Real modest, Bob. One of these days, you're gonna wind up dinner."

Another smug quack. The rest of the flock circled in slowly, feathers ruffling, beaks dipping. The water rippled in lazy rings. Calmer now.

I let out a breath. A real one. Not the shallow kind I'd been surviving on lately.

I hadn't planned to speak today. Most days, I didn't. I kept to my routines—coffee, feed the ducks, fix what needed fixing. Avoid people. Avoid their noise, their small talk, their endless appetite for drama. My brothers were the only people I needed.

It was better this way. Lonely, maybe. But safe.

Then she'd arrived.

Frankie Bellamy.

The moment I saw the gap in the fence, saw her standing there with my ducks spilling into her yard like they'd staged a feathered mutiny—something in me snapped.

And she hadn't even looked sorry. No, she'd looked amused.

Worse—unbothered. Like duck anarchy was just another Tuesday.

Probably one of those people who breezed through life with noise and opinions, playlist always too loud, coffee cup always in hand, collecting loyalty cards she'd never use. The kind who had a Pinterest board titled Vibes Only, full of neon quotes, chaotic travel photos, and plants she forgot to water.

Frankie Bellamy screamed chaos.

And now she was next door.

Perfect. Just fucking perfect.

I stood, brushing corn dust off my jeans. My shoulders ached in that clean, earned way. The kind of soreness that came from digging, lifting, building something with your hands. The kind of ache I chased daily to forget the other ones I couldn't.

I liked that kind of pain. It was honest. Predictable. Unlike most people.

My gaze drifted toward her house as I walked to mine.

I'd wondered why Mabel Simmons had suddenly decided to paint her old southern monstrosity. Now I knew—she'd sold it. The house was probably older than the damn town. Wraparound porch circling it like a tired belt. Railings sagging. Columns leaning. Shutters clinging on with pure spite. Wood siding, once a faded but dignified white, was now suffocating under a coat of fresh paint in a godawful shade of pink that tried too hard to be charming.

The damn thing looked haunted by the thought of other renovation plans in its future. Like it couldn't decide if it wanted to be saved or left alone.

I understood that feeling, too.

It had been vacant for a year. Mabel was too old to take care of it anymore; her kids weren't worth the breath it took to curse them.

I'd liked having that house empty. No neighbor. Ducks could wander without interruption.

Now?

A walking disaster named Frankie Bellamy had moved in.

I scowled. Someone should've landmarked the place—then maybe it would've been protected from people like her.

Inside, my house was dim. Quiet. The same as it had been for years. I stepped over creaky floorboards and glanced at the photo on the mantle.

Willow—my twin sister, not the duck. Sunlight had caught her auburn curls in the picture. She was laughing, a duckling perched on her shoulder like some weird little badge of honor. Her laugh had been loud. Constant. Impossible to replicate. Sometimes I stared at the photo too long and realized I'd forgotten what her voice had sounded like.

Other times, I swore I still heard it.

She'd been the only one who had ever really understood why I left New York. If she were still here, she'd understand why I hid behind my ducks—then again, I might not have them at all if she were still alive because she'd be forcing me to *people*.

The others hadn't asked why I had tucked tail and hid from the man I used to be. Or maybe they had, but by then I was too far gone to answer.

I rubbed a hand over my beard, half-damp with sweat after this humid day. I needed a shower. Needed to repair the patched fence, otherwise Bob would find another way out. Needed to figure out how to coexist with a woman who thought peony pink was an acceptable house color.

She could host craft parties or start a cult of houseplants. As long as she stayed on her side of the fence and didn't spook the ducks, I didn't give a damn. I lacked the bandwidth to care—the guilt I carried from my past took up enough space in my head. Letting her glitter-bomb personality have free rent there couldn't happen. Not when the city kept creeping back in. When the headlines I tried to forget flickered behind my eyelids like old film reels.

When you build a company from the ground up, the people who work for you assume you know what you're doing. That the stress rolls off you. That perfection isn't a weight, just a badge of honor.

I pushed too hard. Missed the signs.

One of my team—a kid. Twenty-two. Smart, eager, terrified of letting me down.

He'd let himself down instead.

They had never printed my name. For that, at least, I was thankful. It had meant that I could come back home with relative anonymity—people here knew me as the child and teenager I was, but not the failure that was the adult me.

The fallout nearly broke me, though. Would've, if it hadn't been for Nate calling me, saying nothing for six full minutes until I finally spoke.

I left everything behind after that.

The company. The press. The glass box of an apartment where I couldn't sleep.

Sold my shares, donated more than half of the profits, bought this house through a shell LLC and disappeared into the town that raised me.

Nate had shown up with a twelve-pack and tried to fight me. Jamie cried. Hank had just grunted, like grief was a flat tire and he didn't have a spare. And Caleb made a quick appearance but vanished again soon after. He used the Army as his avoidance tactic, much like I used my ducks. After losing our sister Willow, we were all fractured in some way or another. They'd managed to find something to lessen their pain. I'd only found more.

And even though I didn't understand why I came running back to our hometown when the shit hit the fan, I stayed anyway, and I dug the pond. By hand. It was marginally therapeutic.

It started with one duck. Willow. Then came Bob, Cluck Kent, Eggsy, and the rest of the feathered freeloaders. Each one earned. Each one loud in its own annoying, grounding way. They didn't ask questions. Didn't care what I used to be. They just wanted water, corn, and a steady hand.

That, I could give.

I stepped into the bathroom and twisted the faucet. Let the scalding water roar. I should have been outside repairing the fence better than I had, but I needed to get away from the chaos that was my new neighbor.

Steam blurred the mirror. My reflection disappeared in the fog. Good.

I didn't need to see that guy today.

The first hit of heat burned my shoulders. Hissed against my back. I welcomed it. Let it scald me. Let it scrub her off. But the ache behind my ribs didn't ease. The knot in my chest only pulled tighter.

Something about her clung to me. Damned if I knew why. I'd barely met her—not even half an afternoon of noise and nerve and those eyes that looked straight through me. Like she knew exactly what kind of man I was and didn't give a damn.

That voice. That laugh. That grin—careless, sharp-edged, like life was a game she'd already figured out. It scraped against something in me that I didn't like having scraped.

I was here to be left alone, but Frankie Bellamy had gotten under my skin.

Not because she was loud. Not because she was a walking violation of every HOA code we didn't have.

Because she'd *looked* at me. Really looked. Like she saw past the silence. Past the beard and the work clothes and the duck poop. And didn't flinch.

That was dangerous.

I finished the shower, red-skinned now but no calmer, and dragged myself into jeans and another Henley. Sunset painted the sky in shades of blood and cream that spilled through the windows into my room. Across the yard, her house was lit up like a damn lighthouse. Windows glowing. A shadow moving. Too much life for a house that had looked half-dead a mere week ago.

I closed my eyes recalling the sign I'd seen propped by the front window earlier. Chipped wooden frame. Big, looping script that read *Shelf Love: An Indie Romance Bookstore*.

A bookstore—of course.

Of course, she'd drag that circus here. Book clubs. Story hours. Cars clogging the road. Selfies on the porch. I told myself it was the noise. The disruption. That she'd nearly killed my ducks—not really, but I wanted to be madder than I was.

I made my way out back and sat on the porch with my coffee and watched her shadow move from window to window. Bob hopped up beside me like he owned the place.

"Don't say it," I muttered.

He quacked once.

"Yeah. I know." I glanced over at him. "But she's too loud. Too nosy. Painted the house pink."

Bob stared up, patient. Maybe it was me who needed the advice.

I scrubbed a hand through my hair. "It's gonna be a long summer."

And somehow, this girl next door, who laughed too loud, had cracked open something I wasn't ready to name.

I told myself it was curiosity. The same way you watch a fire you know you shouldn't touch.

It wasn't. It was her and maybe even the start of something I hadn't felt in a long time.

Interest in someone…

God help me, it was going to be a very long summer.

I woke before dawn. As usual. Habit now.

Coffee first—always. Feed the ducks. Check the perimeter. Fix whatever needed fixing—especially the fence that I never got around to fully securing yesterday.

I didn't want the ducks getting out or her getting in.

I moved through it all on autopilot that morning, but there was an itch under my skin I couldn't scrub out. No amount of strong black coffee dulled it.

My gaze kept drifting toward the pink house next door.

Damn thing looked worse in daylight. Like a sundae someone had left out in the sun—melty, sticky, too sweet for its own good.

I was halfway through my second cup when I caught something, rather, some*one* in the house next door's kitchen window.

Her curtains were open, and our houses were just close enough for me to see clearly. Frankie.

Barefoot. Pajama pants—plaid, sagging low on her hips—and cropped T-shirt that I was pretty sure read, I like my men morally gray.

Of course she'd wear that.

She padded across her porch, clutching a houseplant like it was a newborn. And then—hell if I wasn't seeing this right—she started talking to it.

Out loud.

I stared. Coffee mug halfway to my mouth, forgotten.

She carried it across the yard and set the plant on the fence post —*my* fence post—and tilted its pot, adjusting the leaves like they were tiny arms. A slow smile curled at the corner of her mouth as she spoke to the thing, her voice lost in the air but it must have been animated—her hands moved like punctuation marks.

I didn't know what unsettled me more—her talking to the plant or the fact that I… didn't hate watching it.

She tipped her head, laughing at something the plant had apparently "said."

I ran my hand over my beard. This woman was going to be a problem.

She stretched then, arms overhead, T-shirt rising just enough to reveal the edge of a tattoo curling along her ribcage. A flash of ink and skin that sent a bolt of heat low in my gut—uninvited.

Damn it.

I turned away. Set down my coffee cup and gripped the edge of the counter until my knuckles whitened.

Not your business. Not your problem.

I kept to myself for a reason. This life I'd built—quiet, simple— was the only thing that kept the ghosts at bay. And now?

Now I had a neighbor with a duck-disrupting smile and a dangerous ability to make a dead house look alive again.

The ducks were already curious. Bob, especially. Every time I passed the fence this morning, he had waddled over and stared at it like it owed him answers.

Maybe it did, or maybe he was plotting ways to escape again. I sighed, grabbed my toolkit. I wasn't going to seek her out. Wasn't going to start a conversation.

I was going to fix the fence. Then I was going back to my silent, very duck-filled, very non-Frankie life.

That was the plan.

And I always stuck to the plan.

Except when I didn't.

CHAPTER 3

HOT MESS ON AISLE THREE

FRANKIE

I WEDGED my phone between my shoulder and ear, juggling a basket of supplies in one arm while squinting at the never-ending wall of wood stain samples.

Twelve shades of brown.

All of them looked like slightly different cups of over-steeped tea.

Twelve options. For a damn fence.

"Tess, swear to god—if I pick the wrong stain and end up with a fence that looks like someone's tea disaster, you are personally driving out here to repaint it."

Tess's laugh burst through the phone. "Babe, I will drive down there just to see that happen. And you know I'll bring wine and judge in person."

I smirked, grabbing a can of Truffle Brown and putting it into my basket. "You think I'm kidding. You didn't see the crime scene that was my side yard three days ago."

"I saw the pictures you sent. Literal duck parade."

"Duck rebellion," I corrected, shifting the basket to my other hip. "One of them glared at me like I'd insulted its mother. And then Bob—yes, the infamous Bob—tried to eat my shoelace."

"Bob sounds like he has excellent taste."

"Mm-hmm. Taste and attitude."

I turned the corner of the aisle, basket balanced, list in hand. Fence nails—check. Sandpaper—check. Paint—check. Stain— God help me—check.

Power drill? Maybe. Probably. Beckett had definitely muttered something about proper tools when he stalked off mid-duck-rescue.

And Beckett… yeah.

I shook my head, lips twitching before I could stop them.

"And then there's my neighbor."

"Ooooh," Tess practically purred. "Now we're getting to the good part."

I rolled my eyes, but my heart kicked a little faster, anyway. "Tess," I scolded.

"Frankie. You can't tell me you moved next door to a lumberjack duck dad and aren't at least a little tempted."

"It's called self-preservation."

"It's called being repressed," Tess shot back. "Spill."

I sighed, thunking the basket down on the floor and leaning against the shelving. "He's hot, okay? There. I said it. Are you happy?"

"Beyond."

"Tall. Built like manual labor is his therapy. Beard that says 'don't talk to me,' voice that says 'talk to me and regret it.' And those eyes." I rubbed my forehead. "Storm gray. Like 'rain about to ruin your entire picnic' gray."

"Sexy."

"Infuriating," I corrected. "And absolutely allergic to conversation. Or smiling. Or being remotely neighborly."

"That's called being just your type."

I snorted. "Apparently. Because my brain is helpfully supplying all kinds of mental images I do not need."

"Do tell."

"Not in a hardware store." I grabbed my basket again and started walking. "Besides, the whole thing was a disaster. I wrecked his fence. His ducks staged a breakout. I basically introduced myself as the new neighborhood menace."

"You were being authentic. I respect that."

I grinned despite myself. "Remind me why I love you?"

"Because I remind you that it's okay to want things again. Even if those things are tall and grumpy and possibly smell like cedarwood and pond water."

I stopped dead in the aisle. "How do you know what he smells like?"

Tess cackled. "I know you. And I know that if you're noticing the voice, you have definitely noticed the scent."

I groaned, covering my face with one hand. "I hate you."

"You absolutely don't. Now tell me—what's the gossip on this Beckett guy? Small towns always have gossip."

I hesitated, fingers drumming on the handle of the basket. "Nothing concrete. Just whispers. People call him the pond guy. Oz says he's from here—went away and then came back. Bought the place a few years ago—that it had been his childhood home or something. No one knows much about the adult version of Beckett Ford. All *I* know is that he keeps to himself."

Tess hummed thoughtfully. "Mysterious. Even better."

"Stop." I shook my head, strolling toward the checkout. "I am not getting involved with my hot, grumpy neighbor. I have a bookstore to open and a fence to un-wreck."

"And yet you're in the hardware store thinking about him."

"Because I need nails."

"Because you need nailed. Preferably of the door-slamming, clothes-removal variety."

I burst out laughing, nearly dropping the basket. "You are the worst."

"The best. Now buy your stuff and go flirt with the man."

I opened my mouth to reply—then stopped cold.

Outside the glass storefront, a sheriff was leaning over my truck. Not admiring it. Writing a ticket.

"Oh, you have got to be kidding me," I muttered. "Tess, hold on."

Without waiting for a reply, I set my things down and strode outside, boots thumping across the sidewalk. "Sheriff!" I called.

The man looked up over the brim of his sunglasses, pen still poised. And damn was he hot—there must be something in the water in this town because this guy was like the BookTok porn of cops. "Mornin', Miss Bellamy, I presume? This your truck?" He jerked his chin toward my beat-up Chevy.

"The one I love more than life itself? Yeah." I looked down at the curb. The ancient, nearly invisible yellow line looked more like a suggestion than a warning. "Seriously? Are you actually writing me a ticket for being the only car on the sidewalk?"

He gave a slow, apologetic shrug. "I don't make the rules. Just enforce 'em. And you're parked illegally." He pointed to a "No Parking" sign.

I blew out a breath, hands on my hips. "Really setting a warm tone for the new girl in town."

Tess's voice came through the phone still clutched in my hand. "Frankie. Are you arguing with a cop? Please tell me you're arguing with a cop."

I brought the phone back to my ear. "I'm having a spirited conversation with Sheriff—" I leaned in and glanced at his name tag. "Ford."

"Hank Ford at your service." He smiled faintly, leaning against the hood of my truck. "You're the gal who bought the old Simmons' place, right? Over by the pond?"

I folded my arms. "That's me."

"Yeah, Beckett—mentioned the new… resident fence-wrecker and hot mess in town."

I blinked. "Resident fence-wrecker and excuse me—hot mess?"

Hank grinned, holding his hands up. "His words, not mine. Though he's not wrong."

I tilted my head, smirking. "Are you flirting with me, Sheriff?"

Tess practically screeched through the phone. "You better be flipping your hair right now!"

I laughed and whispered into the phone. "Mentally, I am."

"Sure. And this ticket is my way of asking you out." He tucked the ticket under my windshield wiper with a wink. "Welcome to Peachtree Bluff, Miss Bellamy."

"Fuck me sideways. You really gave me a ticket. Don't suppose you'd consider changing that to a warning, would ya?"

"No can do, ma'am. Wouldn't want you to think I was trying to get something in return." He winked again. "Plus, you ain't my type."

"Wow—talk about wounding my fragile ego. And no worries. I'm not interested in dating you or anyone else." Though quick rebound bed games with him wouldn't be out of the question.

"Good," Hank said, sobering just a touch. "Your neighbor doesn't need another reason to retreat further into his cave."

I blinked. "Wait… are you two friends?"

He chuckled, pushing off my truck. "I'm his brother."

My eyes flicked to the name tag I'd just read, registering the last name. My eyebrows shot up. "Seriously? You're related to my six-foot-something neighbor?" I asked, surprise lacing my tone. This flirty cop was Beckett's kin? I shouldn't have been surprised, because their resemblance was uncanny now that I'd looked closer at him. He was slightly older than my neighbor, with a hint of gray lacing through his dark hair, but just as gorgeous.

"Six-four. And yeah, same haunted gene pool—but I'm the older, sexier version." His smile faded, turning thoughtful. "Look, I know he's not exactly sunshine and puppy dogs. But go easy on him. He's been through more than most people know. He's not hiding out because he's rude. He's hurting… Deeply."

I opened my mouth, then closed it.

Hank nodded toward the street. "He won't talk about it. Not to anyone. But it's written all over him if you know where to look." My chest ached unexpectedly at his words. "He notices more than he says," Hank added, echoing that same line. "And he's watching. Even if he pretends not to care."

As Hank sauntered off, I picked up the phone again. "Did you hear that?"

"Every word. Broody Duck Man has layers. Called it. Was the cop at least hot?"

I shook my head, re-entering the hardware store. "Or maybe Broody Duck Man is just annoyed. And of course the sheriff was hot. Their parents won the lottery with looks on those two men."

"Either way—a duck daddy or a hot cop, maybe let yourself be part of something real again. Even if it's messy."

I took a deep breath, my shoulders loosening. "Maybe. The one in uniform definitely has that sex appeal thing down."

"That's my girl. Now buy something unnecessarily large and intimidating. Like a power drill."

"Why?"

"Because nothing says, 'I'm not afraid of you, duck man,' like showing up on your porch with hardware."

I laughed again, the weight in my chest easing. "God, I love you."

"You know it. Now go make trouble."

I ended the call, grin lingering as I headed for the checkout.

I couldn't help the smirk as I set the basket on the counter. I could just picture the look that must have been on Beckett's face when he'd seen the pink peony paint going on the siding. Or when I'd started painting the porch yesterday a deeper shade of pink. Those two pinks, combined with the sage green color I'd just bought for the trim and shutters and the Truffle Brown stain for the new fence I wanted to put up, were sure to send him off the rails. I mean, if painting the rest of my house borrowed trouble? Well. I was already in debt for the pinks.

Avoiding trouble? Yeah. I wasn't sure that was even an option anymore.

Not with Beckett Ford glaring across the fence line—and me grinning like the hot mess I absolutely was. And Hank's words stuck with me as I loaded my supplies into the truck.

He's not hiding out because he's rude. He's hurting… Deeply.

Interesting.

Very interesting.

I caught my reflection in the glass—messy hair, faded band tee, a smirk I couldn't quite shake.

Hot mess? Sure.

But I was a hot mess who loved a good challenge.

And Beckett Ford was definitely that.

CHAPTER 4
COFFEE, DENIAL, AND DUCK-FREE ZONES

BECKETT

I HATED WALKING AROUND TOWN.

More like—I hated peopling.

I tolerated it when absolutely necessary. Hardware store runs. Duck feed. Occasional vet visits. Otherwise, I stayed home. Too many people. Too many eyes. Too much damn noise.

But this morning? My coffee tasted like burned disappointment and the inside of a water trough. I needed something stronger than regret and rainwater.

Which was how I found myself at Steam & Bean, standing in line behind two tourists debating whether "duck lattes" were real and why this small town didn't sell pond-themed croissants. Joey's eye twitched behind the bar. I felt it in my soul.

At least the coffee here was solid. Even if there were duck puns on the menu. No trendy bullshit like there was in the Big Apple. Only some "Live, Laugh, Quack" mugs, caffeine, sarcasm, and floors that creaked with judgment. My kind of place.

Until I glanced out the front window.

There she was.

Leaning against her rusted-out truck like she belonged in a country music video. Laughing at something Hank said. Tossing her hair back like she hadn't upended my entire life in seventy-two hours of duck-related destruction.

And Hank—my own damn brother—was eating it up.

Grinning. Flirting. Probably handing her his card like a Hallmark side character trying to get laid before Act Two.

My jaw clenched.

"Staring's free," Joey said behind the counter. "Coffee's not."

I didn't look at him. "Wasn't staring."

"Sure. And I'm the Easter Mallard."

I cut him a sharp look. "Don't."

Joey smirked. "I've seen that look before."

"What look?"

"The one that says, 'Why is my duck-defiling menace neighbor laughing with my brother instead of crying over the fence she wrecked.' That look."

"She's annoying," I muttered. "And loud."

"She's also funny. And hot," Joey said, like he was listing groceries. "And Hank's single."

I scowled. "She's a menace."

"You keep using that word," Joey said, sliding a cup across the counter to another customer. "But your eyes say something else."

"What? They say I don't trust new people."

Joey's smile turned sly. "That all they say?"

I growled and stared at the espresso machine like it might offer salvation.

"Ah," Joey nodded. "There it is. The Ford jealousy glower."

"It's not jealousy."

"Then why are you glaring like she stole your duck and made it wear glitter?"

Because she kind of had. Bob was definitely developing brand loyalty to her now. The feathery bastard.

Joey leaned closer, his tone softening just enough to thread through the noise. "Look, man… I know you don't want anyone poking around your business. But people already know who you are. They just don't care the way you think they do."

My gut twisted. "They should."

"No one here gives a shit about the headlines. They give a shit about *you*. And whether you're gonna let them in before you drink yourself to death on black coffee and pond fog."

I didn't answer.

He kept going. "You lost your parents. You lost Willow. You nearly lost yourself. And I get it. But it's okay to let someone—anyone—in. Doesn't have to be her. But it could be."

I hated how much that hit. Joey didn't talk about my sister. No one did. It was the quiet agreement this town had made when I moved back into the house—nobody would touch the grief I hadn't finished bleeding from.

Until now.

"Maybe you could start with your damn neighbor," he added.

"She's painting her porch pink."

"Brave," Joey said, pouring my usual.

"It's an offense to wood."

"Tell her. Start with that. It's practically foreplay."

I groaned, taking the cup.. The truth was—I had noticed her. Too much. The sharp wit. The curve of her mouth. The way she talked to that damn plant like it was an old friend. And yeah… the pink house.

That annoyed me most of all.

"She's good for this place, you know," Joey said quietly pulling me from thoughts of her. "Shakes up the dust. Reminds people that life doesn't have to be polite to be good."

I didn't say anything. Just shoved a five across the counter and headed out the door.

And ran right into Hank. He was leaning against the wall, sipping from a travel mug like he hadn't just tried to flirt with a walking box of glitter and chaos in a rattletrap truck.

"Fancy seeing you out in the wild," he said.

"Funny. Thought you only gave tickets, not commentary."

He grinned. "Frankie's got quick reflexes. And nice legs."

My scowl deepened. "You're not funny."

"I'm hilarious."

"You're interested?"

Hank chuckled. "I'm married to the job. But yeah—if I weren't your brother, and she weren't secretly interested in you like you're made of smut and brooding potential? I might've asked."

I said nothing.

"Relax," he said, nudging my shoulder. "I lied and told her she wasn't my type. Besides, I like my nose where it is. But she's something else. And I think she sees past your crap. Which, if you ask me, is a miracle."

I rubbed a hand over my face. "She talks to her houseplants."

"She named her aloe vera. I know. I was charmed."

I shot him a look.

"Look," Hank said, stepping in front of me, tone leveling out. "I know what happened back then… how what people said fucked you up. But this town? Your family? We're not them. No press. No boardrooms. No co-founders throwing you under buses. No deaths that weren't your fault. Just people who've seen you dig that damn pond with your bare hands, who left casseroles on your porch when our sister died, and who pretend not to notice when you fall apart in the back of the bakery on Willow's birthday."

The silence that followed felt louder than the street noise.

I looked away.

"She's not gonna break you," he added. "But you might break yourself trying to pretend you don't want something to feel good again."

"You're one to talk." I snapped at him, but in true Hank fashion, he just smiled.

"Yeah… well, we're talking about your trauma not mine." He

clapped my back and walked off like he hadn't just emotionally sucker-punched me in the chest.

I stood there for a second. Coffee cooling. Jaw tight.

Then I turned and drove home. By the time I pulled up, Bob was missing.

Again.

I found him in Frankie's yard ten minutes later, as if he'd planned the whole thing to torture me.

Frankie was holding a hose. And—god help me—playing with that traitorous bastard.

My duck. My self-proclaimed agent of chaos. Who had apparently staged yet another jailbreak from my yard and was now waddling circles around her as she laughed and spritzed the hose toward him in teasing arcs.

She was barefoot, humming a song I didn't recognize but suddenly hated on principle.

Bob was smiling—that smug duck bastard.

And Frankie?

She glanced up, saw me watching, and grinned.

I didn't grin back.

She waved anyway. "Hey, neighbor!"

I raised my coffee in salute. "You're stealing my duck."

"He defected," she called back. "Says I'm a better cook."

"He eats bugs."

She shrugged. "Maybe I season them better."

I didn't laugh. Not out loud. But the edge in my chest shifted. And god help me… I stayed right there. Just watching.

Because even if I didn't trust her, didn't understand why she was here, didn't want to want anything again…

There she was. Laughing in her backyard. Making mine feel less haunted.

She was dangerous.

And I was in trouble.

CHAPTER 5
FEATHERED HOME INVASION

FRANKIE

I HAD FACED DOWN WORSE things than an IKEA bookshelf.

Or so I told myself as I knelt in the middle of my living room, my new screwdriver clenched in one hand, assembly instructions in the other, trying not to cry from frustration—or sheer rage.

Step Five: Insert cam lock bolts into panel B, align with pre-drilled holes on panel C...

"Who the fuck writes this shit?" I muttered under my breath.

Some sadist, clearly.

Half the bookshelf was strewn across the floor like the aftermath of a wood-and-metal explosion. The other half mocked me from the instruction page with its neat little diagrams that looked nothing like the disaster in front of me.

I sighed, pushed my hair out of my face, and sat back on my heels. A sheen of sweat clung to the back of my neck—the humidity was already flirting with triple digits. After I got back from the hardware store, I hooked up my new hose to water a few plants and then ended up squirting water at Bob—and I hadn't remembered to turn on the old house's window AC.

A bead of sweat slid down my spine, sticking my tee to my skin.

"Perfect," I grumbled. "One more thing."

Somewhere behind me, a rustle sounded.

I froze. Mouse? No. Please no. Not in my new-to-me house.

Heart kicking hard, I twisted—and stopped cold.

There, standing in the wide patch of afternoon sunlight spilling across my hardwood floor, was a duck.

Not just any duck.

Bob was back.

The buttery-colored little shit who belonged to my storm-gray eyed, shirtless-image-inducing, infuriating neighbor named Beckett Ford.

Bob blinked at me. Tilted his head. Blinked again.

"Son of a bitch," I breathed. "How did you get in here?"

Bob gave no answer. Just stood there like he'd been invited to tea.

I scanned the room. Back door? Closed. Windows? Secure. Front door… ah. I'd left it cracked open to haul in bookshelf parts earlier.

And that little feathery bastard had seen his chance.

"Alright, ninja duck. Party's over."

I rose to my feet, brushing dust off my bare knees. "Out you go."

Bob watched my approach, head bobbing with each slow step I took.

"I mean it. One more step and I'm calling animal control."

Bob flapped once. A single, insolent quack escaped him—and then he was off. Waddling at an alarming speed to hide behind the couch.

"Oh, hell no."

I lunged, reaching for tail feathers—and caught air.

Bob juked left, slipped between a stack of boxes, and reappeared by the bookshelf pieces, leaving a trail of muddy web prints on my freshly cleaned floor.

"Goddammit, Bob!"

And so began a full-blown comedy of errors.

I darted and lunged, cursed and skidded. Bob led me on a merry tour of my living room, flapping and quacking like he was enjoying every second of the shit show—literally. Duck shit was everywhere.

Every time I thought I had him cornered, he'd flap onto a box or squeeze behind something too small for me to follow.

At one point, he launched himself onto the low bookcase I'd just stocked with vintage paperbacks, knocking over half the stack with an indignant quack.

I gaped at the mess.

"You did not just touch my Judith McNaughts."

Bob blinked innocently.

"Oh, you're asking for it now."

Two near-misses later, I was panting, red-faced, dangerously close to throwing a hardcover at my uninvited guest.

And then… I gave up.

Hands on hips, chest heaving, I glared at the feathered interloper.

"Fine. You win this round. But if you keep shitting on my floors, Beckett Ford is paying to have them refinished."

Bob quacked smugly.

"Asshole," I muttered.

Enough was enough. This wasn't my problem anymore. Oh no. It was Beckett's problem.

And the grumpy bastard next door was about to get an earful.

I stormed across the lawn, barefoot, fury fueling every step. My oversized tee clung to my damp skin, my hair had half-fallen from its clip and hung in wild waves down my back.

I didn't care. Beckett was going to hear about this. And he was going to collect his fucking duck.

I pounded on his front door.

No answer.

I hit it again, harder. "Beckett! Open up!"

Still nothing.

My temper flared hotter. I raised my fist to bang again—when the door suddenly opened mid-swing.

I stumbled forward—and nearly swallowed my own tongue.

Beckett Ford stood there. Shirtless.

Apparently fresh from a shower, hair damp and tousled. Bare, broad chest gleaming in the sunlight streaming through the doorway. Low-slung jeans hanging off lean hips. Bare feet.

Veins roped his forearms, muscles flexed as he leaned casually against the doorframe. I watched a single drop of water slide over one pec then continue until it disappeared below the waistband of his jeans. Every inch of him was pure sin in denim.

My brain short-circuited.

Hormones screamed, *Danger!*

His storm-gray eyes flicked over me, faintly amused. "Something wrong?"

For three full seconds, I could only gape. Then adrenaline surged.

"Your fucking duck is in my house."

Beckett blinked, entirely unbothered. "Bob?"

"No. The Pope, obviously. Yes—Bob!" I jabbed a finger at him. "He broke in. Tore apart my books. Waddled across my floor like he owned the place. I've been chasing him for twenty goddamn minutes. And don't get me started on the poop."

A faint quirk tugged one corner of his mouth. The closest thing to a smile I'd ever seen on him. "Sounds like Bob."

"Sounds like—? Are you kidding me?"

He exhaled a low chuckle. "Frankie. He's a duck."

"He's a fucking nuisance. And if you don't come collect him, I swear to god I'll—"

I trailed off as Beckett shifted, leaning deeper into the doorframe, muscles flexing even more with the movement. The scent of cedarwood, clean soap, and dark coffee drifted toward me. My pulse stuttered.

He tilted his head, eyes gleaming. "You'll what?"

"I'll…" I swallowed, cursing the wobble in my voice. "I'll call animal control."

One brow lifted. "You'd sic the town's overworked animal warden on a duck?"

"I'll do worse. I'll teach him to like the bookstore."

At that, Beckett laughed. Low and rough. The sound curled straight through my gut.

"Fine." I stomped my foot. "I'll call your brother," I snapped. "Yeah, that's right. He already wrote me a ticket today, and I'm really tempted to call him again and tell him Bob's trespassing. Maybe see if he wants to handle your mess since you clearly can't. And then maybe I'll take him out for coffee for being my hero."

Beckett froze. The lazy glint in his eyes flickered. The faintest tick of muscle worked in his jaw before he huffed a dry, almost bitter laugh. "Low blow," he said, voice darker now. "You're not calling my brother."

I blinked. "Didn't realize Hank was off-limits."

"He's not. Just… leave him out of this."

Something about his tone made me pause—but only for a second. Then his storm-gray eyes locked on mine again, and that maddening amusement was back.

"You're an overgrown man-child," I shot back.

"You're dangerous," he murmured.

"And you're irresponsible," I returned, grasping for indignation. "You let that little shit roam wherever he wants."

"I don't let him. Bob has free will."

"Well, tell your little anarchist to use it outside my house."

Beckett pushed off the doorframe in one lazy roll of muscle. "I'll grab a shirt." His voice dropped, amusement warm and dark. "Hopefully he won't redecorate while I do it."

As he retreated inside, I fumed on the porch, arms crossed. Do not think about wet hair. Do not think about abs. Do not… Moments later, he emerged in a fitted black tee that didn't hide a damn thing. Tugging the hem down absently, he gave me an unreadable stare. "Lead the way."

I spun and stalked toward my house. He followed at a lazy prowl, every step making me hyper-aware of my own.

In the living room, he surveyed the chaos. Toppled books. Feathers. One smug duck perched on the paperbacks. And a trail of droppings where he'd roamed around the room.

"Classic Bob," Beckett murmured.

I shot him a glare. "Get him. Now."

He crouched, voice softening. "Come on, buddy. Time to go."

Bob quacked, fluttered—and launched himself behind the couch again.

I groaned. "See? Menace."

Beckett's mouth twitched. "Good taste in books, at least."

"He knocked over my McNaughts! That is a capital offense."

"He's not coming out willingly," Beckett said.

"Fix it."

He glanced up. "Ask nicely."

My jaw dropped. "You want me to sweet-talk a duck?"

"Maybe you should threaten him with confetti."

"Unbelievable," I muttered.

He stood, towering over me. "You always this worked up over houseguests?"

"Only the feathered, freeloading kind."

His eyes dropped to my mouth for one beat too long. Heat coiled low in my belly.

"I'll trade you," he said.

"Trade me?"

"You stop glaring at me like you want to commit murder. I'll wrangle Bob."

"Fine. Deal."

He brushed past me—close enough to stir every nerve—and crouched again, murmuring something low. Moments later, Bob waddled out, calm as can be, and Beckett scooped him up like it was nothing.

Broad chest, gentle hands, soft voice.

I was so screwed.

"Satisfied?" he asked.

I swallowed. "He's your problem now."

"Always has been."

At the door, he paused beside me. Voice low. "By the way… you look good when you're riled up."

My breath caught.

Before I could speak, he was gone.

I stood there, cheeks burning. *You look good when you're riled up.*

Asshole. Sexy, maddening, broad-shouldered asshole.

I groaned and grabbed my phone.

Frankie: Beckett's duck broke into my house. I chased it like a lunatic. He showed up shirtless. I hate everything. Send wine.

Oz: You hate it, huh? Yet you're thirst-texting us about Duck Daddy.

Tess: DUCK DADDY STRIKES AGAIN 🦆 🔥
Pics or it didn't happen.

Frankie: Go to hell.

But even as I typed it, I couldn't stop the grin. And deep down, I already knew—

This? This was only the beginning.

CHAPTER 6
DAMMIT, BOB!

BECKETT

"DAMMIT, BOB."

I didn't talk to many people.

But I talked to my ducks.

Unfortunately, most days they didn't listen worth a damn.

Especially Bob.

I stalked across the yard, bare feet against cool damp grass, the feathered bastard tucked securely under one arm. Bob let out an occasional indignant quack like he hadn't just staged a fucking home invasion.

"You couldn't stay put for one afternoon," I muttered, voice low and steady, like talking to a rogue hacker bent on testing my firewall. "No. You had to go rogue."

Bob blinked up at me. Innocent. Too innocent.

I narrowed my eyes. "Don't give me that look. You know what you did."

Another blink. Unrepentant.

I sighed. The ridiculous part was—I respected it. The sheer audacity. Bob had always been the ringleader. I could secure every gate on the property, double-check every damn fence.

And somehow—some way—Bob still found a way through. Over. Under. Around.

Today's crime spree? Sneaking into Frankie Bellamy's living room.

And now, the image of her—flushed, wild-haired, barefoot, furious—was burned into my mind with high-def clarity.

A force of nature. Sharp-tongued. Tattooed. Maddening as hell… and too damn beautiful for my peace of mind.

I didn't need that distraction. Not now. Not ever.

I reached the gate, undid the latch one-handed. "Stay in the yard," I warned quietly. "One more stunt like that and you're getting GPS-tagged."

Bob flapped once, let out a soft, smug quack, and waddled toward the pond with zero shame.

I secured the gate, double-checked the latch—twice—then stood there, fingers curled around the rough wood, staring at nothing.

The conversation with Frankie had stirred something I didn't like. Not just her fire—though that damn near lit me up—but her nearness. Her scent. The tremble in her voice—half rage, half something else.

And worse—the way I'd responded.

You look good when you're riled up.

Reckless. Stupid.

I wasn't built for this kind of complication. Not anymore.

Jaw tight, I turned and stalked back inside.

The house felt too quiet. Cool air hummed through the vents. Faint scent of cedarwood and coffee lingered, not quite enough to mask the hollow thrum building under my ribs.

I wiped my bare feet on the doormat, scrubbed a hand through my hair, and crossed to the kitchen.

Two steps in—my phone buzzed.

Unknown number.

I froze. The weight hit instantly, familiar and sharp. Don't answer.

Like an idiot—I answered, anyway. "Yeah," I said flatly.

"Beckett."

That voice. Too smooth. Too practiced. Silk over poison.

"Daniel."

Ice slid through my veins.

"Don't sound so happy to hear from me."

Daniel Maddox's snicker skittered under my skin like barbed wire. The last person I ever wanted to hear from.

I should've hung up. Should've thrown the phone in the damn pond.

But curiosity pinned me in place. Why now? After all this time?

"How'd you find me?"

Daniel chuckled. "Come on. You know me better than that. I've always been persistent."

My teeth ground together. "Lose my number."

"I'll get to the point," he said, tone sharpening. "There's an opportunity. A new firm. Massive backing. We could—"

"No."

"You haven't even heard—"

"I don't need to," I cut in, voice cold as stone. "I'm done with that life. With you."

A pause. Then darker, quieter. "You think you can hide forever in that little town of yours? Playing pond dad to a flock of ducks?"

My grip tightened on the phone. Knuckles white. Gut twisting.

How the hell did he know?

I'd buried my name. Bought this place under a shell company. Erased every damn trail.

Daniel pressed on, voice like a blade. "Sooner or later, someone's going to figure out who you really are. You can't stay off the radar forever, Beckett. And when it hits? Your little quiet life? Gone."

The words landed like a gut punch. Harder than they should've.

Breath shallow, as old fury clawed up from the dark. Anger. Guilt. Disgust. Shame.

I forced steel into my voice. "If you ever call this number again, I'll make damn sure you regret it."

A cold laugh. "Suit yourself."

The line went dead.

I stood frozen, phone clenched in a shaking fist. Chest tight. Heart hammering.

Daniel's voice still echoed, every word a scar reopening. *You can't hide forever.*

I tossed the phone on the counter, scrubbing a hand down my face.

Damn Daniel. Damn that whole fucked-up chapter of my life.

I paced the kitchen once, twice. Restless. Wired. No calming the storm under my skin.

And then—against every instinct—I stalked into the office.

The space was sparsely furnished. Wide desk. Dual monitors. Battered leather chair. Willow's photo on the small side table, her smile the only thing grounding me.

I exhaled hard and flipped open my laptop. For a long moment, fingers hovered over the keys. Don't do this to yourself. I typed anyway.

Beckett Ford media scandal.

Beckett Ford founder lawsuit.

Beckett Ford betrayal.

The results to each search loaded fast.

Punches to the gut, one right after another.

I hadn't looked in over a year. But there they were—headlines still screaming.

Billionaire Tech Genius Implodes After Internal Power Struggle

Scandal Rocks Cyber Titan — Founder Forced Out Amid Betrayal Claims

Beckett Ford: From Golden Boy to Ghost

I clicked through them one by one. Photos of me—clean-shaven, suited—filled the screen.

Cold eyes. Tired smile. Trapped.

I scrolled by snippets.

> *"Sources say Ford had grown increasingly unstable during the company's meteoric rise…"*

> *"An anonymous insider reports Ford was difficult to work with and refused key acquisition terms…"*

> *"Sources close to the board suggest the remaining partners had no choice but to act for the good of the company…"*

Lies and half-truths.

I clicked for a deeper dive.

> *"The scandal has raised questions about Ford's future in the industry. Once hailed as a visionary, he now faces an uncertain road ahead."*

A photo of me leaving the courthouse, ducking my head, surrounded by cameras. My hands curled into fists. I could still hear the bulb flashes, the shouting. The betrayal still stung after all this time. Daniel's smile behind closed doors. The board turning on me.

Willow—gone… she'd been my anchor, my shield in the shit-storm that was my life.

I slammed the laptop shut.

You can't hide forever.

I rubbed the back of my neck, trying to shake off the cold creeping in.

Here, in Peachtree Bluff, I was Beckett Ford. Grumpy duck man. Recluse. No one looked twice. But one hungry journalist—and it could all unravel.

And worse—it made me think of her.

Frankie. Bright. Sharp. Fearless.

If this blew up, she'd be caught in it. Her bookstore. Her new start. All because I hadn't been careful enough. A bitter laugh escaped me. I'd wanted my hometown to be a safe harbor. A place to heal. Maybe even hope.

But shadows had sharp teeth. And Daniel was right about one thing—some ghosts don't stay buried. I shoved to my feet and turned toward the kitchen to grab a bottle from the cabinet I rarely opened.

And that's when the knock came.

Three quick raps. No hesitation. Just enough weight to piss me off. I frowned. No one knocked at this hour. Not unless something was on fire or dead.

I opened the door and… Nate Ford. My little brother stood there, his smirk visible beneath the night sky.

Well—"little." He stood at six feet even, covered in soot-smudged tattoos, still half in uniform and acting like I was his favorite problem.

"Evening, sunshine," he said, brushing past me into the house without waiting for permission.

I stared after him. "What the hell are you doing here?"

"Nice to see you too," he called over his shoulder, already moving toward the kitchen like he owned the place. "Hank told me to come kick your ass."

I shut the door. "Of course he did."

Nate tossed down the dirty gloves he'd been holding. I watched as he grabbed two glasses from the cabinet, found the bottle I hadn't reached for yet, and poured two fingers of whiskey into each. "He said—and I quote—'If that stubborn bastard won't listen to me, maybe he'll listen to you. Or maybe you'll just punch him and call it even.'"

"I'm not in the mood and you shouldn't be drinking—you're on duty."

Nate slid a glass across the counter. "Yeah, I got that from the hundred-yard scowl and the tension in your shoulders. And one little sip isn't going to hurt me unless you tell on me.."

I didn't touch the drink. "Seriously. What are you doing here?"

He dropped into the kitchen chair across from me. "I had a call two blocks away. Electrical fire. We cleared it fast. And I figured —what the hell. I'll drop in on my favorite emotionally consti-pated brother. The guys are outside waiting so I won't be here long… You can relax."

I ran a hand down my face. "Nate—"

"Beckett." His voice shifted—less cocky, more steady. "You slammed the door on the world three years ago. I get it. We all did. After Mom and Dad… and then Willow… I wanted to disappear too. Hell, I did for a while. Caleb is still hiding."

Silence.

"But you didn't just pull back. You vanished. You bought this house like a bunker, dug a damn pond like it was a moat, and you filled it with ducks like they could keep the ghosts out.”

I looked away.

“You’re not the only one who lost them,” Nate said, softer now. “You’re just the only one still pretending it didn’t break something in you.”

I turned to the window. Moonlight caught the ripples on the pond. Bob floated near the dock, head tucked under his wing. Peaceful. Untouchable.

“I’m fine.”

Nate snorted. “You are about as fine as that fence you rebuilt with duct tape and spite after the pink tornado next door moved in.”

My lips twitched.

He leaned in. “You think none of us care about what happened in the city? The headlines were everywhere, Beckett. We cared—a lot. But we just never brought it up because we knew you’d rather eat glass than talk about it.”

My gut tightened.

“I don’t care what they said about you. I know the truth. You worked yourself to the bone building that company. You trusted the wrong people. And they burned you.”

I clenched my jaw.

“And then you lost Willow, and everything else snapped.” Silence stretched long. “She was my sister too, you know,” he added, quieter. “Not just yours. And I know it’s different because you two shared that twin thing, but I hurt the same, Beckett.”

That one landed deep. Right in the ribs. I closed my eyes, swallowing hard. Nate didn't press. He waited. Let the truth settle. After a long beat, I finally spoke.

"I don't know how to come back from it."

Nate leaned back in the chair, looking older than I remembered. "Maybe you don't have to 'come back.' Maybe you just… move forward. One inch at a time."

I shook my head. "It's not that easy."

"No," he said, draining his glass. "But hiding's not working either."

I didn't answer.

"She's good for you, you know."

My head jerked up. "Who?"

Nate smirked. "Frankie. The one you pretend not to watch from the window. The one Bob now worships like a feathered cult leader according to what Hank tells me."

I rolled my eyes.

"You need someone who'll shove back when you snarl. Someone who'll throw your damn ducks back at you and not flinch when you glower."

"She's loud."

"She's alive."

That stopped me cold.

Nate stood, stretching. "Just think about it. Maybe it's time to let go of the wreckage. Doesn't mean you forget. Doesn't mean it didn't matter. But it means you stop letting it define every damn breath."

He grabbed his gloves from the counter. "And Beckett?"

"Yeah."

"Next time Bob breaks into her house, maybe say thank you instead of growling at the universe."

I snorted. "I'll add it to the list."

He clapped me on the back. "Tell her about Willow someday. She'd get it."

And with that, he was gone. The silence he left behind wasn't as sharp as before.

I stood there for a while. Then finally, slowly, I picked up the glass he'd poured for me. The whiskey hit like fire and memory.

I didn't head back to the office. I didn't reach for the laptop. Instead, I walked upstairs, shut off the lights, and flopped onto my bed, staring at the ceiling.

And for the first time in months… I thought about what it might mean to let someone in.

Even if it was just one inch at a time.

I rolled off the bed, walked to the window that looked out on the pond. It gleamed silver beneath the moonlight. Bob sat near the edge, feathers fluffed, content. I shook my head, a dry smile tugging despite it all. "You're lucky," I murmured. "No headlines. No betrayal. Just feathers and mud."

My gaze drifted, unbidden, toward the window that faced her bedroom.

A single lamp burned behind her curtains.

Frankie's silhouette moved past the window. Quick. Restless. Pacing.

She's wound up too, I thought.

The knot in my chest cinched tighter. She didn't need my mess bleeding into her life. No one did. But damn it—tonight, with her voice still echoing in my head, her laugh lodged somewhere it shouldn't be—the quiet didn't feel like enough.

I shoved my hands deep into my pockets, jaw locked, and forced myself to turn away.

The quiet was all I had left. The only thing untouched.

And I'd be damned if I let anyone—especially Daniel—take it from me.

Not now. Not ever.

The stillness in my room felt wrong now. Too thin. Too brittle. I left the lights off, letting the dark settle around me as I crossed my room, back to the bed. Stripped off my shoes and pants, kicked them to the side. I sat down and blew out a breath. Sleep wouldn't come—I knew that from past experience, not with the pulse still pounding in my ears, the weight of old words pressing against my ribs. Forcing myself to lie back, I let my head hit the pillow. I lay in the dark, staring at the ceiling, my breaths slow but jagged at the edges, and tried to think of anything but Frankie Bellamy.

Failed.

I tried to think of anything but Daniel's voice on the phone.

Failed harder.

Minutes stretched thin, and the quiet pressed in. Then—faint, through the open window—soft laughter. Her voice was low, hushed—barely a thread of sound carried in the night air. Too far to make out the words. But enough to drag my gaze back toward the window. A sliver of lamplight glowed like a beacon I found myself unable to ignore.

She was still awake, too.

Probably wound up because of me. Because of Bob.

I let out another slow breath through my teeth. This was dangerous ground. And I was already slipping. I shoved a pillow over my face.

I told myself to forget it.

Forget her.

Forget the way her voice had trembled. The fire in her eyes. The laugh that wouldn't leave my head. And the way—for one impossible second—I'd wanted to chase that sound.

Not your life anymore, Ford. Stay in your lane.

I told myself that again and again as sleep finally dragged me under.

But even in the dark—her voice followed me.

CHAPTER 7
SAGE ADVICE AND AGGRESSIVE PARKING

FRANKIE

I WAS on my second cup of coffee and my third curse word of the morning, muttering them all under my breath as I yanked weeds out of the skinny little garden bed that lined my driveway.

I'd spent all week laying the border, turning the soil, planting herbs and wildflowers—my small *fuck you* to the concrete and chaos I'd left behind in Atlanta.

This garden wasn't big. It wasn't fancy. The wildflowers leaned sideways in the Georgia sun, and the basil looked vaguely offended by the clay-heavy soil. But it was mine. Just like my needs-a-little-attention house. Just like the bookstore taking shape piece by piece inside.

And irrational or not, I was stubbornly proud of both.

The sun was already creeping higher, heating the back of my neck and making the backs of my knees stick to my cutoffs. Sweat slicked my temples. I was cursing my own perfectionist streak—who weeds at eight in the morning on a Saturday, really —when the low growl of a truck engine snapped me out of my thoughts.

Too close.

I glanced up.

Beckett Ford's pickup rumbled past the street sign and swung into his gravel driveway. But instead of pulling into his usual spot, he rolled halfway across the invisible line between our properties—tires grinding to a halt dangerously close to the very edge of my newly planted garden.

I narrowed my eyes.

The man had a whole damn yard. And today—while I was sweaty, covered in dirt, and trying to have a wholesome morning —he'd decided to play bumper cars with my sage.

I rose, brushing dirt off my hands. "Seriously?" I called, voice sharp enough to carry. "You park that monster an inch closer and we'll be having roasted duck for dinner."

Beckett stepped out of the truck and I thought again of a romance novel cover model, this time a grumpy lumberjack who hadn't gotten the memo about personal space. Gray tee stretched across broad shoulders, worn dark jeans, boots that had seen more mud this morning than I'd dealt with all week.

He looked over at me. Impassive. Calm as his pond on a windless day.

"It's not on your side," he said.

"It's hovering over my side," I shot back.

He closed the truck door with a solid thunk. "It's not a hovercraft, Bellamy. It's parked."

I crossed my arms. "So is my sage. Right under your rear tire."

His jaw twitched, just a little. "Didn't realize I needed a zoning permit to park in my own driveway."

"You don't. But you're not parked in *your* driveway. You could try using some awareness of your surroundings. Like, I don't know, the woman swearing in the dirt ten feet from your grill."

"Not my fault you decided to cosplay as a landscaper in the middle of a driveway," he said, completely unbothered, moving toward the back of the truck to grab something—bags of feed or seed, no doubt. Duck supplies. Probably bribery for Bob's next great escape.

I blinked. "Wow. Did you practice that level of passive-aggression, or is it just your factory setting?"

He paused, reached for a bag. "Your garden looks fine."

I blinked again. That almost sounded like… Nope. I wasn't falling for it. Or maybe I was… "That sounded dangerously close to a compliment," I said, pointing my garden trowel at him.

"It wasn't," he replied without looking back. "Just a fact."

I watched him for a second longer. I was annoyed. Flushed from heat and frustration. And okay—maybe from something else, too.

The man moved with aggravating ease, like carrying fifty-pound bags was just part of his Saturday routine. His shoulders flexed, back muscles rippled through that thin gray tee as he hoisted a bag over one shoulder and strode away.

The show-off.

"Next time," I called, "I'm putting up one of those little gnome signs that says *This is not your damn yard*." I muttered a string of words that would've gotten me excommunicated from any respectable church potluck and then shoved my gloves into my back pocket.

Before I could stomp toward the house, my phone buzzed.

Oz: Library's slow. Come meet me for caffeine therapy?

I glanced toward Beckett, who was now hauling a second bag, rolling his shoulder like it was no big deal.

Frankie: Absolutely. If I stay here I'm gonna throw mulch at my neighbor's truck.

Oz: Meet me at Steam & Bean? I'll order for us.

Frankie: Be there in 10. I need something with espresso and vengeance.

I jogged inside, scrubbed the dirt off my arms, changed into a clean tee, and twisted my hair up with a pencil. My brain still buzzed with Beckett's smug tone as I walked the two blocks to Steam & Bean.

But my frustration had shifted. Simmered into something… more dangerous.

I wasn't sure what to call it. And frankly, that pissed me off more.

The place was already buzzing with the Saturday morning crowd. Locals, tourists, a few bookish types hoarding outlets for their laptops. The scent of roasted beans and cinnamon made my stomach growl. I scanned the interior for my best friend.

I spotted Oz through a window. He was out back on the patio at a shaded table under the crepe myrtles, a paperback in one hand and a coffee in the other. Making my way through the café, I pushed open the rear door.

"Saved you the good chair, grabbed you a coffee and placed our regular order," he said, kicking the chair for me out with his foot.

I dropped into it with a sigh. "You're a saint."

He eyed me over the rim of his iced chai. "You look flushed."

"Because my neighbor parks like a narcissist and pissed me off."

Oz perked up. "Ooooh, Beckett again?"

"He nearly murdered my sage."

"I thought Bob was the wild one."

"He is," I said, grabbing my cold brew and taking a long, fortifying sip. "But apparently grumpy duck dads have no spatial awareness, either."

Oz tilted his head. "Or maybe he's just trying to get close to you."

I choked on my drink. "Please don't start."

He grinned. "I'm just saying. You argue with him a lot. You know what that means."

"It means he's impossible. He's either glaring or pretending I don't exist."

"That's foreplay for a man like him."

I groaned. "I'm changing the subject. What's happening at the library?"

Graciously, he let me pivot. Launched into a story about someone trying to return a copy of Outlander with three pages stuck together. I didn't ask. I wasn't asking.

Some things were sacred.

By the time our food arrived—egg sandwiches and cinnamon muffins, and we had a shared mini-crisis over whether a patron had swiped a signed Colleen Hoover, I was almost relaxed again.

Oz was one of the two people who'd stuck with me through every storm. He'd known me since college, back when we bonded over fanfiction and a mutual caffeine addiction. He was fierce and nerdy and the best kind of loyal. And probably the only guy alive who could say *Beckett foreplay* with a straight face and survive.

Then the bell over the door to the patio jingled.

Beckett.

Stepping out of the café, he held a brown paper bag in one hand, coffee in the other.

I froze mid-bite.

Oz didn't miss it. "You've got it bad."

"I don't have anything but indigestion and stress diarrhea," I whispered.

Oz snorted. "You've got heat in your cheeks and murder in your eyes. That's something."

Beckett looked up. For one second—just one—his gaze caught mine.

And stayed.

I lifted my cup in a lazy salute, heart thumping.

He raised a brow.

Then—cool as you please—he nodded once and walked on in the direction of home.

Oz's jaw dropped theatrically. "Did you two just… acknowledge each other without insults?"

"Shut up."

"You're doomed." His laugh drew glances from nearby tables.

I stabbed my muffin with my fork. "I will never fall for a man who parks like a jackass and glares like it's his job."

"But what if he also bakes duck-shaped cookies and looks so hot in a T-shirt?"

"I hate you."

"No, you don't. But you might hate how much you're into Grumpzilla."

I buried my face in my hands. "I question why we're still friends."

Oz leaned forward, voice mock-serious. "Because I'm the only one who will hold your hair back when you inevitably spiral into a full-blown, duck-induced existential crisis. And because I know exactly what to order to bribe you with cinnamon pastries and hot men."

"Tempting. But I'm not spiraling."

He raised a perfectly shaped brow. "You chased a duck through your house. Threatened your neighbor with violence. And you're now mood-weeding before sunrise. That's a spiral, darling."

"It's productive spiraling," I muttered.

"Mm-hmm." He sipped his chai. "Tell me, are you planting emotional stability next to the sage, or just more denial?"

I reached across the table and stole a chunk of his muffin. "Eat your carbs and mind your business."

"I would, but your business is just so goddamn entertaining. I feel like I should be taking notes. Or selling tickets."

"Hard pass. I'm not letting you write gay fanfic about me and the duck man."

Oz wiggled his brows. "Too late. Working title: Pecks and Wrecks: A Love Story."

"Oh, my God."

"You're the one feeding the romantic tension. I'm just narrating."

I groaned. "One of these days, I'm gonna actually kill you."

"You say that, but who's going to organize your spice shelf and remind you which coffee beans give you heartburn?"

"You're lucky you're pretty."

"Obviously." He leaned back, satisfied. "Now drink your coffee. You'll need the energy to repress everything you're feeling emotionally until it explodes in some spectacular bookstore-adjacent meltdown."

"That's my plan," I said sweetly. "Right after I teach Bob how to use a paintbrush so I can redecorate Beckett's truck in passive-aggressive pastel."

"Oh, if that duck learns to hold a brush, I'm filming it and selling merch."

"Already brainstorming sticker designs," I deadpanned. "One says: My neighbor's a grump, but his duck has taste."

Oz slapped the table. "I love us."

Later, walking home, the sun high and hot, I spotted Bob waddling down the sidewalk like he owned the town.

He stopped. Stared up at me.

I stared back. "Are you seriously following me now?"

Bob quacked once. Loudly.

"Tell your dad he owes me a new sage plant. And maybe a damn apology."

Bob blinked.

I sighed. "I need new boundaries. And possibly a duck restraining order."

Still—when Bob trailed me all the way to the edge of my porch, I didn't stop him.

And when I sat down later with my notebook and coffee, I left the front door cracked just enough for a certain smug little duck to waddle inside.

Because apparently, boundaries were for other people.

CHAPTER 8
SPECIAL DELIVERY OF RAGE AND ROMANCE

BECKETT

I HAD A SYSTEM.

Quiet mornings. Black coffee. No unexpected variables.

Especially not on a fucking Tuesday.

Which made the boxes sitting on my porch a personal assault on that system.

It wasn't the boxes themselves—though they were bad enough.

It was the glittery tape on each one.

I glared at the box on top. At the neon-pink sticker screaming "Smut Shipment: Handle with Care."

And the winking alien cowboy stamped right across the side like a smug little bastard daring me to open it.

I stared at it. Hard. Like maybe, if I focused hard enough, it would vanish into the void from whence it came. And take the rest of the boxes with it.

It didn't.

No one had knocked. No text. No warning. They were just *there,* waiting for me when I'd innocently opened my front door this morning, intending to enjoy my own damn coffee on my own damn porch.

Which meant Janet at the post office had seen this… this *thing* stamped on the box, recognized it, and—wisely—dropped the boxes and retreated.

Smart woman. Except she'd dropped them on the *wrong damn porch!* Yeah they had my house number on the label, but it clearly read Frankie Bellamy.

I exhaled—long, slow, already tired—and raked a hand down my face.

Craning my neck toward the pink abomination, I could see that Frankie's front door hung open.

An empty coffee cup was balanced on her porch railing. The faint hum of some cheerful, bouncy song drifted out—each beat a personal offense to my soul this early in the day.

Because of course she would be blaring sunshine music while the universe delivered soft-core alien porn to my porch.

I crouched, slicing the top box open with my pocketknife.

Books. Dozens of them. Bright covers. Glossy finishes. Titles in metallic fonts that practically shouted: Read me. With wine. No judgment required.

The kind of books that belonged anywhere but my porch.

I pulled one from the top.

I Got Abducted by Aliens and Now I'm Trapped in a Rom-Com.

I blinked.

A glittery bookmark slipped out—pink foil, delicately printed with Beam Me Up, Daddy. I stared at it hard. My pulse ticked once. Then again. I was ten seconds away from tossing the entire box straight into the pond.

But principle—and sheer stubborn male pride—stopped me.

She'd done it again.

Or rather, her mail had. But to me? Same damn thing.

And this? This was the last straw.

I slid the bookmark back into the paperback and stared down at it like it had personally insulted me. Then—with a groan of defeat —I grabbed my phone and hit *Hank* in my contacts.

It rang twice.

"Good morning brother," he answered, voice dry.

I didn't waste time. "Hypothetical question."

A pause. "Should I be sitting down for this?"

"Is it illegal to knowingly, intentionally drop off someone's misdelivered mail at their house instead of returning it to the post office?"

Another beat. Then a very slow exhale. "Jesus Christ, Beckett. What did you do?"

"I didn't do anything," I growled. "But *someone's* mail got dropped at my door. And it's not normal mail, Hank. It's… themed. Like aggressively themed."

"You mean the alien porn?"

I stiffened. "How do you know about that?"

Hank laughed. Actually *laughed*. "Janet called me. Said she needed moral support. She thought if she left the boxes on your porch without warning, you'd either implode or start an intergalactic incident."

My eye twitched. "This town needs less gossip and more boundaries. Did she say why she left the boxes on *my* porch?"

"Nope. But she did say that the tape sparkled," he continued, unbothered. "Something about alien daddy ranch hands and a surprise baby box set? I didn't ask for details."

I dragged a hand down my face. "It was labeled *Smut Shipment*, Hank. In holographic font."

"So… technically that's just misdelivered *merchandise*. Not first-class mail."

"There are seven boxes of the same smut, Hank."

"You *counted*?" he said, choked on a laugh.

"Can I file a harassment complaint?" I muttered. "She's violating my porch space."

"She's violating your composure, more like."

"I will hang up this phone."

"Do it. But I'm telling Nate you've got a girl next door who reads about tentacle cowboys and you're still single."

"She is not my girl next door."

"Oh? So the scowl you wore at Steam & Bean yesterday when she smiled at me like I was the second coming of coffee wasn't personal?"

My jaw clenched. "That wasn't a scowl. That was my normal face."

"That was your *I'll rip your spine out if you keep flirting with her* face. Pretty sure Joey flinched."

"I hate you," I muttered.

"No you don't. You're just grumpy because someone delivered unresolved sexual tension to your doorstep in a glittery box and you don't know what to do with it."

I stared at the wall. Dead-eyed. "I'm hanging up now."

"Say hi to the alien groom for me."

I ended the call in the middle of his laugh.

Asshole.

I grabbed the opened box, straightened to my full height, and stalked across the gravel. Boots hitting stone with deliberate force. Jaw clenched.

I didn't think about how this would look.

Didn't think about how the last time I'd crossed this yard, I'd ended up trying not to stare at her legs while she'd smirked like she'd won a prize.

This wasn't that.

This was war.

"BELLAMY!"

She appeared almost instantly—hair up in that damn messy knot, oversized tee slipping off one shoulder, bare legs tanned and tempting and very, very visible.

And smiling.

Of course she was.

"Morning, sunshine," she called, voice like a damn caress. "Come to borrow some thyme? Or are your ducks staging a coup again?"

I held up the box like a cursed relic. "The post office left this, along with six other similar boxes on my porch."

She tilted her head, grinning wider. "Is that… oh! That's my preorder. I was wondering where it landed." I watched as she scanned the label.

"You need to get this delivery shit straightened out," I growled.

She leaned against the doorframe, radiating smug amusement. "It's a stock delivery. You don't want to know what they're sending next week. I'll get it straightened out eventually, you prude."

She winked.

I nearly ground my teeth to dust.

I shifted the box to my hip, yanked the top book out and read the title aloud, each word tasting like pain. "*I Got Abducted by Aliens and Now I'm Trapped in a Rom-Com.*"

She beamed. "It's excellent. Girl gets dropped on a strange planet, falls for not one, but two aliens."

I stared at her. "No one in their right mind reads this."

"Well, thank god I've never claimed sanity," she said breezily, that voice scraping something raw beneath my skin.

And that's when it hit me.

It wasn't just the damn boxes. Or the books. Or the way she stood there looking like the sun had personally kissed her skin.

It was *her*—bright, flushed, alive—while I stood here with concrete lodged in my chest.

It was her making this whole place feel less empty—and I couldn't fucking afford to notice that.

And yet.

I noticed everything about her.

The curve of her mouth when she teased.

The freckle on her collarbone.

The faint scent of citrus and warm skin that wrapped around my neck like a fucking noose every time I got too close.

I shook it off. Barely.

"This is not normal mail," I said, voice rough, as I put the damn book back in the box.

"It is for me," she sing-songed.

"It's—" I opened the box's flap wider, scanning more titles, "tentacles and cowboys and—" I yanked out another book. "*Morning Glory Milking Farm.*" I blinked. Then looked at her. "Seriously?"

She covered her mouth, eyes sparkling. "Okay, that one is sooo good. It's about—"

"Stop. I don't want to know." I held up my hand like a traffic cop in hell. "You order this stuff… why?"

Her voice shifted—softer, surer. "Because they make me happy. Because life gets heavy, Beckett. And sometimes it's nice to read something ridiculous and fun and full of hope. Gives you a reason to smile."

I didn't want to hear it. Didn't want to hear hope spoken like it was still a thing people deserved.

Didn't want to admit that for half a heartbeat... I wanted to ask her what it felt like to believe that way.

"I'm returning this circus," I said flatly, dropping the open box on the porch, then turning on my heel. "Come get the rest of your depraved reading material."

She followed—barefoot, fast, close enough that I could hear her breathing. Feel it.

I stomped up my porch steps, grabbed my coffee cup from the porch railing and went in. She could carry her own damn boxes of smut.

Except she followed me into the house. Infuriating woman!

Her eyes swept my space.

"You really do live in a cave," she said softly. "No color. No plants. One couch. Functional. Depressing."

"I like quiet," I said.

"You like walls."

I stiffened. "Not your business."

"Then stop making mine yours," she shot back, fire flashing behind those eyes.

"You left your damn books on my porch."

"The mail left them."

"Same difference," I growled as I stomped out to the porch, grabbed another box, brought it into the house and dropped it on the coffee table. I cut through its scandalous glitter tape and grabbed the book on top. "*Galactic Groomzilla.*"

She actually sighed dreamily. "That one has amazing banter."

"People can't be into this trash."

"You keep saying that. But here you are—still holding it."

I dropped it like it burned. "You need to grow up."

Her smile faded. Just a breath. "And you need to loosen the hell up."

Our eyes locked. The air between us snapped taut. It wasn't about the books anymore or the porch or the mail or the goddamn aliens.

It was *her*—standing too close. Breathing too deep. Daring me to notice the want tucked behind my every word.

And me—feeling her pull like a tide ripping through my gut. "You think I don't know how to live?" I asked, voice rough. Revealing things I didn't want to divulge.

She swallowed. "I think you've forgotten."

For a beat, neither of us moved. And fuck, I wanted to.

Wanted to close the space between us and find out if her fire burned as hot as it looked.

Wanted to lose myself for one reckless second.

But I forced a step back. The air felt too thin.

"Get your boxes," I said, voice harsh.

She lifted her chin. "Fine." Her fingers brushed my wrist as she plucked *Galactic Groomzilla* from my hand.

And Christ. For one flash of a second, my whole fucking heart stuttered like I'd taken a hit to the ribs. She returned the offensive book to the offensive box, picked it up and spun toward the door.

At the threshold, she paused. "For the record," she said softly, "it's not just porn. It's fantasy. Some of us still need that."

Then she was gone.

The door swung shut.

I stood there.

Chest aching.

Jaw locked.

Her scent—citrus and coffee and heat—still lingered in the room.

I turned and saw that one book remained on the table.

Ice Planet Barbarians.

I stared.

The cover was a goddamn crime. Half-naked blue alien, woman clinging to him like her life depended on it. I made a low sound. Part scoff. Part growl.

What the hell was the world coming to that smart women like Frankie Bellamy were reading this shit?

I grabbed the book. Grip tight enough to leave indents. Should've tossed it. But I couldn't.

Because under every muscle and scar and wall I'd built, one truth burned through me like a brand… I couldn't imagine her not living next to me anymore.

Couldn't imagine tomorrow without her voice drifting through the air. Without the wild tangle of her pink hair. Without the sound of her laughter gutting me when I least expected it.

Without wanting her in ways I didn't dare admit.

I dropped onto the couch, still holding the damn book.

"Goddammit," I whispered.

And still—still—I wasn't throwing it out.

I stared down at the paperback clutched in my hand, my fingers flexing against the glossy cover like it held answers I didn't want to questions I didn't want to ask. Was afraid to ask.

I should've tossed it. But the truth burned through me, undeniable now.

I could handle the pink house and even pinker porch. The ducks. The fence. The damn books.

What I couldn't handle…

Was the fact that for the first time in years—someone had walked into my life, kicked the door wide open, and made me *want*.

And that scared me worse than any scandal or headline ever had. Or could.

CHAPTER 9
DUCK POND DISTRACTIONS

FRANKIE

I WAS ABSOLUTELY NOT GOING to think about Beckett Ford today.

Nope. No chance in hell.

It'd been days since the boxes debacle. I was outside this beautiful Saturday morning for one perfectly wholesome, practical reason. Building a knee-high fence to protect my garden. Not replaying the last time I'd stomped out of his house, clutching a box of my own damn books while he stood there, glaring at me with prudish eyeballs like I'd committed a federal crime against masculinity and interior design.

And I was definitely not thinking about the way he'd looked in that moment—hair mussed, arms braced on the coffee table, chest rising like he was holding back a storm. Or the way his voice had gone low and rough when he had growled: *"You need to grow up."*

I stabbed the post hole digger into the soil with more force than was strictly necessary. Over and over and over.

The whole encounter sparked beneath my skin like a nascent fire. The slow-burning kind that kept flaring hotter the longer you tried to ignore it.

How *dare* he dismiss what I loved like that. Like my joy—my lifeline—was something embarrassing. Like hope was for people who hadn't survived shit.

I told myself that those boxes would be my last interaction with him. I'd reclaim my space. My calm. My fucking dignity. And yet here I was. Every muscle wired tight. Every heartbeat too fast. All because of him.

Because beneath my righteous fury was something more dangerous.

Something that had noticed the way his jaw flexed when he lost his temper. Something that had noticed the way he looked at me —like I'd exposed a part of him that he hadn't let breathe in years. Something that *wanted*—for just one second—to see what would happen if I pushed him over that edge.

"No," I muttered aloud, hammering the next post into the hole I'd just excavated. "Absolutely not."

This fence? It was mine. Literally and metaphorically. It would separate me from the chaos, the questions, and the dangerously magnetic man living across the gravel.

Pickup trucks rolling over my thyme? No. I stabbed the digger into the sandy southern soil and pulled out the loosened dirt.

Escaped ducks eating my basil? Nope. Another stab of the digger. More dirt removed.

Grumpy neighbors with smoldering eyes? *Hell. No.* Last fence post pounded in.

I was tired and a dirty mess by the time I had the small fence erected, but too angry to quit.

I knelt in the grass, painting each board a muted sage green. I originally bought Truffle Brown for the fence, but had since changed my mind. This green reminded me of vintage book covers. Of calm. Of a woman who definitely didn't fantasize about a certain neighbor's mouth.

Focus on the color. Not the voice. Not the forearms. Not the way he said *You look good when you're riled up* like it wasn't meant to ruin me.

The problem was simple.

I *hated* him.

From the moment we'd met—him glowering at me like my moving truck had insulted his damn pets—I'd hated him.

But my brain? That bitch betrayed me daily.

Reminded me of how Beckett looked when he thought no one was watching him. Quiet. Haunted. Like the kind of person who had survived something and hadn't figured out what to do with the rest of his life.

Moody. Arrogant. Unavailable.

Been there. Married that. Had the legal fees to prove it.

I stood and stretched my aching back. I was about to go back to painting when motion caught my eye.

And then… I froze.

From this angle, beyond the fence, I could see Beckett thigh-deep in the duck pond.

Absolutely nothing on his magnificent chest except the suspender straps of the waders he was wearing.

My heart skidded sideways and then slammed into a wall marked *Bad Decisions Ahead.*

Sunlight skimmed across his bare shoulders, catching in the waves of his long-ish hair—damp and shoved back, like he'd run a hand through it without thinking. He turned, and his entire torso was bronzed and dripping, a slow sheen of water sliding down his chest like some kind of cruel visual torture. His pecs flexed as he pulled the net across the pond's surface, the muscles in his arms rippling under golden skin. A few drops clung to his collarbones before trailing over his ribs and disappearing beneath the lip of those low-slung black waders.

I stared.

Fully and shamelessly.

I slid my phone from my back pocket. Using my camera app, I zoomed in to get a better view. And God, what a view it was.

His body was the kind you didn't just notice—you *felt* it in your teeth. Even the little silver streaks at his temples caught the light and somehow made the whole thing worse. Unfair. Rude.

His back was beauty in motion, muscles rippling from shoulder to waist in a fluid, powerful rhythm. Broad. Solid.

His neck—that thick line of muscle running from shoulder to jaw, his traps alternately taut and relaxed as he turned his head. The veins that popped on his forearms. The way his biceps flexed with every pull was a goddamn Calvin Klein ad that had decided to take a detour through small-town Georgia.

I could practically hear my ovaries firing up like they were clocking in for overtime.

This was not safe. This was *visual arson.* Incendiary.

His face was tilted slightly down, jaw shadowed with scruff, lips parted just enough to show concentration. And those storm-gray eyes? I could picture them. Focused. Intense. Completely unaware that they were the cause of ninety percent of my current suffering.

My thighs pressed together of their own volition.

I bit my lip. Hard. *Click.* The sound of my phone's camera made me blink. Shit! Now I had this pond porn in my gallery. I shoved my phone back in my pocket.

That helped absolutely nothing, because I continued to watch.

Every survival instinct within me screamed *Look away! Stop!* Told me to grab my phone, delete all proof of this moment, and go make bad decisions with ice cream and air conditioning.

But I didn't.

Because *Beckett Ford,* six-foot-four of shirtless, scowling temptation, was the kind of man you didn't walk away from. Not literally. Not visually. Not emotionally. Not unless you wanted to lie awake every night remembering how the sunlight hitting the grooves of his abs was like a fucking romance novel cover.

I could already hear Oz, *You're so fucked.*

And honestly? He wouldn't be wrong.

My breathing was shallow. Skin felt flushed. Every nerve strung tight like a well-tuned guitar string.

It was the heat. The humidity. The lack of sex in the last… well. Let's not count.

It was the fact that this man looked like something I'd conjured from the backlist of my favorite filthy fantasy books.

But it was more than that, and I hated how *aware* of it I was.

It was his strength. His stillness. That *wounded wildness* in him that made me want to touch and curse him in the same breath. Heal him. He wasn't just sexy. He was *undone*. And something primal in me wanted to see what he looked like when he *finally broke*.

I was in a dangerous place. Not physically—I was relatively safe here, albeit sweaty—but *mentally* I was vulnerable. Teetering on the edge of decisions that started with *It was just a conversation* and ended with *Oops, he's naked*.

I'd never wanted to climb someone and simultaneously hit them with a garden hose so badly in my life.

I muttered a swear.

This wasn't a crush. This was a *crisis*. A tall, shirtless, duck-wrangling, emotionally unavailable crisis with a mouth that could start wars.

My phone buzzed.

> Tess: How's Project Fence? Pics or it didn't happen.

God help me.

I grabbed my phone. Aimed. Quick snapshot. Just the fence. Definitely not the duck daddy thirst trap behind it.

Sure.

I looked at the image.

Shit.

> Frankie: Project Fence proceeding. Minor distractions included.

> Attachment: Photo.jpg

> Tess: OH MY GOD. IS HE SHIRTLESS. YOU ARE A LUCKY BITCH.

> Tess: This is why I believe in you. Weaponized thirst and spite.

I choked on a laugh and went to respond, but—

QUACKQUACKQUACKQUACK

My head jerked up.

Bob.

The feathered agent of chaos was waddling toward me like he owned the place.

"Shhh!" I hissed. "Be cool, Bob. Don't narc."

Bob did not stay cool. He quacked louder. Then louder again.

Traitor.

I dropped flat onto my ass, fumbling for my phone and the brush. Maybe if I lay down and played dead—

For a few minutes I thought my ploy had worked. But no…

Rubber legs squeaked as they slipped past each other. Rubber boots crunched the gravel. Slow. Heavy. Lethal.

And then there was a shadow. Wide. Broad. Blocking out the sun.

"Everything alright over here?"

I opened one eye. Regretted it instantly.

Beckett. Arms crossed. Still shirtless. Smirking like sin.

"I… dropped something," I said weakly.

He tilted his head. "Looks like you dropped *yourself.*"

"Your duck startled me."

He looked at Bob. Bob blinked, innocent.

"Good instincts," Beckett said.

"Good instincts for ruining my entire life, maybe."

He looked me over—dirt on my legs, paint-streaked arms, hair a mess—and something in his eyes shifted. Heat. Recognition.

"Nice color," he said. "Green suits you."

I wanted to throw the paint can at his face.

Instead, I smirked. "Figured it would pop nicely when it was framed by shirtless trespassers."

His grin was slow. Dangerous. "Wasn't trespassing. Pond is in my yard."

"You were very *visible.*"

"You looked."

"Reflex."

"Hmm."

That was all he said. But the sound of it curled inside me like warm honey laced with poison. He turned, slow and smug, and I stared at his retreating back like my eyes hadn't signed up for any of this shit.

"Enjoy your pond," I muttered.

"Always do," he called.

I flopped back in the grass, chest heaving.

Why?

Why did I want him dead and naked at the same time?

Bob waddled by. Smug. Judging.

"Don't look at me like that," I said. "I know I'm in trouble."

And the worst part?

I didn't want out.

CHAPTER 10
FEATHERS, FILES, AND F*CK THAT GUY

BECKETT

THE SUN HAD SHIFTED by the time I returned to the pond.

And no—I wasn't avoiding the house. Or thinking about the way Frankie Bellamy had looked earlier.

Flushed. Intimidating. Gorgeous in that wild, stubborn way of hers.

Bare legs streaked with dirt, paint on her cheeks and arms, hands fisted like she was ready to punch God in the throat and look good doing it. The kind of woman who made your blood heat even when you told yourself to stay cold.

Definitely wasn't thinking about her.

I was just finishing what I'd started—clearing the pond.

The water lapped warm against my forearms as I worked. The sun was brutal on my back. Sweat rolled down my spine, clung to the waistband of the waders. Every muscle in my arms burned from dragging the net again and again through the muck.

But I needed the pain. Needed the rhythm.

It settled the noise in my head.

Until Bob quacked like a little bastard.

I looked up, half-smirking—then froze.

Frankie was facing down some asshole in a golf-club sweater vest and loafers. His BMW was parked at a slant behind him like it owned the zip code.

Everything about the guy screamed money and smug entitlement. Too clean. Too slick. The kind of man who thought he could buy silence and slap forgiveness on his breath with a gold card.

Frankie jabbed her finger into his chest. Her whole body was tense, like a storm coiled tightly inside her skin.

Then he said something—I couldn't hear it—but her face crumpled for half a second before snapping back into fury.

He grabbed her arm.

Hard.

I moved.

Didn't think. Didn't weigh it. Just moved.

Water surged around me as I bolted from the pond, heavy boots hitting the earth hard. I moved as fast as I could in those fucking waders. My heart kicked like a war drum. I didn't care. Didn't feel anything but the red haze building behind my eyes.

She tried to yank free—but he held on.

Not on my watch.

Not *ever*.

I shoved through the gate and was across our yards and in his face before I'd fully drawn breath.

"Let her go."

My voice didn't rise. Didn't need to.

It hit like a brick dropped from a rooftop.

The man startled, looked up, sneered. "Who the hell—"

He froze.

Recognition hit him. And the way his mouth curled after he made the connection caused something primal and *violent* to ripple through my chest.

"I know you," he said, eyes narrowing. "Beckett Ford. Jesus, she downgraded harder than I thought."

Frankie's head jerked toward me, startled.

I didn't blink. Just grabbed the front of his cashmere-soft shirt and slammed him against the side of his overpriced car with a solid, satisfying *thud*.

"Touch her again," I said, voice grinding like gravel under pressure, "and I'll break your fucking arm before the cops show up to sweep what's left of your smug ass off this driveway."

He barked a bitter laugh, despite the shaking I could feel vibrating up from his knees. "You gonna code me into submission, Ford? That what this is? Some small-town redemption arc for a washed-up, disgraced billionaire?"

I stilled.

Something inside me went razor-sharp and *cold*.

He smirked. "You think hiding behind ducks erases the headlines? You're a joke. A walking scandal in waders."

I shoved him harder.

His voice wobbled but kept going. "Christ, Frankie. You go from the Atlanta investment circuit to this? No wonder your dad cut you off. You're surrounding yourself with charity cases and broken toys."

That did it.

I *snapped*.

My knuckles grazed the side of his collar, one beat from slamming him to the concrete. Only the sound of Frankie's gasp stopped me.

Just that.

Not her begging me to stop.

Not a scream.

Just her breath catching. Hurting.

I looked at her—and saw that the fear in her eyes wasn't for him.

It was for me.

I let go.

Hard.

The man stumbled, nearly falling into the driver's seat when I yanked the door open.

"Get in your car," I growled, voice shredded. "Now."

He did. Because cowards like that only fight when they're sure someone else will lose.

As he started the car, he muttered through the open window, "This isn't over, Bellamy."

I leaned down and smiled. It wasn't a nice smile.

"It is if you don't want a second round, asshole."

Then I straightened. Watched him scurry away like the rat he was.

My pulse thundered.

My hands shook.

The pond was behind me, but I felt like I was still waist-deep in something I couldn't quite clean out.

I turned.

Frankie was standing there—chest rising too fast, hair wild, eyes blazing.

"You didn't have to do that!" she snapped. "I had it handled."

"Didn't look like it." My voice was flat, controlled.

"I didn't ask for your help."

"No," I said softly. "But you needed it."

She threw her hands up. "God, you arrogant—damn—grumpy pond man!"

I blinked. "Grumpy pond man?"

"You stormed over here like some damn avenging duck daddy! Now he's gonna come back twice as pissed!"

"He put his hands on you."

"I know!" Her voice cracked. "And I was handling it. I've handled worse."

That ripped through me like a blade.

Worse?

She saw my expression—went pale. "Don't."

"Frankie—" My hands curled into fists at my sides. "He won't touch you again," I said roughly.

"No." She spun away, pacing hard. "You don't get to come charging in and fix things just because it makes you feel useful. This—this is *my* life."

"He put his hands on you."

"And I handled it."

"No. You *froze.*"

She flinched.

I swallowed. Fuck. "I didn't mean—"

"God, I can't—" she spun away, pacing, running both hands through her hair. "You can't just do that. You can't just—get involved. You think this is about me being saved?" She snapped, spinning back. "I've been saving myself since the day my father said I was an embarrassment. Since my ex tried to turn my name into a legal footnote. Stay out of it, Beckett."

The words cut deep.

Then she was gone. I stood there, muscles still taut, heart still racing. The words echoed. *Stay out of it.*

But the heat in her voice, the fear under it—I'd seen too much. Heard too much. That bastard was her ex. I'd bet my fortune on it. And there was no way in hell I was staying out of it now.

I turned slowly, my gaze hardening for a moment until it found my damn duck watching me from the pond's edge, head tilted.

I exhaled. "Yeah," I murmured. "I know, Bob."

I stalked back to my house, body still vibrating with leftover adrenaline. If she wasn't going to tell me what was going on… I'd figure it out myself. I might have left the fast-paced corporate world behind, but one thing remained. I was a fucking tech genius, and I'd get to the bottom of whatever she was keeping from me one way or another. I ditched my waders by the back door. Inside, the familiar cool quiet hit me like a wall. Usually, I welcomed it. Today, it was suffocating.

I strode through the kitchen to the laundry room, where I peeled off my sweaty socks, shorts and boxers. Grabbed last night's bath towel and wiped the wetness off me. Found clean-enough shorts and a T-shirt. Headed back to the kitchen, then through the living room, then to my office. The laptop was still on the desk from the night before. The memory of Daniel's voice tried to creep back in, but this time, it wasn't Daniel's words echoing through me.

It was Frankie's. *Stay out of it. I've handled worse.*

I dragged a hand through my damp hair, ground my molars together. *Handled worse.* What the hell did that mean? And why did it bother the fuck out of me more than anything she'd said to me yet?

I sat down hard, fingers already moving before my brain could catch up. I wasn't going to pry. Wasn't going to stalk. I just… needed to understand. Enough to know how bad this could get. Enough to be ready if that smug bastard came back.

I opened a private search tab and started typing.

Frankie Bellamy.

Hits came fast and I narrowed my search after scanning the first few.

Frankie Bellamy Atlanta.

A profile photo popped up—a local magazine feature from years back. Frankie in a sleek black cocktail dress, smiling tight for the camera, hair smoothed into perfect waves. The caption read,

> *"Francesca Bellamy Monroe, daughter of Harold and Margaret Bellamy, attending the Atlanta Society Arts Gala."*

My brows lifted.

Bellamy. I knew I'd recognized that name… it meant something. Old money. Atlanta elite circles. I'd run in enough of those worlds to recognize it.

I clicked deeper. More articles. An only child. Prestigious private schools. Social features. Wedding announcement. Charity events. Her father ran an investment firm; her mother chaired half the arts organizations in the city.

But the trail stopped cold about two years ago.

Time for a new search.

Francesca Bellamy Monroe.

Nothing new.

Francesca Bellamy Monroe divorce.

Bingo.

Francesca Bellamy Monroe vs. Christopher Monroe.

Divorce finalized eleven months ago. Acrimonious.

I clicked through the public docket listings. Some were sealed. But what remained painted a picture. Frankie had received almost nothing in the settlement. No alimony. No division of property. Her parents had sided publicly with her ex, cutting her off. Financial statements confirmed it.

> *"Petitioner using personal savings and small inheritance to fund independent business project."*

I frowned, heart spasming. I dug deeper. She'd cashed out an old investment account left by her grandmother—about forty grand. Not much, in the world she was used to. Enough to cover startup costs and first months' mortgage on a small-town shop.

She'd done this whole damn thing alone.

No safety net. No trust fund.

And now…

My fingers stilled as I landed on a linked public crowdfunding page.

> *DonorFund Campaign: "Help Frankie's Bookstore Thrive!"*

Raising money for essential inventory, repairs, and upgrades.

My gut twisted. The page showed photos of the shop—her front window with handwritten chalk signs, an old oak counter, a few shelves half-stocked. Her words beneath were direct and vulnerable.

> *"I dreamed of this store for years. It's the one thing I've built entirely on my own. Every dollar helps us stay afloat while we build community support."*

The donation list wasn't large. What I assumed were a few friends and maybe some locals.

My throat tightened. She shouldn't have to do this alone.

I clicked further.

The latest court update stopped me cold.

> *"Petitioner's ex-husband is contesting the legality of inheritance funds used to open said business."*

The bastard was trying to claw it back. The only money she had. My hands clenched on the desk. I almost clicked the attached documents—then paused.

One file caught my eye.

> *Medical Records—Closed—Sealed by Court Order.*

I stared at it as a wave of coldness swept through my chest. A single click would open it.

Don't.

This wasn't about curiosity. This was her life. Her pain. Not mine to take. I exhaled hard and forced myself to close the tab. But the rest? That stayed burned in my brain.

She'd walked away from everything. Built this life from scraps. And now that bastard was trying to take that, too. My pulse thudded as I clicked back to the DonorFund page. I didn't think about it. Didn't weigh the optics.

I just typed.

Anonymous Contribution: $250,000.

I clicked submit before I could talk myself out of it.

The page refreshed. The new total jumped. Frankie's campaign now sat well past its goal. I leaned back in my chair, exhaling a shaky breath. It wasn't enough. I could never undo the damage that piece of shit had done.

But it was a start.

I'd been down the rabbit hole a while and night had fallen. I stared out the window, toward the dark line of her house. The light was on in her front room. A single silhouette moved past the window—fast, restless.

She'd be furious if she knew. I accepted that. But this wasn't about pride. Not anymore. I couldn't stop caring. I wouldn't pretend she wasn't under my skin—because despite ignoring her, she'd crawled right under and burrowed in deep.

I scrubbed a hand over my face and whispered to no one, "Too damn late for staying out of it."

CHAPTER 11
PEGGING, PETTY, AND PROBABLY DOOMED

FRANKIE

BY MID-MORNING, I'd rearranged the front display three times, threatened the stepladder twice, and stabbed myself with the tape gun once.

Progress.

The bookstore smelled like lemon cleaner, dust, and cheap optimism—the good kind. The kind I'd been clinging to with both hands since I found out yesterday that my ex was still actively trying to ruin my life.

Again.

Which was why I wasn't letting myself think about Beckett Ford today.

Or his bare chest. Or the way he manhandled Chris like he was unloading a sack of mulch.

Nope. Not today, Satan.

I was halfway through restocking a paranormal romance endcap when the bell over the front door jingled. I didn't look up. "I'll be with you in a second."

QUACK.

My head snapped toward the entryway.

And there he was. *Bob*.

Feathered home wrecker. Winged agent of chaos. Beckett Ford's feathery second half.

He waddled in like he owned the place—beak high, feet loud against the floorboards.

I groaned. "Do you have a tracker on me, or are you just emotionally codependent now?"

Bob ignored me. He padded straight for the counter, flew up, circled the register once, then plopped down like it was his personal throne.

I stared. "Okay. Fine. You want to hang out? Great. But you're listening."

Bob blinked.

I grabbed my tablet and pulled up the crowdfunding dashboard to check if anyone had donated overnight. I needed a morale boost.

What I found instead? An anonymous donation for *$250,000*.

My breath locked in my throat.

I stared at the number. Refreshed the page. Stared again.

Still there.

"Holy shit," I whispered.

Bob blinked. Again. Very calm. Too calm. I paced in a circle, heart racing.

"Someone just dropped a quarter of a million dollars into the campaign. That doesn't happen. That's not *real.*"

I turned toward Bob, pointing. "*Was it him?*"

The duck stared.

"Don't play innocent with me. I know he talks to you. I've seen it. You're like his emotional support animal and unlicensed therapist. You're probably listed on the deed to his house."

Bob tilted his head. "Was it Beckett?" I demanded. "Because if it was, I *swear* I will smuggle you to the café and replace your morning cracked corn with oat milk and judgment."

Bob stood. Quacked. Waddled two steps forward to the edge of the counter.

"Okay, now you're just being smug about it."

I dropped into the nearest chair and ran both hands down my face. "I don't know whether to scream or cry or throw this tablet at a wall. Who the hell *does* that? $250,000 is a lot of freaking money. I swear to god if I find out your human did this I'll—"

Bob fluffed up like that was his cue.

I glared. "Don't you dare defend him. He's impossible. He has the emotional range of drywall and the charm of a tax audit."

Bob quacked once. Loud. "Right. Duck logic. Clear as ever."

I stood and paced, energy vibrating under my skin.

"Is he some sort of *broody billionaire Batman in waders?*" I jabbed a finger at Bob. "And don't get me started on what he did to Chris. He didn't even hesitate. Just… stormed over like a six-foot-four vengeance golem, all shirtless and glaring."

My breath caught. Damn it. Not again.

"And the worst part? The *worst* part? I liked it. I *liked* that he did it. That he got mad on my behalf. That he looked at Chris like he wanted to destroy him."

Bob waddled in a slow, deliberative circle.

"I'm not proud of that. I'm… conflicted. And angry. And also—fine. A little turned on."

He stared.

I crossed my arms. "What would *you* do if some grumpy, gorgeous pain in the ass just might have given you a quarter million dollars out of nowhere? And where in the hell would he have even gotten that kind of money?"

Bob flapped his wings once, then plopped his butt back down like he was settling in for popcorn and drama. "You're not useful."

I rubbed my temples. "I need to do something. I want to *rattle* him as much as he rattles me, damn it."

Bob perked up. "I want him to regret thinking he can steamroll into my life, play silent savior, and get away with it."

And then… the idea hit me.

Slow. Vicious. Brilliant.

I turned toward the storage room. Opened a box marked *in-store smut bundles* and pulled out the most unhinged, *NSFW-drenched*, laugh-out-loud, filthy, illustrated romance I had: *Pegging the Pirate King*.

Complete with a glittery sticker sheet and a limited-edition *Captain Peg Me* enamel pin.

I pulled a sticky note from the counter and scribbled.

> Thanks for the unsolicited help.
> Here's something just as hard to forget.
> — F.

I found a perfectly sized cardboard box and lined it with tissue paper. Nestled the book and the pin inside. Closed the box and wrapped it in tissue paper, then tied it with a pink satin bow before slapping on the note.

Bob quacked in approval.

"Oh, you like that one?" I smirked. "Maybe I'll read it aloud next time you sneak in."

He jumped off the counter, flapped once and stomped out like his mission was complete.

I held up the package. Tomorrow, before sunrise, I'd leave it on Beckett's porch. *Let's see how the duck daddy handles* this *particular delivery.*

Because I might be grateful.

I might be reeling.

I might even be halfway to something terrifying and real.

But right now?

I was going to win the petty war.

And *that* felt damn good.

CHAPTER 12

PORN, POULTRY, AND PETTY VENGEANCE

BECKETT

IT WAS TOO EARLY for bullshit.

The sun hadn't cleared the tree line. The coffee hadn't brewed. And Bob was already pacing outside my back door like he had crimes to commit and no time to waste.

I opened the door.

He quacked once—short, smug, and patronizing.

"Whatever it is," I muttered, stepping outside, "no."

He turned. Waddled toward the front of the house. Reluctantly, barefoot, half-asleep, I followed. That's when I saw it. A box. Small. Wrapped in pink paper. Bow tied dead center like it was waiting to sucker punch me with whimsy.

I stopped cold.

Bob sat beside it like a little feathered herald. "No," I said again, slower this time. "Absolutely not."

He blinked. I stared at the package like it might detonate.

Stomped up the porch steps. Craned my neck to read the neon-pink Post-it stuck to the top, the handwriting sharp and looping.

Thanks for the unsolicited help.

Here's something just as hard to forget.

— F.

My jaw flexed. I looked at Bob. "Did you… did you *watch* this happen?" He blinked. "You're complicit."

Bob preened. Bastard. I picked up the box. Something inside rustled. The pink bow made a mockery of my soul. I ripped it off and then the paper, and tore into the box.

And inhaled so sharply I choked.

Pegging the Pirate King.

I had to slow blink twice to take it all in. Full-color cover. Glossy. A buff, shirtless man in *very* snug leather breeches clutching a ship's wheel with one hand and a woman's thigh with the other. The title font was—God help me—*tentacle-shaped.*

I stared. There was a pin nestled in layers of yet more pink tissue paper. I nudged it with a fingertip until I could read it—*Captain Peg Me.*

A corner of… something was peeking out from below the book. I used two fingers, like tweezers, to slowly pull it out, certain it was going to bite me. As soon as my mind could make sense of it, I tossed it back into the box. A sticker sheet featuring riding crops, nautical ropes, and what I *hoped* was an eggplant with a hook for a hand.

Then I stood there, staring at the sky like it owed me an apology.

Bob quacked.

I pointed at him. "You're not even pretending to be neutral."

I stomped back into the house and tossed the box and its obscene contents onto the kitchen counter only to learn that it wasn't enough for her to wrap it in girly paper. Nooo. She'd also dumped glitter in the bottom. Glitter that exploded out of the box when it landed on the counter. I refused to call her. Or acknowledge it in any way, shape or form. Or let it get under my skin. Except my skin was already humming. And the smirk in her note echoed louder than it had any right to.

Unsolicited help.

Like I hadn't been trying not to think about her since yesterday. Since her ex grabbed her. Since her voice cracked when she told me to stay out of it. Since I walked away without saying a word. Since I donated enough money to save her store. Now she was thanking me with pirate porn. And I didn't even know how the hell I felt about that.

Half of me wanted to storm over and tell her to take her glitter and her stickers and her goddamn pink bow and—

The other half?

The other half was still staring at that pin.

I grabbed my phone and dialed the only person who'd advise me without needing context.

Hank picked up on the second ring. "What."

"She sent me *Captain Peg Me.*"

He paused. "I'm gonna need more to go on."

"A book. A *matching* lapel pin. With a note. On my porch."

Another pause. Then a suspicious snort. "Please tell me that's not a euphemism."

"It's not funny."

"It *is*. Lemme guess?"

"Frankie."

His laughter irritated the hell out of me. "I'm assuming she got you back for something. What'd you do?" I didn't answer. "Beckett… what did you do?"

"I may or may not have donated a hefty sum to her donor fund last night. But I did it anonymously. Surely she doesn't know it was me—I'm not even sure she knows about that part of my life." I sighed, then it hit me. "Fuck!"

Hank made a low, incredulous sound. "What?"

"Her ex was here yesterday, and he knew who I was."

"Which means that if she didn't know before, she probably does now." Hank chuckled. "And then you went and donated money… I feel like you're leaving out a big part of this story, brother."

"It doesn't matter. I did it anonymously for a reason. I didn't want a thank you."

"No, you just wanted to broody-savior your way into her subconscious. Mission accomplished."

"I swear to God, Hank—"

"She gave you pirate porn as a warning shot. That woman is terrifying. And perfect for you."

"I'm hanging up."

"Wear the pin, Beckett. You'll never get this kind of fan mail again."

I ended the call and threw my phone on the couch. Bob quacked from the windowsill, watching with great interest. I glared at the box on the counter. I was not reading the note again.

I was not picturing the way her lips probably curled when she wrote it. I was not imagining her laughing to herself while she wrapped it in that damn tissue. Or sprinkled in that damn glitter.

Except I was. All of it. Every second.

And worse?

I liked it.

She wasn't afraid of me. Or of the silence I wore like armor. She pushed. Smirked. Sent duck-insulting smut to my front door with a glittering vengeance. And my dumbass wanted more. More of her teasing me. Laughing at me. Looking at me like she was two seconds from kissing me or killing me and wasn't sure which she wanted more.

I wanted the chaos.

And I wanted *her*.

But first?

She was going to pay for the glitter. I slipped my phone out and called Nate.

"What's up big bro?"

"You off today?" I glanced out the window toward her house.

"Yep."

"Meet me at my house. I need your help with something."

"With the ducks?"

"Jesus. No! Not with the ducks. Something else."

"Oh. Mysterious. This sounds like fun… I'll be there in a few hours."

That left me just enough time to expedite a delivery that would surely give me a one up. By the time Nate pulled into my driveway, I had the items needed for my plan. His eyes widened in surprise when I told him about this morning's box.

"This is a bad idea," Nate said, arms crossed, iced tea in one hand, judgment in the other.

"That's your opinion."

"It's also a *correct* opinion." He gestured toward the carefully arranged weapons on my porch like it was a literal crime scene. "You're going to get glitter bombed. Again. And this time? You're going to *deserve* it."

"She started it."

"Oh, here we go. Full fourth-grade energy."

"She did. She smuggled intergalactic pegging porn onto my porch with a *bow*."

"And a note."

I glared at him. "Don't make it worse."

"You're the one who sent a smut fairy into cardiac arrest by donating a quarter mil and then ghosting her."

"I didn't ghost. I just… did it anonymously. And haven't mentioned it yet."

Nate arched a brow. "She thanked you with *Pegging the Pirate King,* a pin that says *Captain Peg Me* and a sticker sheet, man."

"Exactly. Which is why she deserves this."

Nate took a long, slow sip. "Okay. So explain this again for posterity."

I pointed to the wooden crate sitting neatly on the top step. "Inside: a dozen rubber duckies, each with a hand-painted accessory. Some have pirate hats. Others have tentacles. One with a tiny peg leg. All nestled around a pristine hardcover copy of *The Art of Not Minding Your Own Damn Business.*" Same day delivery was the greatest thing since sliced bread, even if it did cost me a small fortune. "And on the top? A card that reads, *Thought you could use some new coworkers. XO, Duck Daddy.*" Nate made a strangled noise. "You actually signed it *Duck Daddy.*"

"She earned that."

He shook his head, grinning like a bastard. "And you're leaving it *where?*"

"At her front door."

"You know she's going to kill you."

"She'll try."

Nate clapped me on the back. "Cool. Let's go, but don't say I didn't warn you."

"Chicken."

Nate had the audacity to hum the *Mission: Impossible* theme under his breath as we snuck across the front lawn. "You're enjoying this too much."

"I'm *terrified* for you and enjoying it. Different flavor," he joked.

Frankie's shop wasn't open yet—she was still doing renovations, but the lights were on. I could hear music inside—something bouncy, probably covered in glitter and feminism.

I crouched low, set the box squarely in the center of her doormat, knocked once, and retreated like I'd just lobbed a grenade made of duck puns and pride issues. Nate was laughing so hard he was wheezing as we slid back up the steps to my house and sat watching from the front porch.

"You are a petty little pest," he wheezed. "She is going to *end you.*"

And that's when her front door flew open. Frankie stepped onto the porch, looked down, and froze. Then—slowly, dangerously—she bent, picked up the card, and read it.

I watched from my chair, not breathing. She turned. Saw me. And smiled.

Not a nice smile.

A smile that said *Oh, you want war?*

Then—because she was *Frankie*—she reached into the box, pulled out the duck with tentacles, and gave it a little shake. One of the tentacles *wiggled.* She held it up over her head like a trophy.

I watched as she tossed it back into the box, turned then waved. With *both* hands. Like she was thanking me for the trauma.

Nate snorted. "She's *so* into you."

"Shut up." I grunted.

"She's going to burn your house down with glitter napalm."

"She wouldn't dare."

"She's the kind of woman who keeps industrial glitter and a label maker next to her vibrator, Beckett. She would *absolutely* dare."

I stared at the shop, heart thumping like I'd just won—and lost—something in the same breath. Because yeah, I wanted to rile her. But I also wanted to see that fire again. Wanted her storming across the lawn, all fury and wild hair and words that hit like sparks.

I didn't want to want her.

But I did.

And something told me she wasn't going to let me pretend otherwise much longer. I opted to clean the pond again, trying to put her vicious smile out of my mind. Nate sat on the back porch, a beer in his hand while I was elbow-deep in pond filters. It wasn't long, though, until I heard the gate open, then footsteps, heavy at first as they crunched across the gravel before being softened by the grass. Nate let out a slight chuckle, causing me to look up.

Frankie stood at the edge of the dock, holding a cake box like it was a weapon of mass destruction. She was in a black tank top, cut-off denim shorts, and boots that looked like they could kill a man *and* attend brunch. Her hair was up, her sunglasses perched on her head. And her mouth?

Set in a line that made my blood pressure spike. "I come bearing gifts," she said sweetly.

"I'm a little scared." I dropped the shovel I'd been shucking out the pond with onto the ground beside me.

"You should be." She handed me the box. I opened it.

Inside?

Twelve iced cupcakes.

Each one decorated with a different, perfectly piped *emoji*.

Eggplant. Peach. Fire. Duck. One said "Daddy?"

My ears went red.

Nate—who had absolutely *not* left, who had sauntered down to look over my shoulder at the cupcakes—choked on his beer. Frankie leaned in, smiling up at me like she hadn't just detonated a thirst trap made of buttercream and aggression.

"Next time you call yourself Duck Daddy," she said, "just remember. Now I *have merch.*"

My pulse kicked. My jaw locked. "You baked these?"

She shrugged a shoulder. "I bribed the woman in town."

I looked at her.

Looked *hard*.

And maybe it was the sugar in the air, or the sun making her skin glow like a sin I was dying to commit—but I took one step forward.

Close… Too close.

Her breath caught.

"You gonna keep poking the bear, Bellamy?" I murmured. "'Cause I bite."

Her lashes swept up. Bold. Defiant. So fucking *her.* "Maybe I *want* to get bitten."

The air between us snapped.

Behind me, Nate groaned. "For the love of God, just make out already."

Frankie and I didn't move.

Didn't blink.

But something shifted. Something deep. And I knew, right then, that the next time she crossed that fence? There wouldn't be a war.

There'd be *wreckage*.

And we'd both burn in it.

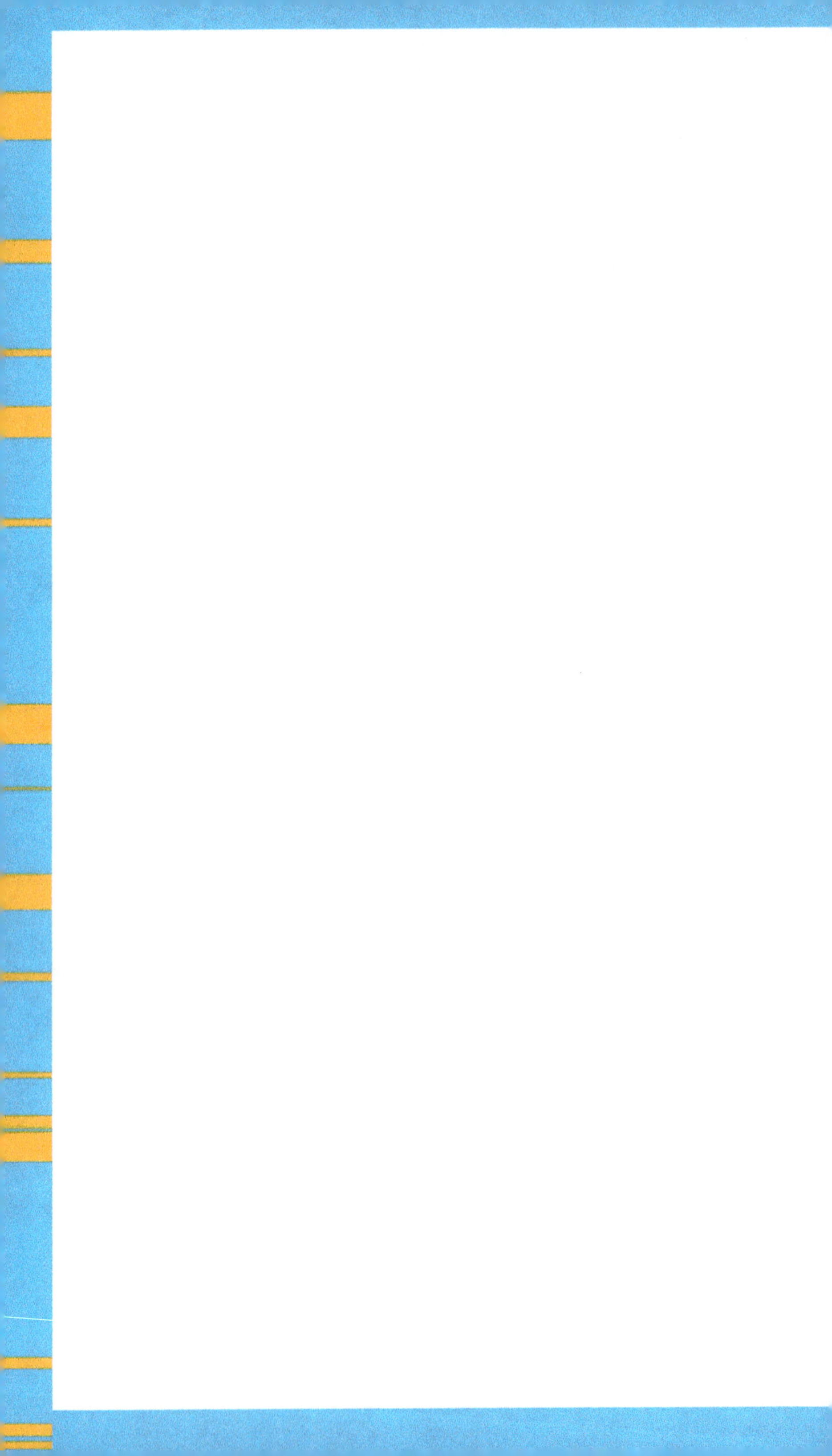

CHAPTER 13

DUCK OFF, I DON'T LIKE HIM

FRANKIE

THE PICNIC TABLE under the big oak in front of the library had become one of my favorite spots in Peachtree Bluff. Warm sun, dappled shade. Quiet corner of Main Street where I could steal an hour and pretend the world didn't have sharp edges. And today, it came with lunch and Oz Ramirez, which was about as good as things got lately.

"Seriously, Frankie," Oz said, waving his half-eaten crust for emphasis, "you are killing it. The new time-travel romance display? I walked past your shop window yesterday and I almost blushed."

I grinned around my straw. "That was the goal."

I sipped my iced coffee—blessedly strong, double shot—and leaned my shoulder against his. We sat side by side on one of the weathered benches, an open pizza box on the table in front of us. Oz had charmed Greta into making one of her ridiculous sourdough crust pies, and the results were worth every bit of the guilt I'd feel later.

"You're the one who told me to lean in," I reminded him. "'Own your brand, Bellamy,' remember?"

Oz flapped a hand dramatically. "And look at you now. Tattooed romance goddess who is going to have the cutest bookstore in town. I take full credit."

"You should also take partial credit for me moving here too," I added, nudging his shoulder again. "I still think you sent me that newsletter as part of your whole escape plan for me."

His grin turned soft. "Maybe I did. You needed out of that city. Out of that whole mess."

I glanced away, eyes on the bright line of storefronts across the street. "Yeah. You weren't wrong."

Oz bumped my knee. "And look at you. You've got your store, your sassy mugs, your grumpy neighbor…"

I groaned. "Don't start."

Oz laughed. "I'm just saying. Your comeback arc is looking excellent."

I shook my head but smiled. It was good being here. A little lonely sometimes. And terrifying. But mine. Every inch was mine.

Oz had been an anchor through the worst of it—the divorce, the family fallout, the court mess.

Lunch breaks like this felt like a tiny piece of the life I was fighting to build.

I snagged another slice, about to change the subject—when I heard the bell over the hardware store door across the street jingle. I looked up automatically—and almost choked on my bite.

Beckett strode out into the sunlight, broad shoulders filling out a plain black tee, faded jeans hugging long legs, a brown paper sack tucked under one arm. He didn't look at anyone. Just stalked down the sidewalk like he owned the damn thing, headed home no doubt. Jaw set. Dark hair pushed back from his too-sharp face.

Oz followed my gaze—and grinned. "Well, well. Speak of the devil."

I scowled. "I wasn't speaking."

"But you were thinking, and the universe heard you."

I tore my eyes away. "Nothing to think about. He's impossible."

"Uh huh."

I jabbed my straw into the ice with more force than strictly necessary. "I'm serious. The man is made of scowls and bad moods. And ducks."

Oz leaned his chin on one hand, eyes twinkling. "I am dying to know what's going on there."

"Nothing," I said firmly. "Absolutely nothing."

Oz arched a brow. "You sure? Because your face is very… expressive."

I groaned. "Fuck off, I don't like the man."

He laughed. "Okay, okay. But you do talk about him a lot."

"Because he drives me crazy!"

"Which is very different from being ambivalent."

I cursed softly and yanked a napkin out of the box. "You want to know what he did this week? I'll tell you."

Oz perked up. "Please do."

I slammed my palm lightly onto the table. "He mowed his lawn. At six-thirty in the damn morning. On a Sunday."

Oz blinked. "Oh."

"Right? Who does that? And I had a massive order to unpack Saturday night—I didn't get to bed until two. So there I am, finally sleeping good, and I wake up to the sound of his grumpy ass riding around like it's a NASCAR event."

Oz cackled. "Maybe he's an early riser."

"He's a prick," I grumbled. "And I know he did it on purpose."

Oz's grin widened. "Did he glare at you afterward?"

"He always glares. I don't think his face does anything else."

"Maybe not. But I've heard he looks very good shirtless while cleaning a duck pond."

My cheeks went hot. "You're evil."

"I'm just observant. And so are you, apparently."

"I wasn't spying!"

Oz gave me a look. "You sent me photographic evidence."

I covered my face with one hand. "That was a weak moment."

"A weak moment? Please. You can't honestly tell me that you haven't re-read the text chain about four times." He arched a brow waiting for me to deny it.

I groaned. "I really hate you."

"No, you hate that you don't hate him as much as you want to," Oz said gently.

I froze.

He reached over and tugged my hand down. "Frankie. It's okay."

I swallowed hard. "It's not. I can't… I can't afford that. Not with everything else."

Oz squeezed my fingers. "I get it. I do. But maybe—just maybe—your grumpy neighbor likes you more than he lets on."

I snorted, but it came out shaky. "Yeah, right."

"He got involved with your ex, didn't he?"

My breath caught.

"He was protecting you," Oz said softly. "I heard about it from Greta. Half the town has. It doesn't surprise me though, not really."

I stared at the now-empty pizza box, throat constricted. I hadn't wanted anyone to know. Hadn't even wanted to think about that moment, about the raw fury in Beckett's voice when he'd shoved Chris against the car. About the way my heart had stuttered, not with fear, but with something stupid and warm and terrifying.

"He shouldn't have done that," I whispered. "I didn't ask him to."

"Doesn't mean he didn't want to."

I shook my head. "I can't go there, Oz. Not with him. Not with anyone."

"Look, Beckett was always protective of his sister, Willow. When he lost her, he became someone else. You're good for him, Frankie—even if you don't mean to be." My friend's smile softened. "I'm not saying you should go there. I'm just saying… maybe stop fighting so hard against what's already happening."

I blinked. "What do you mean?"

Oz winked. "You talk about him. You watch him. You care when he does stupid things—or good things."

I opened my mouth to argue—and closed it. Because dammit, he was right. And that scared me more than anything.

Oz's phone buzzed a few minutes later, dragging us both out of our comfortable bubble. He glanced at the screen and winced. "Inventory delivery's early. I gotta run."

I smiled, though it felt a little forced. "Go. Save your precious non-fiction section."

Oz laughed and stood, brushing crumbs off his jeans. "You good?"

"Yeah." I tried for breezy. "Just gonna finish my coffee. Maybe glare at a few more unsuspecting townsfolk."

He squeezed my shoulder. "Text me later. And remember—just because a certain grumpy neighbor makes you crazy doesn't mean you have to hate it."

I rolled my eyes. "Goodbye, Oz." But my voice lacked heat.

He winked. "Goodbye, Frankie."

I watched him jog up the library steps, then picked at the rough wood of the table. The breeze rustled through the leaves above me. Somewhere down the block, Greta was shouting at someone about a pie order. And across the street… no one lingered at the hardware store.

Beckett was gone. But the echo of him lingered in my chest. My pulse hadn't quite settled since Oz's words. *Your grumpy neighbor likes you more than he lets on.*

I wanted to scoff. To shake it off. To text Oz something snarky and stubborn. But when I closed my eyes, all I saw was Beckett —broad and furious, shoving Chris back. His voice a dark growl. His eyes locked on mine like I was the only thing that mattered in the world for that one breathless second.

And beneath the memory, a quieter truth hummed… I didn't hate it. Didn't hate him.

And that scared me more than any ex, any court case, any risk I'd taken yet.

I blew out a shaky breath and sucked up the last of my iced coffee. "Not happening," I whispered to myself. "Can't happen."

But even as I said it, some stubborn part of my heart refused to listen.

Just then, a low quack dragged my gaze sideways. I blinked. "You've got to be kidding me."

Bob.

He waddled across the grass as if he owned the whole damn town, paused beside the picnic table, and looked up at me like he was about to deliver a sermon. My mouth dropped open. "What the hell—do you have a tracker on me or something?"

Bob quacked again and flapped once, entirely unfazed.

I shook my head, laughing despite myself. "I am not talking about this with a duck."

Bob waddled closer and settled beside the bench like a bored therapy animal. I looked around to make sure no one was watching, then leaned down with a sigh. "Did he send you? Is this some Beckett Ford duck-based surveillance scheme?"

He blinked. Twice. Assessing me.

I scoffed. "Don't look at me like that. You saw the cupcakes."

Bob tilted his head.

"Oh, don't play innocent. I bet he *laughed* after I left. You know he did. Probably took a photo. Framed it."

Bob quacked again. Short and smug.

"And don't act like you don't *live* for the drama. You show up every time I'm about to have a meltdown." I pulled out my phone and opened the donation page again. That $250,000 stared back at me like it had teeth. "Tell me he didn't do this. Just say quack if he didn't."

Bob remained silent.

I stared. "That's what I thought."

I rubbed my forehead, anxiety bubbling again. "I should be grateful. I *am* grateful. But… dammit. Why couldn't he just talk to me?"

Bob blinked. Like *You're asking the wrong bird.*

I leaned back with a groan. When I'd gone online and dug into who he was, I had felt like an idiot. I'd grown up in that circle of people but had stuck my head in the sand. Didn't make his donation any less—*irritating.*

"He doesn't do feelings. Just ducks and lawn mowers and turning me into emotional soup."

Bob stood up and waddled in a circle, then stopped like he was ready to charge an hourly fee. "Okay, fine," I muttered. "Maybe I overreacted. A little. But you try living next to a man who could be a Greek god's grumpier cousin and *not* lose your mind—oh, and who may or may not be rich."

Bob quacked. Loud. Rude.

"Exactly." I sighed. "I should do something. Something petty. Something dangerous."

Bob eyed me warily.

I grinned. "Don't worry. No more cupcakes. I was thinking of something more… theatrical. Maybe a glitter bomb in the shape of a duck. Or a commemorative mug that says *Emotionally Constipated Duck Daddy Club*."

Bob waddled closer, nudged my foot.

I leaned down and whispered, "But don't tell him that. It's a surprise."

Bob quacked one more time. Then he turned and waddled off down Main Street like he had errands to run.

I watched him go and shook my head.

Beckett Ford. Duck chaos. Cupcake retaliation. And now, a donation that left me feeling… comforted. Like someone had opened a door in my chest and tossed a blanket over all the sharp, breakable places.

I wasn't sure what came next.

But one thing I did know?

This wasn't over.

Not by a long shot.

CHAPTER 14
DUCK, DUCK... DEPARTURE

BECKETT

I HADN'T MEANT to watch her after I got home from the hardware store. But there I was—sitting on my front porch, half-hidden behind the massive oak tree, eyes fixed on Frankie Bellamy at that damn picnic table in front of the library. The usual sass was gone. She wasn't throwing barbs or flipping her hair in exasperation. She just sat there in the sun, coffee cup in one hand, talking quietly with her friend, looking like the fight had drained right out of her. And that did something to me I wasn't ready to admit.

She looked tired. Not the good kind. Not the earned-it-with-a-day-of-hard-work kind. The other kind. The kind you carry in your bones when everything feels like a fight and the world won't quit swinging. She looked small in a way that twisted something low in my gut. And for a man who prided himself on not giving a damn? That was dangerous ground.

I told myself I wasn't watching. But I didn't move either.

My phone buzzed in my pocket, dragging my attention away. The screen lit up with a contact I hadn't seen in a long time.

Keller Law Group

I hesitated, thumb hovering over the screen. Decided to answer it.

"Yeah?"

"Beckett," Elijah Keller's clipped voice came through. "You need to come to New York."

My stomach dropped. "Why?"

"Maddox is making waves. He's talking to a new round of private investors—trying to position himself as the next big thing in Fintech. And he's starting to throw your name around. There's buzz about a possible countersuit on the IP from the original build."

I paced the porch, blood roaring in my ears. "That won't hold. It's settled."

"It won't hold," my attorney agreed. "But perception isn't about what's real. It's about what people believe. You know that."

I ground my teeth. "Son of a bitch."

"We need you in the city. By tomorrow afternoon. The team's already drafting a counterstrategy."

I exhaled through my nose, every muscle in my jaw tight. "Fine. Text me the brief."

He did soon after he hung up.

I stood up and pocketed my phone, then started pacing like the tension could be walked off. I ended up in the backyard without realizing it, muttering curses under my breath. The pond shimmered in the early evening light, the ducks clustering on the far bank, unaware of the storm clawing up my spine.

I slammed my palm against the nearest fence post, the crack of skin on wood echoing through the yard. Bob squawked, alarmed. I fisted my hair in frustration and tried to pull myself together.

That's when I heard her.

"Everything okay over there, Beckett? Or are you just auditioning for a one-man yelling show? Or maybe Karate?"

I turned toward the gate.

Frankie leaned on a post like she owned the place, arms crossed, mouth curved into a smirk. Her black tee clung to her curves in all the ways I didn't need to notice. Artfully torn jeans, scuffed boots, hair in a messy bun that looked like trouble—and Jesus, I couldn't look away.

I cleared my throat. "Just got an upsetting call… sorry. I didn't mean to disturb you."

She lifted a brow. "I would have guessed, judging by the colorful language. So, not a good call?"

I grunted. "No."

She studied me, head tilting just a little. "You okay?"

Her voice wasn't teasing anymore. It was soft. Real. "I have to take a trip."

That surprised her. I saw it flicker across her face. "You? Traveling?"

I shrugged. "Apparently."

"Where to?"

"New York. Tomorrow morning."

Her brows lifted higher. "Let me guess—fancy tech billionaire business?"

I blinked.

She grinned. "Don't look so shocked. I know who you are, Ford. You didn't exactly scrub your past from the internet. And some of us read more than just blue alien boner books."

That shouldn't have made me laugh, but it did. A short huff. "You've been Googling me."

She grinned. "Only after I suspected you were the one who left me a hefty donation—which you shouldn't have. But we'll come back to that later. So? New York for a few days?"

"Just a meeting. Legal stuff."

She looked toward the pond. "And the ducks?"

That knot in my gut cinched tighter. "I have no idea what to do with them. I could ask one of my brothers to check in on them."

"Well, I've already been babysitting Bob half the time anyway," she said, casual as anything. "I can keep an eye on them."

I stared at her. "You'd do that?"

She shrugged. "Sure. Leave me a key and their food. I'll keep them fed, out of trouble, and away from my bookshelves."

I opened my mouth to say no. But then she smiled—and something in my chest cracked. So instead, I nodded. "Thanks. I'll leave both on the back porch."

She hesitated. Then, softer, "If it's something serious, Beckett, you don't have to deal with it alone… I mean it, don't let it eat you alive."

That hit harder than I wanted it to. Made something under my ribs twist in a way that scared the hell out of me. "I've got it handled."

She held my gaze a beat longer, then nodded slowly. "Call your brothers if you need backup. Especially the firefighter. He looks like he'd enjoy punching someone."

Despite everything, I smiled. "Nate would absolutely volunteer since Caleb isn't around."

"Caleb's another brother?" She raised an eyebrow. "There's *more* of you?"

"Two more. Caleb and Jamie."

"Hmm." She turned to go, then paused halfway down the driveway. Over her shoulder, she called, "Hey Ford?"

"Yeah?"

"Try not to punch anyone in a suit. Unless they really deserve it."

I watched her as she continued walking. Sunlight caught in her hair like fire and god help me—I didn't want to look away. So I didn't. I watched her until she disappeared around the bend of her driveway, the tail end of her hair still catching sunlight like copper sparks.

I told myself to move. Told myself to breathe. But my feet stayed planted, my chest constricted. *Don't let it eat you alive.*

Too late.

It had been eating at me for years now. From the second Daniel stabbed me in the back, from the first headline that called me unstable, reckless, broken. And now the bastard was trying to drag me back under all over again.

I exhaled hard and pushed off the post, stalking back inside.

The house felt colder than it had an hour ago. The shadows stretched long across the floorboards. I paced to the office, yanked my laptop open again. The court briefing Keller had e-mailed sat in my inbox, blinking like an accusation.

I clicked it open, skimming fast. New investors. New press buzz. Potential attempts to reframe the narrative.

I clenched my jaw so hard my teeth ached.

Reframing the narrative—that was lawyer-speak for smearing me again. For dragging the truth through the mud until no one could tell what the hell had happened.

It didn't matter that the acquisition had been clean. Because Daniel didn't want peace. Daniel wanted the damn headlines—wanted to win the public game.

And if I didn't fight back now, I'd lose what little quiet I had left. This trip wasn't optional. I took a deep breath and made a flight reservation for tomorrow morning.

You can't stay off the radar forever. The words he'd thrown at me echoed like a curse. I shut the laptop with more force than necessary.

I dragged both hands through my hair, pacing the first floor, mind racing. Then—instinctively—my gaze drifted toward the window that looked out on Frankie's house.

The light had come on in her front room. A soft, warm glow against the deepening dusk.

I wondered what she was doing. If she'd already regretted offering to watch the ducks. If she'd meant what she'd said—that I didn't have to let this thing eat me alive. And why the hell did it matter that she'd said it?

Why did it stick harder than anything Daniel or my own attorney had thrown at me?

I swore softly and forced myself into motion. My clothes wouldn't pack themselves.

I stalked to the bedroom, grabbed a duffel, tossed it on the bed. Jeans. Shirts. Nothing fancy. I hadn't worn a suit since the last court date and had no plans to start now.

Halfway through folding a flannel, I caught myself hesitating. *I'll be back soon.*

I hoped that was true. But with Daniel involved, nothing was ever clean. The thought made my pulse kick harder again. I zipped the bag shut with a grim breath, then headed for the back door.

I owed the ducks a check-in. And hell—it would ground me. Something normal. Something real. The pond glistened soft and silver under the first stars. The air smelled like damp earth and grass.

Bob waddled over first, quacking indignantly. I crouched low, running a hand over his slick feathers. "I know, buddy. I didn't mean to freak you guys out."

Bob nipped lightly at my sleeve, beady eyes bright.

I exhaled a shaky laugh. "She's right about one thing. I don't leave the pond much." I glanced toward Frankie's house again, voice going lower. "Don't know why the hell it matters that I am this time."

Bob quacked in reply—a soft, almost scolding sound. "Yeah," I murmured. "I know."

Willow paddled closer, her feathers gleaming bronze under the moonlight. She'd always been the calmest of the flock—the one who settled next to me when the world spun too fast. I reached out, fingertips brushing her back. "You'll behave for her, won't you?"

Willow blinked slowly.

I sat back on my heels, gaze drifting over the pond.

It was stupid, really. How attached I'd become to this damn place. To the ducks. To the quiet. And now—to the woman next door who drove me crazy and made me want things I had no business wanting.

You don't have to deal with it alone. The thought echoed in my head.

Maybe not.

But that was the only way I knew.

A soft quack pulled me back. Bob had settled beside me, Willow flanking the other side. I sighed. "You two better be on your best behavior while I'm gone. No jailbreaks. No bookstore invasions."

Another quack. Slightly smug this time. I shook my head, a faint smile tugging despite myself. Then I rose slowly, lingering one last moment as the ducks drifted back into the water.

The house behind me stood silent, my duffel just inside the back door, ready for my crack of dawn departure tomorrow.

And still, I turned and my gaze slid once more toward the faint glow in Frankie's front window.

I won't be gone long, I reminded myself. But for the first time in a long time, I wasn't sure if everything would be the same when I came home.

Wanting something was dangerous.

Wanting her? Even worse. And still, as I headed inside to my bedroom and shut the door, the thought refused to let go.

CHAPTER 15
A DUCK, A THREAT, AND ONE SHIRTLESS LIBRARIAN

FRANKIE

IT HAD BEEN two days since Beckett left town. Two days of unusually quiet mornings and a weird, unspoken sense of… absence. I hadn't expected it to get to me. The man drove me insane. His glares. His voice. The way he loomed, all scowls and broad shoulders and maddening restraint. I'd told myself that I'd enjoy the break—take back my damn porch, my damn fence line, my damn sanity.

And yet.

The first day had been fine… mostly, despite having to gather duck eggs to keep out predators from the backyard. I hadn't realized how many damn eggs a duck laid until I had to gather them for Beckett, which also led me to wonder what he did with all of them.

By the second day, his absence sat heavier. Not that I'd admit it aloud. To anyone. Not even to Oz, who would smirk and lean into it with his whole damn chest.

So when I heard a faint tapping sound that morning—soft and

rhythmic—coming from the living room, my first thought was that I'd finally lost it.

Then came the telltale sound of webbed feet on hardwood.

"Bob, if that's you, so help me—"

I walked out of the kitchen and stopped dead. It was not Bob—instead I was looking at Willow. The calmest, quietest duck of Beckett's odd little flock. Willow stood in the middle of my living room, feathers pristine, soft eyes scanning the space as though she'd been invited in for tea.

I blinked. "How the hell…?"

The back door was closed. The windows were latched. No sign of feathers or footprints through the entryway. My gaze narrowed.

"Bob."

Of course. That little feathered menace had probably staged a jailbreak, herded poor Willow through some secret duck tunnel he'd constructed under the fence or beneath the porch.

I crouched slowly, voice soft. "Hey, sweetheart. You lost?"

Willow blinked, head tilting. Something in my chest melted, a warmth I hadn't expected. "Alright, you can stay for a minute. But only because you have better manners than your ringleader."

Willow quacked softly, almost a hum.

I huffed a laugh and glanced at the mixing bowl on the counter. I'd already started a batch of cookies—something I hadn't done in years. Not since the divorce, when the act of baking, of creating anything soft and sweet, had felt pointless.

But today… today it had felt good to crack eggs, measure sugar, lose myself in the familiar motions. Like taking back a piece of something I'd forgotten I loved.

"Tell anyone I'm making chocolate chip and I'll deny it," I warned Willow, moving back to the kitchen.

The duck followed me, waddling across the hardwood with surprising grace. I preheated the oven, fingers moving on instinct, mind finally settling into something almost calm.

Until my phone buzzed with an incoming message. I glanced at it, smiling absently—expecting Oz, or maybe Tess—or hell, maybe even Beckett checking on his ducks since the man had left his number like these were his children and I was the nanny he'd begrudgingly left in charge of them.

My breath caught.

A chill crawled up my spine as I opened the text.

Unknown number: You think I'm done? Think again. Should've stayed where you belong.

My hands shook. For a long moment, I stood frozen, phone clenched in my hand. The words burned through my chest, sour and sharp and far too familiar.

"Son of a bitch," I whispered.

Willow quacked softly behind me, a grounding presence. I swallowed hard, forced my fingers to move.

Frankie: Hey. Need to talk. Urgent. Can you call?

Tess: Two mins. Hold tight.

By the time Tess's face appeared on the screen, I'd moved to the back step, door cracked open, Willow at my side like a tiny, feathery bodyguard.

"Frankie, what's wrong?" Tess asked, voice sharp.

My throat worked. "It's Chris. I'm pretty sure the text I just got was from him."

"The bastard." Tess exhaled hard. "What'd it say?"

I read the text aloud, voice shaking more than I liked.

Tess's anger was palpable, even from this distance. "You need to send that to your attorney."

"I know."

"Today, Frankie."

"I will. I just—"

Tess's voice softened. "You okay?"

I blinked fast, throat thick. "No. But I'm breathing."

"You're stronger than him. And you're not alone."

I scrubbed my hand down. "Thanks, Tess."

"Call your lawyer. Then call me. You hear me?"

"Yeah."

"Love you, babe."

"Love you too."

The call ended. I sat for a long moment, the phone pressed to my knee, breath shaking. A soft quack drew me back. Willow, watching me with gentle eyes. I swallowed hard. "Thanks, sweet girl."

I stood, gathering myself. One thing at a time. Attorney first. Then maybe… finish those damn cookies. Take back my damn day.

Except—

A chorus of quacks hit my ears.

I stiffened. Stepped onto the porch and stared. The entire duck flock had invaded my yard. Bob led the charge, strutting proudly near the herb beds. The others followed in a chaotic procession of flapping wings and gleeful noise.

My jaw dropped. "You little criminals."

A quick scan revealed the culprit—a board pushed loose at the base of the shared fence.

"Of course." I grabbed my phone again, knowing Oz was off work, and fired off a text.

> Frankie: Oz. Emergency. Duck invasion. Bring tools.

> Oz: Be there in ten.

By the time he arrived, toolbox in one hand, tank top sticking to his chest from the heat, I had wrangled the ducks into a semi-circle using a broom, a bucket, and sheer force of will.

Oz took one look at the scene and burst out laughing. "You are the Duck Queen," he declared.

"I swear to god, if you take a picture—"

"Too late." He snapped one and sent it to Tess. "She'll want evidence."

I groaned. "Help me patch the fence before they overrun my entire property."

We worked in tandem—Oz hammering the board back into place and securing the neighboring boards, and me wrangling ducks and tossing the occasional glare at Bob. At some point Oz had taken off his shirt, complaining that manual labor was not his forte and that I'd owe him my first born for the torture of helping me.

About halfway through repairs, I tried climbing over the fence to adjust a loose top rail.

Oz called, "Careful, Frankie—"

Too late. My foot slipped. I pitched forward.

Oz caught me around the waist just as my foot slipped off the top rail. His arms wrapped around me fast and firm, and I landed chest-first against him with an awkward yelp, fingers clutching the back of his arms for balance. My heart was already hammering when I looked up—only for my gaze to lock not on Oz's warm eyes but on eyes with a completely different kind of impact.

"What in the fuck is going on?"

Beckett's voice sliced through the yard—low, rough, and unmistakably dangerous.

I froze. So did Oz.

There Beckett stood, duffel slung over one shoulder, boots still dusty from the road, jaw ticking, a storm brewing behind his eyes. The wind caught his shirt just enough to outline every inch of tension coiled beneath it—broad chest rising, muscles locked so tight I swore I could feel the pulse of them from six feet away.

And he wasn't looking at Oz. He was looking at *me*. Like I'd just gut-punched him. Like the sight of me in another man's arms was both a crime and a betrayal.

My breath stuttered.

Oz, still clueless, helped me to my feet and grinned. "She's fine. Just clumsy today."

Beckett's eyes didn't leave mine. Something shifted behind them—hotter now, darker. Possessive and furious and far too quiet. It made something deep inside me twist.

"I see the flock's been busy," he said, voice clipped.

I swallowed, trying to find my footing in every possible way. "Fence had a loose board. Bob led a jailbreak."

Beckett's gaze finally slid to Oz. A brief flick. Then back to me.

I could feel the anger rolling off him in waves. The weight of his stare crawled over my skin like wildfire, scorching in its intensity.

Oz, still oblivious, wiped sweat from his brow, slipped on his shirt that'd been tucked in his back pocket, and offered a casual shrug. "I was just patching it up. Your girl here's got a hell of a left hook with a hammer."

Your girl.

Beckett flinched like the words physically hit him, and my entire body seized at the ripple that crossed his face—anger, confusion, something unspoken. His hand choked the strap of his bag. His eyes flashed.

"She's not—" he started, then stopped himself.

I jumped in fast, stomach churning. "You know Oz, don't you? He and I went to college together. He's one of my best friends… more like my *brother*." The explanation came out too fast, too defensive. I hated how desperate it sounded—but I couldn't stop the tumble of words. "He's just—he's been helping."

Beckett's eyes stayed locked on me. And in that look, something burned hot and raw and barely restrained. It wasn't a glare. It wasn't anger.

It was *territorial*.

Like he wanted to push Oz away from me. Like he already had a list of things to say and do that would leave no room for doubt. And god help me—my knees nearly buckled from it.

I crossed my arms to hide the way my fingers trembled. "Nice of you to show up. I've been running duck daycare for forty-eight hours straight."

His mouth curved. Not quite a smile. Something slower. More dangerous.

"Guess I owe you."

My breath caught at the rasp of his voice—just gravel and heat and something that teased too close to a promise.

I lifted my chin, faking a confidence I didn't feel. "You don't owe me a thing."

And then we stood there—just *stood* there—trapped in a current neither of us wanted to break. His stare dragged down my face, from my eyes to my mouth, lingered there for a breath too long. My lips tingled. My pulse pounded in my throat, my ears, between my thighs—in every forgotten place, traitorous and wanting and infuriating.

Oz, thankfully or not, broke it. "Fence should hold for now."

Beckett blinked like someone had snapped their fingers in front of his face. "I'll finish it later," he said, turning away, but not before I saw it—the hardening of his jaw, the stiffening of his shoulders.

He didn't say goodbye. Just stalked into the house like it hurt to stay outside. I stood frozen, heart in my throat, chest heaving like I'd run ten miles.

Oz nudged me gently. "You okay?"

I stared at Beckett's closed door. My skin still burned from where his eyes had landed. My brain still echoed with the way he'd said not a damn thing and yet somehow told me everything.

"No," I whispered. "And also… maybe?"

Oz let out a slow laugh. "Oh, Bellamy. You are *so* screwed."

I let my arms fall to my sides, fingers still tingling. "Yeah," I breathed. "I really fucking am."

And for the first time in a long time, I didn't know if I wanted to run from that truth… or fall headfirst into it.

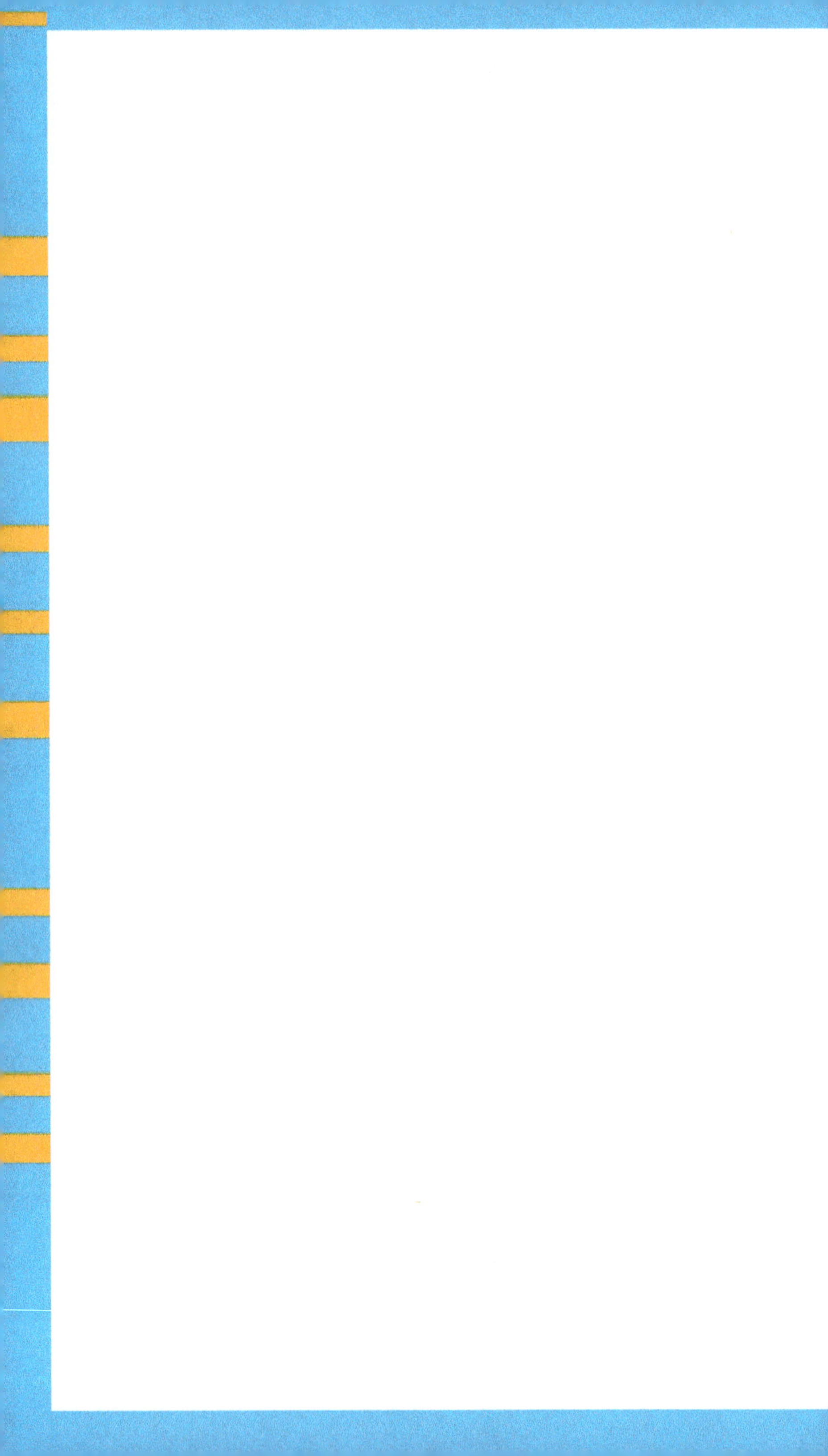

CHAPTER 16
DUCK, DUCK...
BROS BEFORE NOSY

BECKETT

I DIDN'T PLAN on ending up at Hank's usual watering hole, The Rusty Tap, but after the way Frankie had looked at me when I got home—all flushed cheeks, ruffled clothes, and the unmistakable twist of guilt behind her eyes—I needed noise. Something to cut through the echo of that moment. Something that didn't look like her body pressed against another man.

When I'd texted Hank to let him know I was back, he'd apparently read between the lines of and sent a terse response.

> Hank: Get your ass here. You need whiskey or to get laid.

Both, honestly.

The place smelled like old beer, grease from the fryer, and the faint trace of lemon cleaner that never quite covered the scent of regret. Neon signs buzzed lazily above the bar, casting everything in the soft glow of blues and reds. The floor had a permanent stickiness to it, the kind that made your boots hesitate with every step, and the jukebox in the corner hummed a country song that sounded more heartbreak than melody.

I found them near the back—Jamie already halfway into a beer, cap pulled low like he still thought he was avoiding cameras. Nate lounged across from him, long legs kicked out, firefighter hoodie sleeves shoved up, his calloused fingers drumming on the table. Hank looked like he hadn't moved since the bar opened.

"Look what the ducks dragged in," Jamie said, eyeing me with a grin.

"You smell like your pond and bad decisions," Nate added, wrinkling his nose. "That, or you wrestled Bob again."

"If it was Bob, I'd be bleeding," I muttered, sliding into the empty chair. The old wood creaked beneath me.

"You look like you lost a fight with a lawnmower," Hank observed, passing me a full glass of whiskey.

"Fence," I said. "Again."

"Ah," Jamie said, drawing the word out like he was savoring it. "So what really happened? Because that face isn't about splinters."

"It's nothing," I said, lifting the glass. The whiskey burned the whole way down, but not enough to drown the image of Frankie in someone else's arms.

"Uh-huh," Nate said. "That's your 'absolutely something' voice."

Jamie leaned forward, eyes narrowing. "Let me guess. You got back from New York and found your neighbor all tangled up with another man."

My jaw ticked.

"Holy shit," Jamie said. "That's it, isn't it?"

"Oz," I muttered. "Ramirez. He was fixing the fence. She slipped. He caught her."

"Caught her," Nate repeated, dragging the syllables like they tasted sweet. "Did he also whisper sweet nothings in her ear while flexing his biceps?"

"Jesus," I growled.

"I mean, he *does* work out," Jamie said helpfully. "He's got librarian forearms."

"What the hell are librarian forearms?"

"The kind that can shelve the Kama Sutra on the top damn shelf," Nate said, laughing.

"They weren't *doing* anything," I snapped. "He just caught her. It just… looked worse than it was."

"And you didn't like that one bit," Jamie said, eyes gleaming. "Face it, man. You care."

"I do *not.* She drives me crazy. She talks too much. She always smells like vanilla and coffee and insists on putting tiny scarves on my ducks."

"So," Hank said calmly, "you're saying the woman who smells like your favorite things, looks like a walking wet dream, and keeps charming your animals is *not* the reason you look like a kicked puppy?"

"Exactly," I bit out.

"Mhm," Nate said, nodding sagely. "Totally believable. And the fact that you probably could've turned Oz into mulch with your eyes was just… indigestion?"

"It's not like that."

"It's *exactly* like that," Jamie said. "You're not just nuts. You're nuts in love."

"No," I insisted. "She's chaos. She blasts 90s pop at seven a.m., she argues with my ducks like they understand, and she wore a shirt the other day that said *Talk Ducky to Me*."

"You remember what she was wearing?" Nate asked, grinning.

"It was *obnoxious*."

"Sure," Jamie said. "Obnoxiously cute. Admit it, Ford. You're gone. Done. Cooked. That woman has you by the beard."

I sank lower in my chair.

"She deserves better," I mumbled. "I can't even be honest with her. I've been hiding the money. The donation. Everything about me. Although she's figured some of it out."

Hank gave me a look. "So tell her the rest of it. You think she can't handle a grumpy billionaire with a duck obsession? You underestimate her."

"Or overestimate myself."

"Willow wouldn't have let you get away with this level of stupid," Jamie said.

That one hit deep. I tipped my head back and stared at the ceiling.

"She'd have dragged your ass next door with cookies and duct tape," Nate added. "Probably tied a bow on your beard and called it a love offering."

"She always said I'd fall hard." My voice was hoarse. "That I'd fight it. But I'd know it when it hit."

"Maybe this is it," Jamie said. "Maybe she's the one that's supposed to shake your world up. God knows you've been coasting for too long."

I stayed quiet, letting the clink of bottles and the low hum of conversation swirl around us. Someone dropped coins into the jukebox. Johnny Cash. Fitting.

"You went to New York to put out fires," Hank said, his voice quieter now. "But that's not the only reason you look like a man who forgot how to breathe."

"It stirred up everything I left behind," I admitted. "All the reasons I walked away. The press. The betrayal. The way people looked at me like I was a product, not a person."

"And yet," Nate said, "you came back here looking like the only thing you wanted to protect was her."

I blinked hard.

Jamie smirked. "It's like someone handed you the last missing piece and you don't know where it goes, but you know you'll never be the same without it."

"She makes everything loud," I said quietly. "The quiet I built… it doesn't work when she's around."

"Maybe that's the point," Hank said. "Maybe it was never meant to stay quiet."

Jamie raised his glass in a mock salute. "One thing is certain. Your twin would be cackling her ass off right now."

"And to Frankie," Nate added. "Who might just save your dumb ass if you let her."

We drank.

And when I stepped outside into the humid summer night, the air thick with honeysuckle and possibility, I let myself breathe. Really breathe. The kind that made your chest ache and your heart whisper, *Go.*

By the time I pulled into my driveway, the slight buzz from the beer had dulled, replaced by something sharper. Something restless. Something that clawed up from deep inside and settled behind my ribs like a weight.

Frankie's porch light was still on.

The rest of the street was asleep, wrapped in silence and shadows. Moths danced under her light like they were drawn to more than just the glow—maybe it was the warmth. The welcome. The steady hum of life that never quite went silent in her space.

I cut the engine but didn't move. Just sat there, staring at the soft halos spilling through her windows. A silhouette moved past once. Slow. Barefoot, probably. She always kicked off her shoes the second she went inside, like she was allergic to anything that felt like structure. Probably had one of those oversized mugs in her hand. The one that said "Plot Twist: I Like You." I hated how I remembered that.

I blew out a frustrated breath and clenched my fist.

Was she alone?

The question sank low, settling in the pit of my stomach like regret.

Was Oz still in there? Had he stayed after the fence repair, after catching her, after standing where I should've been? Was he in her kitchen, drinking her tea, smiling at her with that easy, open charm that didn't come with baggage or secrets or the kind of silence that made people uncomfortable?

Did she laugh with him? Did she lean into his touch like it made sense?

My chest cracked like it had a damn fault line.

I wasn't like him. I didn't flirt well. I didn't shine in crowds. I didn't fit easily into people's lives. Hell, I barely fit into my own half the time.

She deserved someone who knew how to show up. And all I'd done since the day we met was keep my distance and build walls taller than the fence Bob kept escaping from.

So why did the idea of her choosing someone else feel like suffocating?

She passed by the window again. This time, I caught a better look—hair loose, oversized shirt sliding off one shoulder, book in hand. She was reading. Probably going to curl up sideways on the couch like she always did, legs tucked under her, brow furrowed in concentration. Her lips moved when she read sometimes. I'd noticed that once when she was out back in the sun reading, and now I couldn't unsee it.

I stared harder, relieved when I realized she was alone.

That relief felt ugly. Undeserved. My shoulders sagged like I'd been holding up the world.

I could go over. Just knock. Just… be honest. Tell her everything. About the money. About the stupid LLC. About why I left New York and why I'd stayed gone. About how she made me feel things I didn't think I had left in me.

But I didn't.

I stayed in the truck, fingers clenched around the wheel like it was the only thing keeping me upright.

Because wanting her? That was easy.

Admitting I wasn't sure I was enough? That I didn't know how to *be* enough? That was the part that scared the hell out of me.

So I stayed in the dark.

While she glowed.

CHAPTER 17
FEATHERS AND FURY

FRANKIE

THREE DAYS before the grand opening of Shelf Love, I felt like I could explode with nerves and excitement all at the same time.

The final details were falling into place. The new signage gleamed in the summer sun. My best window display yet shimmered with fairy lights, spines of lush new releases stacked like tiny treasures. Inside, the air hummed with the scent of fresh books and warm sugar cookies, an intoxicating promise of good tomorrows.

I should have been riding that high. Instead, my stomach was a clenched fist of dread.

The texts from the number I was sure belonged to Chris had started again—short, slick threats, each one more venomous than the last. Demands for what he said I owed. Every buzz of my phone sent another cold wave through me. And I hadn't told Oz or Tess about them, about how they were increasingly hateful, nor had I told my attorney yet.

Now, with my shop—the dream I'd clawed into existence—set to open in mere days, the weight in my gut refused to lift.

But I wouldn't let him take this from me.

I scrubbed the front counter until it gleamed. Rearranged the influencer welcome baskets for the fifth time. Adjusted displays that didn't need adjusting. Fake it 'til you make it. Or at least 'til you survive the damn day.

When the knock came, sharp and unexpected, I wiped my hands on my jeans and padded to the door, expecting Oz or a delivery.

The moment I swung it open, my heart stopped cold.

Chris.

He lounged against the frame like he owned it—tailored slacks, pressed polo, a smug gleam in his sharp blue eyes. His smile was oil-slicked, dangerous. Too polished for this town. Too slick for my porch.

"Hello, Francesca." The words oozed from his mouth.

Every muscle in my body tensed. "Don't call me that."

A smirk. "Fine. Frankie. Though it makes you sound like trailer trash."

"What do you want?" My voice was steel. One hand braced the frame, the other curled into a fist so tight my nails bit skin.

Chris's gaze drifted lazily past me, into the house. "I hear you've got yourself a big party coming up. Grand opening, is it? Congrats." Without invitation, he pushed past me and stepped inside.

My pulse jumped. "Get to the point. You're not welcome here."

He leaned in, voice low. "If you want that little fairy tale to stay intact, you'll pay me what I'm owed."

My mouth went dry. "You're owed nothing."

A cold chuckle. "Sweetheart, that inheritance came while we were married. You really think that's yours alone?"

"It was my grandmother's wish. She left it to me and me alone. You lost in court, so I don't get why you're here now." My voice rose. "You have no claim."

His expression darkened. "You think a judge will stop me from getting what I deserve? One call to the right people and your shop burns down before it even opens."

My heart pounded so hard I was sure he could hear it. "You think that scares me?" I spat. "I built this life without you. I'll burn it down myself before I give you another cent."

His grin twisted. "Always so dramatic."

"And you're always a parasite."

The room shrank to the two of us—voices sharp, ricocheting off the walls. Tension so high it hummed in the air.

And then—Bob.

The duck waddled in like a tiny, feathered enforcer, wings puffed wide, eyes blazing. A sharp quack echoed through the room as he flapped toward Chris's loafers.

I startled. "Bob, no——"

Chris's lip curled. "What the hell is this?" With a sneer, he lashed out. His foot struck Bob's side—hard. The small body flew, hit the floor with a sickening thud, and lay still.

Time fractured. A roar filled my ears. Blood pounded in my skull. Without thought, without breath, I launched forward.

My fist connected with Chris's nose—*crack*—pain lancing through my entire arm. I barely felt it through the wildfire of fury consuming me.

Chris staggered back, blood streaming between his fingers. "You psycho bitch!" he gasped as he hunched forward. "You'll regret this."

I stood over him, trembling, rage painting my vision red. "Touch him again and I swear I'll break more than your nose."

He straightened and backed toward the door, eyes narrowed. "You just screwed yourself," he hissed. Then he was gone—door slamming in his wake.

The room shuddered in the aftermath and several nearby books tumbled off the shelf closest to the door.

I spun. "Bob!" I dropped to my knees, gathering the limp duck into shaking arms. Tears blurred my sight. "Come on, baby. Come on. Please."

Bob's eyes fluttered weakly—one shallow breath—but he lay unmoving. My throat closed. My hand throbbed—likely broken—but none of it mattered. Only Bob mattered. Cradling him to my chest, I bolted from the house. Main Street blurred beneath my feet. My breath came in ragged gasps, tears hot on my cheeks. Bob's weight was terrifyingly light against me.

"Please, please, please." The words spilled from my lips in a loop broken only by my sobs.

Shadows of passersby flickered at the edges of my vision, faces turning—but I saw none of them. Just the duck. Just the echo of Chris's venom in my ears.

"You're gonna regret this."

"Frankie!" A voice sliced through the fog—sharp, familiar.

I stumbled to a halt.

Beckett.

He stood on the sidewalk outside the hardware store, bag abandoned to the sidewalk. His storm-gray gaze locked on me, then dropped to Bob. The calm I'd so often resented him for cracked. "Jesus Christ." His voice rasped. "Is he alive?"

My throat worked—no sound. Just a sob.

Beckett was already moving. Two long strides, closing the distance. "Give him to me."

I shook my head, clutching Bob closer to my heart. "He—Chris —he kicked—he—"

"Frankie." His voice dropped, low and rough. "I can't help him if you don't let go."

My arms trembled. Every instinct screamed to hold on. "I—"

"I've got him." His tone was gentle but brooked no argument.

Carefully, his hands brushed mine, coaxed the small, feathered body from my grip. The loss made me sway. Beckett cradled Bob close as he turned and strode toward the vet clinic.

I stumbled after him, breath burning, feet heavy against the concrete. The world shrank to Beckett's broad back and the fragile bundle in his arms. My voice fractured as I continued my desperate prayer. *Please, please, please.*

The clinic door banged open under Beckett's shoulder. "I need help!" His voice rang out, sharp as a whip. A blur of movement

—voices, hands. I hovered on the threshold, unable to move, unable to think.

Beckett and Bob disappeared beyond swinging doors.

And I stood there—arms empty, lungs fluttering, heart in splinters. My hand throbbed, hot and swollen—I must have hit Chris harder than I'd thought—but I didn't care. Bob's limp body haunted my vision. And Beckett… the way he'd looked at me—eyes full of something I couldn't bear to face.

I had to leave. Now.

Spinning on my heel, cradling my injured hand, I fled.

I'd barely made it a block before a voice cut through my haze.

"Frankie!"

I staggered to a stop as Oz jogged toward me, having just emerged from the library across the street. Someone must've told him—his face was painted with worry.

"What the hell happened? Someone said you ran past with Bob —crying."

I tried to speak. The words came out in broken gasps. "Chris— he was at the house—he—Bob—he kicked him—" My voice cracked beneath the sobs. "Beckett has him. He's—at the vet—"

Oz's expression darkened, his jaw flexing. Then his gaze flicked to my trembling, swollen hand cradled against my chest. "Jesus, Frankie. Is that broken?"

"I don't know," I whispered, throat raw.

Oz gently took my elbow. "You're going to the ER. Now."

"I can't—I need to be—I—"

"Frankie." His tone left no room for argument. "You can't help Bob if you're falling apart. Let Beckett handle him. You need to get checked out."

Tears spilled again, but this time I nodded, defeated. "Okay. Okay."

Oz didn't let go of me as we started toward his car. And as the adrenaline faded, the pain in my hand roared to life.

CHAPTER 18
BENEATH THE WILLOW FEATHERS

BECKETT

I PACED the narrow strip of tile outside the exam room, arms crossed over my chest, heart still hammering from the sprint down Main Street. Haunted by the memory of the duck's small body against me—too limp, too still. And Frankie's face… wide-eyed and tear-streaked.

Where the hell was the vet?

The vet had been inside with Bob for nearly twenty minutes now, and every second of the wait had made my heart hammer harder against my ribs. I shouldn't be here. Shouldn't be this tied up over a duck.

But the second I'd seen Frankie running down Main Street, eyes wild, clutching that limp little body against her chest—shaking, gasping, half falling apart—something had cracked wide open inside me.

And once it started cracking, it hadn't stopped.

"Mr. Ford?" My head snapped up.

Dr. Langley stood in the doorway, wiping her hands on a towel, her expression tired but faintly smiling. "Bob's going to be okay."

I exhaled a long breath I hadn't realized I was holding. It punched out of me like I'd been underwater too long.

Dr. Langley continued, voice gentle. "There's no internal damage and nothing's broken. We've sedated him—he'll need rest, warmth, and quiet for a few days, but he should recover fully."

My throat worked. "Thank you."

She nodded. "You can pick him up tomorrow. We'll keep him monitored overnight."

I nodded once, slowly. I should have felt nothing but relief. And part of me did—a massive weight lifting off my chest. But the bigger part couldn't stop replaying the other half of the morning.

Frankie's face. Her panic. The bruises blooming under her eyes from crying too hard. The tremble in her hands. I hadn't seen her since we'd rushed into the clinic. She'd been right behind me—I remembered that much—but somewhere in the blur of techs and voices, she'd vanished.

I moved out to the front desk. The lobby was mostly empty now, a few people lingering with nervous dogs or cat carriers. But Frankie wasn't there waiting. My chest constricted.

I stepped up to the desk. "A woman was with me—did you see where she went?"

The receptionist looked up from her computer. "Oh—she left a while ago."

My pulse kicked. "Did she say anything?"

"Just that she needed to go. She looked… really shaken."

I muttered a rough thanks and strode out into the street. The sun was bright and too hot, glaring against the pavement. I scanned the sidewalk, half hoping I'd spot her.

Nothing.

I turned, stalking toward home. That's when a familiar voice called out. "Beckett?"

I looked up to find Kevin, husband to Joey who ran Steam & Bean, leaning against the front of the coffee shop, an iced drink in one hand.

I crossed toward him fast. "Kevin—you see Frankie by chance?"

Kevin nodded. "Yeah. About thirty or so minutes ago. She was crying pretty hard. Looked like hell. Oz helped her into his car, and they drove off."

My jaw locked. "Which way?"

Kevin pointed toward the highway. "I'm not sure."

My stomach turned. "Thanks," I said shortly, already moving.

I didn't waste time. At home, I grabbed my phone the second I hit the door. My hands shook more than I wanted to admit.

"Hank." My voice came low and rough when my brother picked up.

"You're calling about your girl, aren't you?"

I scoffed. "She's not my girl, but yeah… wait—how'd you know?"

Hank exhaled. "Yeah. Saw Oz and her about ten minutes ago—over at the ER. Something about her hand being busted up. I didn't get a chance to dig more because I was picking up a drunk."

I swore under my breath. "She tell you what happened?"

"Nah," Hank said quietly. "Don't know the details. But she's in good hands."

"She said 'Chris' and 'kicked' when I saw her. He must have kicked Bob… Do you suppose she punched him?" My grip tightened on the counter until my knuckles went white.

"Shit, you serious?" Hank's voice turned deadly. "You need me to—"

"I'll handle it." I disconnected the call.

I stood in the kitchen for a long moment, heart thudding. She'd been hurt. And she hadn't told me. Hadn't even stayed at the clinic. Just vanished into the street like a ghost.

It wasn't about the damn jealousy anymore.

It was about her.

About the way she'd looked holding Bob like her heart was breaking. About the way she hadn't stopped shaking. About the fact that she was probably sitting in a hospital room now, with another man, while I stood here doing nothing.

I scrubbed a hand over my face. Forced myself to move.

Out back, I checked the pen automatically. The ducks clustered near the pond, flapping and quacking in the heat.

Except one. Willow was missing. My pulse jumped. I checked the fence. No gap. No sign of a break. Then I caught the faintest trail of feathers across the grass—small, pale ones that could only belong to her.

My gut twisted. I followed them, moving fast across the shared yard. Toward Frankie's porch. And there she was. Willow sat in one of Frankie's porch chairs, small and calm, feathers fluffed, beady eyes watching the street. Like she was waiting.

My breath caught. The porch was empty. The house was dark. But Willow stayed, sitting perfectly still waiting for Frankie.

Something cracked in my chest. I crouched slowly, my voice rough. "Hey, girl." Willow blinked at me but didn't move.

I reached out carefully, hands steady. When I scooped her up, she came willingly—no flapping, no fight. Just a soft, weary sound in her throat. I sat down in the chair beside hers, Willow tucked against my chest.

And I waited.

Because if Willow could sit here in the heat and hope that Frankie would come back—then goddamn it, so could I. I wasn't going anywhere.

Hours later, the sun had dropped lower, and heat was bleeding from the air. Main Street was quieter, shadows stretching long across the storefronts. I hadn't moved from the chair on Frankie's porch, Willow had remained tucked warm and quiet in my lap, and our gazes stayed fixed on the street.

Still no sign of her.

I shifted once, rubbed a hand gently along Willow's back. The small duck pressed closer, her faint heartbeat fluttering beneath my palm.

"You're not the only one waiting, sweetheart," I murmured.

The sound of tires on gravel finally cut through the stillness. I looked up as Oz's car pulled into the drive, slowing near the curb.

I stood, Willow tucked carefully against my chest. Oz got out first. Came around to the passenger side. My breath caught when he opened the door.

Frankie.

She looked pale, lips pressed firmly together, shoulders locked like she was holding herself together by sheer force of will. A bright pink cast covered her right hand, fingers sticking out stiff and swollen.

My gut twisted.

She barely glanced toward the porch. Didn't meet my eyes. Just shouldered past Oz's careful grip and stalked toward the door. Willow gave a soft sound. I held her a little more snugly.

Frankie's gaze flicked once toward me—fast, sharp as she moved past me. She vanished inside, door clicking shut behind her before I had a chance to speak. Oz lingered by the car for a long beat, then crossed toward the porch. I stayed where I was, Willow still in my arms.

Oz leaned against the railing, arms crossed. He studied me with a protective look that made me squirm. "So," Oz said finally. "You gonna tell me what you're doing here?"

I looked down at Willow, then back up. "Waiting."

"For her?"

I bit the inside of my cheek before answering, "Yeah."

Oz exhaled slow. "Look, man… I'm not here to cockblock anything. But you need to know—she's been through hell. More than you probably realize."

I nodded once. "I know enough."

Oz's gaze sharpened. "Then don't play with her. Don't push in if you're not damn sure about it. Because that ex? He gutted her. And she's only just starting to put herself back together."

I met his eyes. "I'm not playing."

Oz held my stare a beat longer. "You sure?"

"Yeah," I said quietly. "I don't know what the hell this is yet. But I know she's under my skin. And I know I'm done standing back pretending she's not."

Oz's mouth twitched. "You're either brave or stupid."

"Both," I said flatly. "But I'm not walking away."

Oz nodded slowly, a flicker of respect in his eyes. "Well," he said, straightening. "Good luck. You'll need it." My brow lifted as Oz grinned faintly. "Frankie's a ball buster. You want in? You better be ready to earn it."

I gave a faint smile. "I plan to."

Oz pushed off the rail. "Guess we'll see then."

He tipped a nod toward Willow. "That one is her favorite next to Bob. How is the wacky bird anyway?"

"Gonna be fine. I'll pick him up tomorrow."

"That'll make Frankie feel better. She's done nothing but kick herself for what happened—even though the only person to blame is her shithead ex."

"I know." My voice was low.

Oz dipped his chin in agreement and slid back toward his car.

I stayed where I was… waiting.

Because for the first time in five years, there was something—someone—I wasn't willing to walk away from. I took a deep breath, set Willow down on the porch, turned toward the door and walked right inside. Frankie and I had some unfinished business to handle.

CHAPTER 19
DUCK THIS

FRANKIE

I HEARD THE DOOR. A faint click—almost polite. Not loud. Not forceful. But final.

The sound traveled through the floor to where I stood in the living room. Up through my spine, through every locked and brittle piece of my body. I knew and didn't have to look. Didn't have to breathe in the sharp scent of summer-warmed leather and cedarwood drifting faintly through the air.

Beckett.

God. I should've locked the damn door. Should've braced the couch in front of it, jammed a chair under the knob, nailed two-by-fours across the frame if that's what it took.

But I hadn't.

Because no matter how much I told myself otherwise—no matter how hard my stomach twisted with shame—some wrecked part of me wanted him more than safety. The other part wanted an escape hatch. But not from him.

From myself.

Because standing near him… being looked at like I was something worth standing up for… that hurt worse than anything Chris had done.

And my humiliation—my failure to keep it all together—burned too bright. It had teeth now. It sank deep. I stood by the window, arms wrapped across my ribs as tightly as the cast allowed, holding myself together because no one else would. My hands, even the casted one, trembled against the fabric of my dirty T-shirt, nails digging sharp crescents into my skin.

My body was too tense, too wired. My breath came fast, too shallow to fill my lungs.

I felt him drawing closer. Every step. Every movement. His presence was a gravitational pull, impossible to ignore. Like he was taking up too much space in a room I no longer fit inside.

"Frankie."

His voice was smoke and gravel. Low and warm and rough in all the ways I wasn't ready for. It slid across my skin in a shiver of heat that left me shaking harder.

Don't turn. Don't break.

I stayed frozen. Gave him nothing. Only my back. Only my silence.

"Please, darlin'."

There it was. That one word. Darlin'. Coming from him, it wasn't casual. It wasn't polite. It was a vow, a tether, a plea that sank past every defense I'd managed to rebuild.

My teeth sank into my cheek until I tasted iron. The sting gave me something solid to hold onto. A lifeline against the undertow rising inside me.

"You shouldn't be here." My voice was thread-thin, barely audible. "How is Bob?"

"The vet said he'll be alright and I can bring him home tomorrow."

"That's good. Really good. And I'm sorry. It's my fault your duck got hurt."

Behind me—silence. Then the slow, deliberate sound of boots on the floor. He was moving closer. "It's not your fault, Frankie." His voice was steady. Soft. But there was a weight behind it that pressed harder than any shout. "You should know that." Another step. And another. Close enough now that I could feel the heat radiating from his body. "And I'm not leaving until you do."

My breath left me in a harsh exhale. "You can't fix this, Beckett."

"I'm not trying to fix it." His voice gentled. "Whatever *it* is."

My heart thudded hard against my ribs, aching from the strain. "Then what do you want?"

I wasn't sure if it was an accusation or plea, but his answer broke something in me. "I want you to stop shutting me out."

Tears welled again—hot, bitter. I squeezed my arms tighter around myself, shoulders hunched. "You think I don't want to let you in?" The words spilled out, cracked and raw. "You think I don't—" I broke off on a choked breath. "God, Beckett. I've wanted nothing more than to trust someone again."

I turned halfway, unable to hold the words in anymore. My face was flushed, eyes shining, skin blotched with the tears I couldn't seem to stop shedding. "But every time I do…" My voice shook, crumbled. "Every time I try, it blows up in my face."

I couldn't look at him now. Couldn't bear to see the understanding or the sympathy or—God help me—the anger in his eyes. "Chris won't stop. He's going to ruin everything I've built. And dragging you into this mess is the last thing I want."

"You aren't dragging me anywhere." His voice was low and certain. "I'm walking in on my own two feet."

I shook my head, tears slipping free, sliding hot down my cheeks. "You don't get it, Beckett. He'll keep coming. He'll burn it all down until there's nothing left."

A beat of silence stretched between us, heavy as lead.

Then—my resolve cracked. I turned fully to him, desperate to make him understand. To make him see the wreckage inside me. And his eyes—God. His eyes were oceans. Deep, endless. Filled with something that looked too much like grief. Or hope. Or both.

One moment stretched between us—taut and breathless.

Then everything broke.

He moved.

Beckett crossed the narrow space between us with sudden, raw energy. Hands rough and trembling as they caught my face. His mouth crashed down on mine.

It wasn't a kiss. Not really.

It was hunger. Fury. Helpless longing dragged out from every dark place we'd each tried to bury it. I gasped into him, my body arching instinctively, the last of my defenses shattering like glass. My good hand clawed into his shirt, clinging hard enough to rip the fabric. Because he was heat and solid strength. The only thing tethering me to the moment when the rest of the world had gone spinning.

The kiss bruised and burned. Teeth clashed. Breath caught. A low, helpless sound rose from my throat, swallowed by his mouth. For one wild second, I let myself fall. And when he wrenched away—breathing hard, face wrecked with something wild—I swayed on my feet, dazed and desperate.

"Beckett, I—"

But before I could finish, he was gone. Beckett had spun on his heel, stormed toward the door. Taken one last look—raw, wild, eyes burning. And then—disappeared into the night.

The door slammed shut behind him like a final blow.

I stood there. Trembling. Lips swollen, breath coming in ragged gasps.

What the hell just happened?

I couldn't move. Could barely think. My body still thrummed with the echo of his mouth on mine. My heart pounded so loud it drowned out every coherent thought. Finally—on shaking legs—I stumbled toward the couch. My phone felt impossibly heavy in my good hand.

> Frankie: Tess something happened.

The phone rang instantly.

"TELL ME YOU'RE OKAY." Tess's voice thundered through the line.

I dropped onto the couch with a thud, every muscle trembling. "I… I don't know."

"What happened?"

And then it all poured out. The broken pieces. The jagged edges. "Chris showed up. He… he threatened the store again. Then he hurt Bob. And I hit him."

"Good girl," Tess said fiercely. "I hope you broke his damn face."

A wet, broken laugh escaped that turned into a sob. "Beckett… He kissed me."

Silence. "Wait. Kissed you? Beckett Ford kissed you?"

I covered my face with my cast, voice a bare whisper. "It wasn't just a kiss. It was like… like he couldn't stop himself. And then —he looked at me like he'd set himself on fire. And he ran."

Another beat of silence. "I'm coming," Tess said. Solid. Fierce. "I'll be there tonight. You are not dealing with this alone."

"Tess, you don't have to—"

"Frankie. You are my person. Of course I do. And you've got a grand opening in a few days. I was coming for that anyway. A few extra days is nothing. You're going to get through this. We're going to get through this. Got it?"

I swallowed hard. "Got it."

"Good. Now breathe for me. And for the love of God—don't lock that man out unless you're sure."

A choked laugh escaped. "No promises."

We hung up a few minutes later. I sat motionless on the couch, staring at the door. And what scared me the most wasn't the kiss. It wasn't even that he ran. It was the unbearable ache twisting inside my chest. The hunger I couldn't silence. That I wanted him to walk back through that door more than anything in the world.

I could still feel him—every place his hands had touched me, every hard, unyielding line of that kiss burned into my skin. The house was too still. Too empty.

And then—

A soft sound.

My head whipped around.

Willow blinked up at me from the folded afghan, her little head tilted. Soft feathers ruffled like she could sense something wasn't right. The sight of her—small and helpless, a silent witness to this whole mess—split something wide open inside my chest.

Damn it.

I pressed a shaking hand over my mouth, throat thickening. Because Beckett hadn't just left. He'd left me. He'd left Willow.

Tears burned down my cheeks, but this time they weren't helpless. They were furious.

"Fuck this," I whispered. Grabbing my phone, I shot off a text to Tess letting her know that I was going over to his house to give him a piece of my mind and to return his damn duck.

> Tess: K. I'll let myself in if you're 'busy.'
> winky face

I shook my head. But I wasn't about to let him get away with kissing me senseless and then running like a little bitch.

My heart was pounding so hard it hurt.

Willow gave another soft peep. I crouched, scooped her up

gently, cradling the small body against my chest as well as I could.

"You're coming with me," I said under my breath. "If he wants to run—fine. But he's going to damn well look me in the eye when he says he's going to."

And with that, I stormed out the door, Willow warm and light in my arms, fury and heartbreak giving wings to my steps as I headed straight for Beckett's house.

CHAPTER 20
FEATHERS AND FOOLS

BECKETT

I HADN'T MOVED from my chair on my back porch. Not since I had landed there after slamming Frankie's door behind me like a damn coward. Not since I'd stood on her front porch, chest heaving, heart racing like I'd just walked out of a war zone. Not since I'd bolted like my ass was on fire. Not since I'd grabbed the bourbon and a glass and plunked myself down out here.

So here I was, long past dark, legs braced wide, a half-empty bottle beside me.

The glass was still half full but felt cold in my palm. My pulse was colder.

What the hell had I done?

I hadn't meant to kiss her. Christ, I'd walked in there ready to tell her she wasn't alone. That I wasn't going to let Chris take another thing from her.

But the second she turned and looked at me—eyes wide, raw, too

189

full of everything she wasn't saying—I'd lost every bit of sense I had left.

And now?

Now I couldn't go back. Couldn't undo it. Couldn't breathe without the taste of her still burning on my tongue. A sick, aching weight settled behind my ribs, sharp enough to leave me restless and wrecked. Was I having a heart attack? I'd fucked up and now I couldn't erase the pain I'd put into the universe.

The crunch of footsteps across the yard snapped me out of it. I looked up, slow, as I set my glass on the table.

And there *she* was. Storming across my yard like a goddamn force of nature, her hair even more wild around her face than when I'd kissed her moments ago. Her cast-covered hand clutched Willow awkwardly against her chest.

My pulse kicked hard.

I rose fast, the bourbon long forgotten.

"Frankie—"

"Save it," she snapped.

She marched straight to me, shoved Willow into my arms harder than was necessary. "Here. Take your goddamn duck."

Willow quacked softly, flapping against my chest. I steadied her with shaking hands, heart hammering harder than before.

Frankie stood there, vibrating with fury. "You want to tell me what the hell just happened in my living room?" she demanded, voice sharp as glass.

I opened my mouth, but nothing came out.

Her laugh barked out—bitterness and hurt laced the sound. "That's it? No snark? No grumpy little grunt? Christ, Ford, the one time you actually touch me, you run like the house is on fire."

I exhaled hard. "Frankie, I'm sorry."

"Don't you dare." She jabbed her cast-covered hand toward me. "Don't you dare apologize like it was some accident. You walked in there. You kissed me like your life depended on it. And then you left."

Her voice cracked at the edge of the words, and it damn near undid me.

"I didn't mean to—"

"Oh please," she spat. "Don't insult me. You wanted it. And you think I didn't?" Her breath hitched, sharp. "I wanted it," she said flatly. "God help me, I did. But you know what I don't want? An emotionally unavailable man who thinks walking away to keep from screwing me up worse is some noble act."

I flinched.

"You think I don't see it?" Frankie went on, voice shaking now. "You're already writing this off. Already building your little walls again. 'Poor broken Beckett, can't be the man she needs, better shove her away first.'"

"That's not fair."

She laughed again—a brittle, angry sound that barely masked the ache underneath. "You know what's not fair? That I have fought tooth and damn nail for this life. For my store. For a future where I wasn't someone's second choice or punching bag." Her eyes burned. "And now you—you—kiss me like that, like you mean it, and then you run? No. I don't have room for this shit anymore."

Every word felt like a blow. I'd walked into this one with my eyes wide open. And I'd still managed to screw it up.

"I'm not the man for you, Frankie."

Her chin lifted. "No shit."

The words landed sharp, but I didn't stop. Couldn't. Because if I didn't rip the truth out now, I'd never survive watching her hope for more.

"You think I don't want you?" My voice came rough, almost a growl. "Hell, I do. I wanted you the second you opened that damn bookstore. But I can't give you what you want. I don't have it in me anymore."

Frankie blinked, thrown off by the edge in my tone.

"My business partner—someone I trusted like family—gutted me from the inside out. Stole everything we built, dragged my name through the mud, left me with nothing but ashes and lawsuits. I thought that was rock bottom." I dragged in a harsh breath. "Then my sister… my twin… she died. Drunk driver took her out on a rainy night and left me standing at her graveside wondering how the hell I was supposed to keep breathing when half of me was gone."

The words came fast now, years of silence breaking loose like floodwaters.

"So, yeah, Frankie. I can kiss you like I'm drowning. I can want you so bad it makes me insane. But giving you more? Giving you all the things you deserve? I can't. I'm hollow. There's nothing left in me to give."

Her face wavered—anger and hurt tangling with something softer I didn't want to see.

"You think you're protecting me by saying that," she whispered. "But all you're really doing is protecting yourself from feeling again."

I clenched my jaw, pulse hammering. "Better that than dragging you into the wreckage that's my life." Frankie's mouth twisted. "You think *you* get to decide what I deserve? How dare you."

My jaw clenched. "I can't give you what you need."

"You don't *know* what I need." Her voice broke now, soft but sharp. "You didn't even stay long enough to ask."

Silence dropped between us like a hammer. Willow shifted faintly in my arms, quacking once, the only sound in the thick night. Frankie stared at me—eyes blazing, lips trembling, shoulders shaking like she was holding herself together with fraying string.

Then she took a step back.

"You know what hurts the most?" she whispered. "That for one second, I thought maybe I was wrong about you. That maybe you were the one person in this damn world who wouldn't run or try to control me."

Her voice cracked, and it undid me.

But before I could speak, before I could move, she turned on her heel. "Don't follow me," she said, voice rough.

And she walked away—without looking back.

I stood frozen in the dark, heart pounding so hard I thought it might crack in two.

Willow shifted against me. "I'm sorry, girl," I whispered. "I'm sorry."

But the words weren't for the duck.

And deep down, I knew there weren't enough apologies in the world to undo what I'd just done. I moved without a second thought and plopped back down into my chair. I sat on the dock long after Frankie's footsteps had faded into the night.

I'd barely touched the bourbon I'd poured an hour ago.

Couldn't.

Every time I closed my eyes, I saw her face. The hurt in her eyes. The words she'd flung at me—and the ones she hadn't been able to say.

I thought maybe I was wrong about you.

Christ. The worst part was that she hadn't been. But I'd proved her right anyway. My phone buzzed sharply against the table, breaking the silence. I jerked upright, heart already pounding.

It was the Boston area code I knew too damn well—one I hoped I'd never deal with again.

I exhaled once, hard, then answered. "Yeah."

"Beckett. It's Keller."

My attorney's voice was always calm, even when the world burned. I appreciated that about him.

I sighed. "Didn't expect a call this late."

"Apologies," Keller said. "But I figured you'd rather hear this now."

My stomach sank. "Go on."

There was a pause. Then, "We've been monitoring Maddox's channels. Press contacts. Social media plants. For now—it looks like he's pulled back."

I went still. "What the hell does that mean?"

"It means the pressure campaign we expected hasn't materialized," Keller said. "His legal team's gone quiet. He's canceled a series of media appearances this week. It looks—for now—like he's shelving the plan to go public and try to smear you some more."

My jaw locked. "I don't trust him."

"I wouldn't either," Keller said smoothly. "This has all the feel of a pause. Not a surrender."

I exhaled through my nose. "Calm before the storm."

"Exactly." Another pause. "But it buys us time. A little breathing room."

"Breathing room doesn't mean safe," I said flatly. "He won't stop. He'll wreck what's left of my life—and all because he needs me to do his damn work."

Keller was quiet for a beat. Then his voice came more carefully. "Beckett—you know I'm going to say this again."

I leaned back, eyes on the ceiling. "Don't."

"You should tell the people you've built a life around what's going on. The people you've let in can help you."

"I haven't let anyone in," I said, too fast. Too sharp.

Another long pause. "You and I both know that's not true anymore," Keller said quietly. "And the longer you wait, the harder it'll be."

I closed my eyes. "It doesn't matter."

"It matters more than you think."

My voice came low. "Let it go, Keller, and stick to your job."

Keller sighed. "Alright. I've said my piece."

I sat forward again, rubbing at the back of my neck. "Stay on it," I said. "Watch everything. I want to know the second Maddox moves."

"You will," Keller promised. "But Beckett… be ready."

"I am," I said. "I always am."

I ended the call and set the phone down hard on the table. Then I sat there, breathing rough, hands curled tight around the edge of the wood. The quiet pressed in again. Truth was, I wasn't ready. And worse—deep down, I wasn't sure if I ever would be.

Not for the ghosts coming for me.

And God help me, not for Frankie Bellamy.

CHAPTER 21

THE GREAT PANTY CAPER

FRANKIE

I SAT on my wraparound porch the next morning, feeling exactly as wrecked as I looked.

I'd barely slept. Every time I closed my eyes, it was the same damn loop—Chris's voice, the sickening sound of Bob hitting the floor, the flash of my fist connecting with his face.

And then Beckett.

His mouth on mine. The raw, furious kiss I hadn't been able to stop wanting even as he tore himself away. Now I sat in the morning air, a mug of too-strong coffee cradled between my palms, trying to focus on the sunshine and not the tornado still spinning inside my chest.

At least I wasn't alone.

Tess sat beside me, legs curled under her, oversized sunglasses perched on her nose. My best friend had arrived in a flurry of caffeine and righteous fury a little after midnight.

In silence, we stared over the damn fence that separated my backyard from Beckett's. More specifically—at the seven ducks currently milling around the pond. Beckett must have already brought Bob home.

Tess squinted. "So… let me get this straight."

I sighed, knowing she was about to launch the inquisition she'd spared me from when she arrived.

"You've got a hot, broody, emotionally constipated man living next door."

"Yep."

"Who also runs a duck sanctuary."

"Apparently."

Tess shook her head slowly. "I feel like I'm missing a chapter here."

I let out a small, tired laugh. "You're not. That's just… him."

"That's insane."

"I know."

We watched in silence as Bob clambered lazily onto a rock near the pond, fluffing his feathers like royalty.

"And you like him," Tess added.

My heart twisted. "I didn't mean to."

Tess slid her sunglasses down, gave me a pointed look. "Frankie. You punched your ex. Ran down Main Street with a duck, sobbing. And then kissed your hot neighbor."

I groaned. "Don't remind me."

Tess grinned. "I mean, hot mess vibes aside—that must have been one hell of a kiss to crack your list."

A shaky laugh escaped me. "I can't do this, Tess. I can't afford another man who wants to change me. Or worse…. won't stay. I've spent the last year figuring out who I am. I don't need Beckett or any other man to derail my new life. Not when I'm finally getting it back on track."

Tess's smile faded. "I know, babe. But…" She nodded toward the yard. "He's literally raising ducks. The man may not know how to stay with people yet. But he knows how to stay."

I swallowed hard. Looked away. We were quiet for a beat.

Finally Tess sighed. "Alright. Tell me about the opening. How are you feeling?"

I latched onto that—thank God for something practical. "Nervous. Exhausted. Obsessed with checking the window displays every three hours."

Tess smiled. "Sounds about right."

"It's in two days. I keep thinking something else is going to go wrong."

"It won't."

"I hope not." I sipped my coffee. "I need this, Tess. I need something good to happen."

"It will." Tess nudged my knee. "You've earned it."

I was about to answer when movement caught my eye. I glanced toward the front door—and froze. Bob waddled out of the house. Holding something pink and lacy in his beak.

For a second, my brain didn't compute—not even a minute ago Bob was at the pond. I shrieked when it finally registered. "Bob! You little shit!"

Tess blinked, then gasped. "Is that—"

"My underwear!"

Tess lost it. She laughed so hard she nearly tipped her chair. "Oh my god. This is the greatest thing I've ever seen."

Bob quacked smugly and took off down the porch steps, pink lace trailing behind him like a victory flag.

"GET BACK HERE!"

I launched myself after him, Tess right behind me, cackling.

Bob flapped and waddled, fully recovered and clearly delighted with his new toy. I chased him across the yard. "Bob! Drop it!"

"Should've set boundaries earlier," Tess called, doubled over with laughter.

Beckett stepped out just in time to see me barreling toward his porch. I'm sure my cheeks were flushed, my hair flying. He blinked. "Frankie—?"

Bob spotted an opportunity—the open side door to Beckett's house.

My heart stopped. "No. NO—" Too late. Bob darted inside, still clutching his prize. "Control your damn duck!" I shouted.

I stood there, chest heaving, eyes squeezed shut, counting to ten.

Beckett looked stunned. Tess sauntered up behind me, still grinning.

He glanced at her, wary. "Do I even want to know?" He looked between her and me, his eyes briefly flicking down to my cast.

Tess tilted her head. "Honestly? You probably don't."

He ran a hand down his face. "What the hell is going on?"

"Your goddamn duck is what happened. I can't do this today." I spun and stomped down the front steps. "Fuck this—let's go, Tess. I have shit to do and it's not dealing with hot lips."

I heard Tess shout, "Look. Let me say one thing. You're an idiot." Turned to see whether she was talking to Beckett… or to me. She was pointing her index finger at Beckett, so I waited. His mouth pressed into a thin line as Tess folded her arms. "You kissed my best friend like she was the last thing you'd ever get—and then you ran."

Beckett's throat worked. "I know."

"Drop it, Tess." I stomped my foot. "This isn't worth your breath." I gave him my back and started across the yard, but not before I caught my best friend's grin.

"Enjoy Bob's gift, by the way." She snorted as she followed me back to my house.

I stormed inside like a woman possessed, Tess following behind at a slower pace, still shaking with laughter.

"I cannot believe that damn duck!" I fumed, pacing the length of the living room. "He stole my underwear. Out of my laundry basket. What kind of psychotic bird—"

"Duck," Tess corrected, flopping onto the couch.

I spun on her. "Same goddamn difference, and don't you dare defend him."

"I'm just saying—I've heard ducks can be… enterprising."

I flung my arms wide. "He waltzed out of my house like he was going to present a prize at the county fair!"

Tess grinned. "It was very pink."

I groaned, dropping onto the armchair. "I can't. I literally cannot. First his owner kisses me like he's starving, then ghosts me, then sends his damn duck over to steal my underwear."

"You think Beckett sent him?"

I scowled. "I don't know! Maybe! He's weird enough to train them. I wouldn't put it past him."

Tess laughed. "Frankie."

"What."

"Breathe, babe."

I glared. "I am breathing. Through pure rage."

Tess leaned forward, resting her elbows on her knees. "Look. I get it. You're pissed. You're hurt. You're mortified."

I groaned into my hands. "Mortified doesn't begin to cover it."

"But." Tess grinned wider. "You have to admit—when Beckett sees what his duck just delivered to him? He's going to shit himself."

A snort escaped me despite myself. "Good. I hope he chokes while he's doing it."

Tess tilted her head. "You're gonna survive this."

I exhaled, my shoulders slumping. "I hate that I want him."

Tess smiled gently. "No, babe. You hate that you want more than just the kiss."

I covered my face again. "I do not have the bandwidth for this. I've got a grand opening in two days. I can't afford to be distracted by a man who can't decide whether to kiss me or run for the hills."

"Then don't be," Tess said simply.

I blinked. "That easy?"

"It's a choice," Tess said. "You focus on what matters. You remember that a man—any man—doesn't get to derail this dream you're building. Least of all one who's too dumb to stay after the best kiss of your life. And probably his."

I groaned. "God, it was the best kiss."

Tess cackled. "Of course it was. You attract the complicated ones, remember?"

I shook my head. "You know, I used to think Beckett Ford was safe to hate. Simple. Easy."

"And now?"

I leaned back, sighing. "Now he's complicated and frustrating and entirely too hot for his own good."

"And?" Tess nudged.

"And I'm not ready to do this again. Not with anyone."

Tess's voice softened. "That's okay. You don't have to be."

We sat in silence for a long beat, the hum of the ceiling fan the only sound between us.

Finally, I exhaled hard. "Okay. No more duck drama. No more man drama. I have a store to open."

Tess grinned. "That's my girl."

I pushed up from the chair. "Alright—window displays. Final stock check. Coffee station prep. What am I forgetting?"

Tess followed me into the kitchen. "Flowers for the front table?"

"Ordered. Delivery coming tomorrow."

"Ribbon for the door?"

"In the drawer."

"Outfits planned?"

I groaned. "You would ask."

Tess laughed. "Come on—you need something fierce. You're the queen of this opening."

I rolled my eyes but smiled. "Fine. I'll pull a few options."

We moved through the house together, the energy shifting back to purpose, to joy.

By the time we were done, half the prep list was checked off and my chest felt a little lighter.

As we collapsed on the couch again with fresh coffees, Tess grinned.

"You're gonna kill this opening."

I smiled tiredly. "God, I hope so."

"You will," Tess said firmly. "And when you do? That duck-thieving, broody man next door is going to be kicking himself for missing the best damn woman in this town."

My heart pinched, but I nodded. "One thing at a time," I whispered.

And for now—that was good enough for me.

CHAPTER 22
PANTIES AND PUBLIC RESTRAINT

BECKETT

THE TOWN HAD SHOWN up in force for Frankie Bellamy's grand opening.

I could hear it from my damn back porch—laughter, chatter, music drifting across the fence between our yards. I hadn't planned to go. I told myself I wouldn't.

But Willow had started pacing near the pen, quacking low. Bob had flapped up onto the fence rail like a feathered watchdog. And before I knew it, I was grabbing my keys. Muttering under my breath like an idiot. "You guys stay here. I don't need you ruining Frankie's big day."

Bob tilted his head, unimpressed. Squawked once, flapped down to the pond like he had more important things to do. I looked across the yard. I could already see the crowd spilling out from her porch and onto the grass. I was pathetic—I couldn't stay away if I tried.

I crossed the yard, shoulders tense, every step heavier than the last. I wasn't ready to see her. Wasn't ready to look her in the eye after the way I'd kissed her—then run like a goddamn coward.

205

Now I stood at the edge of the crowd, rooted like a damn tree while the whole town buzzed around me. Families, couples, kids eating cookies, retirees holding paperbacks like treasures. Joey and Kevin manned a mobile coffee tent. Greta waved from a bakery table. Hank strolled the crowd in uniform.

And at the center of it all—Frankie.

She moved through them like sunlight, bright and sure, laughing that low, warm laugh I hadn't heard since she'd stormed off my porch. She looked… tired. And beautiful. And so far out of reach it made my chest hurt.

I shoved my hands into my pockets and drifted toward the coffee tent.

I didn't make it three feet before I got ambushed. "Beckett Ford!"

I stiffened. Ruth Simmons and Edna Grayson zeroed in from opposite sides like heat-seeking missiles. Ruth clutched her over-sized purse like it was a battering ram. "There you are. We've been watching for you."

"Yeah," Edna added, eyes twinkling. "Didn't think you'd show your face after that little disappearing act last week."

"Ladies," I said warily.

"Come to support our girl?" Ruth asked sweetly.

"Yeah."

"Good," Edna said, patting my arm. "Because if you break her heart, I swear to God, I will run you over with my Buick."

"And I'll help her hide the body," Ruth added, deadpan.

I blinked. "Jesus."

"Don't look so shocked," Edna said. "You've seen how I parallel park. I've got the aim for it."

"And we've seen the way you look at her," Ruth said, eyes narrowing. "Like a man who thinks he doesn't deserve nice things."

Heat crawled up my neck. "It's… complicated."

"Of course it is," Ruth huffed. "Because men always have to make everything complicated. Y'all act like love is rocket science when half the time it's just showing up and keeping your pants on."

"Speak for yourself," Edna said, grinning. "I read those Ana Huang books. Sometimes the pants part is optional."

"Don't encourage him," Ruth scolded, smacking her shoulder. "He needs the slow burn, not the fast track."

"I—" I attempted a reply, but they weren't done.

"You should be trying to lock that woman down, not scare her off," Edna said.

"And for God's sake, stop brooding on your porch like you're Heathcliff," Ruth added. "This is Georgia, not Wuthering Heights."

"Ladies," I managed, "I—"

"Don't bother," Edna said, waving a hand. "We know guilt when we see it."

"Go read a romance novel," Ruth added. "Learn a thing or two. Then try again."

Before I could respond—not that I had a damn clue what to say—Hank appeared like a gift from God. "Ladies," he drawled. "Giving Beckett here a hard time?"

"Helpful advice," Ruth smiled sweetly.

"He needs it," Hank said, clapping me on the shoulder.

I shot him a glare. "You're not helping."

"They're probably not wrong," he said with a grin.

Edna and Ruth chuckled and wandered off, smug as cats.

I exhaled. "Jesus Christ."

"You were doomed the minute they saw you," Hank said. "They figure they can hook you two up."

"Not what I came here for," I muttered.

"Then why are you here?" he asked, eyes sharp.

Before I could answer, my pulse spiked when my eyes landed on the last person Frankie would want at her opening.

Chris.

That smug bastard moved through the crowd like a shark—pressed slacks, designer sunglasses, too polished for this town. And he was heading straight for Frankie.

Blood roared in my ears.

I stepped forward on instinct, fists already curling—

Hank grabbed my arm. "Don't."

"Like hell."

"You'll make it worse," Hank said, voice low. "Let me handle it."

I forced my feet still. My teeth were clenched so hard my jaw ached. Frankie squared off with her ex near the tent. Her shoulders were stiff. Her chin held high. And even from here I could see how her eyes flashed with anger.

Chris smiled that snake oil smile and started to move closer, but Hank stepped in—his body blocking his forward motion.

Frankie said something that made his eyes widen. Chris leaned in—too close, too smooth. But Frankie spun away, storming back into the shop.

I couldn't move. Could barely breathe. "That man's a piece of work," a voice said softly beside me. I looked down to find the previous owner, Mabel. Small, but sharp-eyed, dressed in lavender.

"Yeah," I said, voice rough.

We both watched the door Frankie had vanished through.

"You alright, son?"

"Not really."

She smiled. "Didn't think so." Then her gaze flicked up, sharp as glass. "You're not as subtle as you think."

I blinked. "What?"

"About her. About yourself."

"I don't—"

She patted my arm. "You keep telling yourself you're just her neighbor. Just a friend. Think that's enough. But it's written all over your face."

"It doesn't matter."

"Doesn't it?"

I swallowed hard. "She deserves more than… what I am."

"And what is that?" Mabel asked gently. "A man with a few ghosts? You think that scares her?"

I shook my head. "You don't understand."

"Oh, I do." She leaned in, voice low. "Let me tell you a secret, Beckett Ford."

Cold slid through me. "Mabel—"

"No one here gives two nickels about the man you were in that hoity toity town," she smiled. "You thought we cared about what happened?"

My throat was dry. "I—"

"You're in the south, Beckett. Did you really think moving to New York would change who you were before? Please, Beckett, you're famous. This town doesn't care. They believe in loyalty and forgiveness. No one cares about your bank account or your name. Least of all that girl."

I could barely breathe.

"Frankie wants one thing," she said softly. "A man who wants her. Broke. Rich. It doesn't matter as long as they're not that piece of shit she was married to." She squeezed my arm, kind and sharp all at once. "Think about that."

She walked away, leaving me feeling gutted. I dragged a hand through my hair and because life wasn't done screwing with me, my brain picked that moment to serve up another image. *Pink lace*.

Bob waddling smugly across my porch two nights ago— Frankie's underwear dangling from his beak like a goddamn trophy. He'd been carrying the damn thing around since he stole it. And he'd decided to present it to me. I could still feel the brush of it against my fingertips.

The taste of her mouth still burned on my tongue from the kiss we shared.

I hadn't touched her since that night. Hadn't let myself go near her house until now.

But it all haunted me. That kiss. That pink scrap of lace. That one breathless second where it felt like maybe I could be the man she wanted. That I had run.

I forced my feet to move and crossed the yard in a blur without saying goodbye to anyone. Once I was at home, safe inside and away from the crowd, I paced the house like a caged animal.

I couldn't stop moving.

Couldn't stop hearing Mabel's voice.

"She wants a man who wants her."

And God did I want her.

Across the yard the festivities had ended and only her windows glowed warm. I stood at my kitchen window for too long, watching the light spill across the grass.

Her silhouette moved by the glass once, twice, then disappeared out of view. I wanted to go to her. I wanted to tell her I was a coward. That I wanted her more than I wanted my next breath.

But I couldn't move.

Couldn't shatter what little was left between us. Ha—that was funny because the only thing left between us was the grass in need of a cut.

By midnight, I had ended up on the back porch. Another glass of bourbon untouched at my side and my thoughts still on the pink lace stuck in the back of my damn drawer.

I hadn't touched it since I'd taken it away from Bob.

But it was there—hidden like some dirty secret.

I tipped my head back, stared at the stars.

"She deserves more."

Why the hell couldn't I stop thinking about Frankie?

For the first time since the day I'd come home, I wondered— What the hell was I still so afraid of?

CHAPTER 23
DUCK ME, PLEASE

FRANKIE

IT HAD BEEN three weeks since the bookstore's grand opening.

Three long, awkward, duck-filled weeks.

I hadn't seen Beckett much since I'd opened. Only an occasional glimpse across the yard. Our paths hadn't crossed except for the day he was getting into his truck as I left the house to get my cast off—and then we'd only nodded at each other. The man was apparently an expert at avoidance. And damn if I hadn't been doing the exact same thing.

Every time I thought about that kiss—hot, possessive, toe-curling—I flushed head to toe and promptly buried myself in a stack of inventory or the never-ending coffee-fueled shelving project. Steam & Bean was practically keeping me alive with iced lattes at this point.

But avoidance? Yeah, it was getting harder, because two of his damn ducks had decided they liked my place better.

Willow and Bob had made themselves at home like they paid rent. Willow had a favorite corner of my living room now—she'd found a cozy sunspot by the floor-to-ceiling window where she could nestle in and watch the world go by. Bob, on the other hand, was a walking menace. The trail of duck poop kept my Swiffer in overdrive, but I couldn't bring myself to ban them from the shop. Plus, he'd developed an alarming obsession with my LGBT and drag queen romance display table. More than once, I'd caught him waddling toward it with intent. I was convinced he was either a closet smut lover, or he just liked knocking over anything pink and sparkly.

I knew I should tell Beckett. I should march over there, knock on that broody man's door, and tell him to come get his damn ducks. But every time I worked up the nerve, the memory of his mouth on mine came roaring back—and I chickened out.

So instead? I let the ducks stay. Sue me.

It was a quiet afternoon, the kind that lulled you into thinking maybe the universe would let you breathe for five damn minutes. The shop was closed for restocking, and I'd been curled on my couch in leggings and a worn "Talk Ducky to Me" tee—thank you, Oz—with Amy Daws's newest release and a mug of cold brew when it happened.

"DAMMIT! WILLOW! BOB!"

I bolted upright, the mug sloshing cold coffee onto my thigh. "Shit!"

Heart hammering, I shot to the window.

Beckett was at the pond, pacing like a caged animal. His shirt was half-untucked, hair wild, and he was shouting—panic clear in every sharp word. My stomach dropped. I barely shoved on my shoes before sprinting across the yard.

"Beckett!" I called. I was breathless by the time I reached him. "What's going on?"

He spun toward me, eyes wild, face flushed. The storm gray of his gaze looked damn near black. "Something's wrong with the pond pump," he ground out. "And I can't find Willow or Bob."

I blinked, taking in the chaos. The pond, normally clear, was murky. Duck feathers were scattered like snowflakes.

My heart twisted. "Shit, Beckett. I—"

"I've checked everywhere," he said, voice cracking. "I've got the rest penned up but those two—they always wander. I should've—"

"Stop," I said firmly, stepping in and grabbing his forearm. His skin was hot beneath my fingers. His muscles were trembling. "Breathe."

He shook his head, looking half-feral. "Frankie, if something happened to them—"

"They're fine."

"You don't know that—"

"Actually," I said, exhaling and stepping away from him, "I do."

His gaze snapped to mine. "What?"

I winced. "They're at my place."

"What?"

"Yeah, um… Willow's been napping in my living room all week. I even bought a indoor pen to keep the duck shit down to a minimum. Bob's been trying to woo my paperback table. I didn't think you'd mind, and then… well, we aren't exactly on speaking terms."

For a beat, Beck just stared, chest heaving. "You let them stay?" he asked, voice low, rough.

"I figured if they wanted a little literary education, who was I to judge?" I tried for a smile. "I think they're partial to the smut section. Official bookstore mascots, at this point."

Something in him broke then—the tension snapping like an overdrawn wire.

He let out a strangled laugh, one hand dragging through his hair. "Jesus, Frankie."

"They're safe. I promise. Come see for yourself."

But he didn't move for a moment. And when he did? It wasn't toward my house. No… he moved toward me. In three long strides, Beckett closed the distance and curled his fingers around my wrist. "I thought they were gone," he rasped. "I thought—"

And then he kissed me. No warning. No time to think. Just heat. Pure, blistering heat.

His mouth claimed mine, fierce and desperate. I gasped against him, hands braced on his chest, ready to shove him away—or maybe pull him closer. My traitorous body hadn't decided.

"Beck—" I tried to mumble his name, but he deepened the kiss, one arm banding around my waist to keep me from moving.

I should've stopped it. Should've reminded us both that we were supposed to be avoiding this—this thing that crackled like wildfire between us. But when his tongue swept mine, when he groaned low in his throat—all resistance burned away. I arched against him, fists curling in his shirt.

I barely registered the lift—his arms strong beneath me, hauling me up as if I weighed nothing. My legs wrapped around his waist on instinct, and I clung to him like a baby koala.

"Beckett, your pond—"

"Safe. You said they're safe." His voice was rough silk as his eyes locked on mine.

The world blurred. I barely noticed crossing the threshold of his house. Because Beckett's mouth found mine again—and everything else ceased to matter.

He kicked the door shut with one booted foot, barely breaking stride as he carried me through the entryway. I caught a blur of deep gray walls, rough-hewn wood beams overhead, the faint scent of cedarwood and soap.

And him.

God, he was hard muscle and desperate heat beneath me.

I should stop this. I *should*.

"Beckett?" I managed, breathless, my voice cracking with his name.

Beckett halted, chest rising and falling like he'd just run a damn marathon. His gaze burned into mine—storm gray, searing, raw. He lowered me slowly, my feet meeting the floor as his body pressed closer.

"I'm not thinking," he rasped. "If I think… I'll stop. And right now, I can't—I don't want to."

The confession shattered something inside me. Because I wasn't thinking either. And I damn well didn't want to stop either.

His fingers flexed against my waist, as if he was barely holding himself back.

I swallowed hard, hands sliding from his chest to his shoulders. "Then don't think," I whispered. That was all it took. The dam broke.

Beckett surged forward, his mouth crashing over mine again—hungry, bruising, desperate. His hands spanned my hips, tugging me flush. I gasped into the kiss, every nerve ending sparking to life.

God, this man kissed like it was a full-body experience.

Like he'd been starving for it. For *me*.

And I was drowning in it.

Somewhere in the haze, I felt him start to walk again—half leading, half dragging me deeper into the house. We stumbled up the stairs, down a short hall, bumping into a wall with a muffled thud that set both of us to laughing, breathless against each other's mouths.

"Sorry," he muttered, voice wrecked.

"You saying you're out of practice, Duck Man?" I teased him, emboldened by the heat in his eyes.

His answering growl reverberated straight through me. "Keep talking. See what that gets you."

I opened my mouth—probably to say something stupid—but Beckett was done with words. One hand tangled in my hair, angling my head as he kissed me harder, deeper. I melted against him, fingers clutching his shirt like a lifeline. God, I'd needed this. Needed *him*. Even if I wouldn't admit it out loud. Even if part of me was still terrified of what this meant. His rough hands moved to the front of my jeans and my breath caught.

Shit. This was happening.

Beckett must've seen something flicker across my face because he froze, arms bracketing me against the wall. His forehead pressed to mine, breath ragged. "We can stop," he said hoarsely. "You say stop, Frankie, and I will."

The sincerity in his voice nearly undid me. That same man who looked like he could break the world with his bare hands… ready to stop because I said so.

God help me.

"No," I whispered, voice trembling but sure. "I swear I will pluck your eyelashes out with my bare hands if you stop this time." I reached for the buckle on his pants. A shudder ran through him. His mouth found mine again, softer this time. And somehow, that tenderness unraveled me more than the inferno between us had.

He stared at me, his gaze roaming over my face like he was memorizing every damn inch. "I've wanted you since the day you crashed into my fence," he said roughly. "And it's been driving me fucking insane."

A helpless laugh bubbled from my throat. "Pretty sure that makes two of us."

"Yeah?" His voice dropped. "Then let me show you."

He reached for me then— his hands skimming the hem of my tee, his eyes asking for permission even as he hovered.

I gave a shaky nod. "Please touch me, Beckett."

The fabric lifted, baring my skin inch by inch to his scorching gaze.

Beckett sucked in a breath, "Jesus, Frankie."

Warm palms spanned my ribs, thumbs stroking the tattoo on my stomach. Every brush of his calloused fingers left a trail of fire. And when his mouth followed—kissing down my throat, nipping along my collarbone—I moaned, arching helplessly toward him.

"Fuck," he groaned, pulling back just enough to look me in the eye. "Tell me you want more. That you want me."

I answered with actions, not words—fisting his shirt and dragging it up, over his head, revealing honed muscle and tanned, inked skin.

My breath caught. "God, you're—" I broke off, heat rushing to my cheeks.

Beckett's answering grin was all wicked male satisfaction. "So are you."

And then we weren't talking anymore.

We were moving—touching, tasting, learning each other in a slow, burning dance. His hands were everywhere, worshipping my every curve. My nails raked down his back, drawing a guttural sound from deep in his throat. At some point he'd stripped me of my shirt, and now his fingers were toying with the button of my pants.

When he dropped to his knees in front of me, taking my jeans and panties with him, I knew I was screwed. As I lifted my feet one at a time, letting him completely divest me of my armor, he looked up and rewarded me with a "Good girl." I felt my eyes widen as a small smile tugged at my lips. Then Beckett's tongue dove between my thighs like a man who knew exactly what he wanted. The scrape of his beard against my legs was pure torture. I fisted his hair and held on as he ate me like he was going for gold in the Olympics.

My body hummed with satisfaction and when he slipped a finger inside me, I lost it. My walls convulsed around his digit and I cried out his name. If the wall hadn't been there to hold me up, I'd have collapsed into a puddle on the floor.

Beckett kissed my clit one more time before slowly standing up. His hands pressed into the wall behind me as he captured my lips with his own. Needing to feel him for myself, I popped the button on his jeans and slipped my hand beneath the fabric. Just like the rest of him, he was big and hard. My fingers barely closed around his girth. His moan of pleasure only spurred me on, but he had other ideas.

"I'm not coming in my pants, darlin'."

CHAPTER 24
BOB CAN QUACK OFF

BECKETT

THIS WOMAN WAS GOING to be the death of me. The way her eyes dilated when I called her a good girl told me she had a naughty side. One I planned to explore. But not yet—for now, I just needed to be inside her like it was my last breath.

I fused my lips against hers as I walked us down the hallway to my bedroom on autopilot. I had stopped thinking. All I knew was heat. Need. Her.

Frankie tasted like something wicked wrapped in sunshine, her soft little gasps feeding every feral part of me I'd been trying to keep leashed for weeks. My hands were everywhere—her waist, her hip, sliding up the soft curve of her back as she arched against me like she'd been waiting just as long.

"Beck—" Her whisper caught in my throat when I kissed her deeper, swallowing every syllable that might remind me to be careful. Screw careful. Careful was for men who didn't spend nights staring at her damn porch light, wondering who she was laughing with.

Her fingers fisted in my hair, tugging me closer like she couldn't get enough either. I growled against her mouth, moving her toward the bed. The way she fit against me? That was going to ruin me. I wanted to savor this moment—burn it into my memory for eternity.

I gently pushed her to sit on the mattress, then stepped back to take off my boots and kick off my pants and boxers. I grabbed a condom from my side table, silently thanking my pushy brother for putting them there, and tossed it toward Frankie on the bed. The look she gave me as I stepped to the edge of the mattress was filled with hunger.

"I don't think you're going to fit." She glanced up at me from beneath her long lashes.

"It'll fit, darlin'. And I'll go slow."

And then—

QUACK.

I froze.

Frankie leaned back a fraction to glance around me, her lips kiss-swollen and eyes wide. "Was that—?"

QUACK. QUACKQUACK.

I didn't even have to turn my head. I knew that smug, demanding tone like I knew my own damn heartbeat.

"Bob," I bit out.

Frankie's laugh burst free, muffled behind her hand as she tried to cover the sound. I swore under my breath as I looked back, and sure enough, there he was—standing in the doorway like the world's smallest, feathered chaperone. Bob tilted his head, one beady eye blinking slowly, as if judging every life choice that had led me to making out with his favorite human.

"Are you serious right now?" I muttered, glaring at him. "You've got a whole pond, Bob. Go be a duck and fuck off."

Bob answered with a low, throaty quack that sounded way too much like *I don't think so, buddy* before waddling closer, wings flaring just enough to make a point.

Frankie couldn't stop laughing. "I think he's jealous."

"Of what?" I growled, trying not to notice how good she looked on my bed.

"Me." She snorted, then added, teasing, "Or maybe you. Bob's a complicated man."

I gave her a look that said we were not about to have a full conversation about my duck's emotional state while I was itching to be buried deep inside her.

"Do not encourage him," I warned.

Bob gave another sharp quack, triumphant, before turning in a slow, smug circle and waddling out of my bedroom like he'd accomplished his mission. Frankie bit her lip, grinning up at me, and for one wild second, I thought about chasing after him just to toss him in the damn pond.

Instead, I scrubbed a hand down my face and muttered, "I swear to God, one day, I'm eating that duck."

Frankie's laughter spilled out again, warm and teasing, her fingers sliding into mine like she had no intention of letting me stew in my frustration alone. "You love him," she said.

I didn't deny it. I just sighed, tugging her closer until her grin softened and her pulse jumped under my thumb. "Yeah. But right now?" I glanced toward the door Bob had waddled through, then back at her, my voice dropping low. "I'd love being inside you a hell of a lot more."

The blush that crept up her cheeks made every second of duck-induced torture worth it, but I didn't want a repeat. I kicked the door shut and moved back to her. Frankie let out a surprised little squeak as I dove between her legs, my patience—and any remaining moral restraint—hanging by a thread.

"Beckett—"

"Don't," I warned, my voice low, rough. "If you tell me we should stop, I'm tying you to my bed and you can argue about it from there. I need to taste this sweet pussy again—take my time with it."

Her lips curved, wicked and daring, and instead of protesting, she tilted her head just enough to brush her mouth against my jaw. "You're bossy when you're frustrated."

"Frankie," I growled.

Her smile was soft this time, but her answer was a whisper that made my control snap in two. "Yes."

I didn't waste another second. My mouth found hers again, slower now but deeper, like I wanted to memorize every sound she made. She tasted like heat and trouble.

I cursed under my breath, pulling back just enough to look at her. Her lips were kiss-swollen, cheeks flushed, and when she bit her lip with a pointed look, my self-control officially died.

Her hands skimmed my chest, nails scraping lightly across my stomach. She hesitated for half a second before she pressed both palms flat, her touch branding me. "Beckett…" Her voice was soft, almost unsure, but her eyes—hell, her eyes burned.

"You have no idea what you do to me," I said, my forehead resting against hers for a beat before I kissed her again, slower this time, dragging it out until she whimpered, her hips shifting against mine.

Then Frankie's hands were in my hair, tugging, urging, and when I moved to flick my tongue over one peaked nipple, she gasped, arching into me. That sound shot straight through me, tightening every muscle until I was seconds from snapping.

"Beckett—"

"Say it again," I murmured against her skin, nipping lightly before soothing the spot with my tongue.

"Beckett." Breathless. Shaky. Fuck, she was going to ruin me.

I kissed a path down her body. The swipe of my tongue against her center earned me a choked moan, her fingers fisting in my hair. "Oh, God—"

"Not God, sweetheart," I muttered, before diving in properly.

Frankie came apart under my mouth again like she'd been waiting years for this—for me. Her breath catching, hips rocking helplessly against my tongue. I held her still, savoring every twitch, every soft, broken sound that told me exactly how good she felt.

When she finally shattered, gasping my name, I didn't stop until she was trembling and tugging at me weakly, trying to catch her breath.

I moved back up her body, kissing her deeply, letting her taste herself on my tongue. She kissed me back, desperate. She pushed against my chest, causing me to lean back to give her room to sit up. I watched as she found the condom I'd haphazardly thrown on the bed.

Frankie ripped open the foil packet and gripped my dick like she wanted it inside her yesterday. As she rolled the latex down my shaft, I had to count backwards from a hundred just to keep from blowing my load too soon.

Once she had me covered in latex, Frankie gave me a firm tug.

"Frankie." My forehead rested against hers, my chest heaving. "If we do this, I'm not letting you pretend it didn't mean something later."

Her wide eyes met mine, no hesitation in them. "Good. Because I'm not pretending. And I won't let *you* pretend, either."

And that was it.

The second I was inside her, every thought, every ounce of restraint, burned away. She was tight, hot, perfect, and the way she gasped my name almost undid me right there.

"Too much?" I rasped, forcing myself to hold still, to give her a chance to adjust.

Frankie shook her head, pulling me closer, her nails digging into my back. "No. Don't stop."

I started to move, slow at first, dragging out every stroke, watching her face as pleasure chased across it in waves. When she moaned, hips lifting to meet mine, I lost whatever control I'd been clinging to.

"God, Frankie," I groaned, my rhythm picking up as she wound her legs around me.

Every sound she made—every soft gasp, every choked whisper of my name—pushed me closer to the edge. Her hands clutched at me like she couldn't get close enough, and when she came again, crying out my name, I followed, burying my face in her neck as I shattered with her.

When it was over, I stayed there, breathing hard, my forehead pressed to her shoulder. Her fingers traced lazy patterns down my back, soft and soothing, and for once, I didn't feel the need to move, to fill the silence.

"Beckett?" she whispered after a minute.

"Mm?"

"You're still never allowed to eat that duck."

I groaned, dropping my face into her neck with a laugh I couldn't hold back. "Son of a bitch. He's going to quack about this for weeks."

CHAPTER 25
BETRAYED BY BEAKS

FRANKIE

I WOKE UP WARM.

Too warm, actually.

The kind of heat that clings to your skin, heavy and lazy, like the air itself is still sighing from what went down a few hours ago. I blinked against the dark, disoriented for half a second before the steady, slow rhythm of breathing beside me clicked into place. Beckett.

Oh, hell.

I turned my head and there was just enough moonlight to see him sprawled on his back, one arm thrown carelessly over his head, the other resting on his stomach. The sheets had been pushed to his hips, stopped from going further by the leg I'd hooked over one of his. He was all hard muscle and soft shadows, and even in sleep, he looked… dangerous. Relaxed, but like one wrong move would have him fully awake, ready to catch me doing something stupid.

Which, conveniently, was exactly what I was about to do.

Because I had to leave.

Not because I wanted to—I didn't. God, I didn't. But this? Waking up in Beckett Ford's bed after we'd spent half the night proving just how good bad decisions could feel? That was a mistake waiting to detonate if I stayed long enough for him to wake up and look at me like that again.

I already felt too much.

Which meant I needed to get out before I said something dumb, like, *Hey, let's do this again forever.*

Slowly, carefully, I slid my leg over his, wincing when the mattress dipped and his breathing hitched. My heart jumped into my throat, but he didn't move—just exhaled deeply, rolling slightly to the side, still asleep.

Good.

Step one: escape Beckett Ford.

I slipped out of bed as quietly as I could and was halfway through step two—finding my clothes, when it all went to shit. I'd snagged my discarded shirt from the floor and tugged it on. My bra had vanished into the Bermuda Triangle of last night's clothing carnage, so… nope, not dealing with that. I found my jeans in the hallway, hopping on one foot to shimmy into them sans underwear, still without making a sound.

I picked up my shoes and gave a last peek into his room to be sure he was still asleep, and… Jesus. He had shifted again and now the sheets were even lower.

Nope. Not looking. Definitely not looking at the man who'd kissed me like I was oxygen, touched me like he'd been starving, and whispered my name like a prayer right before I came apart under him.

Absolutely not.

Time to move on to step three—sneak out the back door. I was dragging my eyes away, muttering under my breath, "Frankie, get a grip," when I heard it.

A soft, unmistakable shuffle.

Then—

Quack.

I froze.

"No," I whispered sharply, turning my head toward the hallway. "Don't you dare." The shadow moved closer, and another quack followed, this one louder, like an alarm going off. "Bob," I hissed. "I swear to God, if you wake him—"

QUACK. QUACKQUACK.

"Oh my God." I tried to shush him with a frantic wave of the hand not holding my shoes, but the little feathered narc was already waddling closer, his beady eyes glinting in the faint moonlight like he'd been waiting for this moment.

"Go back to bed, you little traitor!" I whispered furiously.

He ignored me, quacking louder now, and before I could close Beckett's door and scoop Bob up, a deeper sound cut through the night.

A low, sleepy voice, rough and laced with amusement. "Frankie?"

Shit.

Beckett's voice came again, low and rough with sleep, and I felt it travel all the way down my spine. "You sneaking out on me, Bellamy?"

Crap.

I pasted on my best innocent smile and turned toward him. "Sneaking out? No. Absolutely not. I was just… um… checking on Bob."

"Uh-huh."

The man didn't even sound convinced, and when my eyes landed on him, sitting up in bed with nothing on but a sheet barely covering his hips and a grin that should be illegal, I lost the ability to form coherent excuses.

Beckett Ford looked way too good like that—hair rumpled, chest all hard muscle and sleep-warm skin. He hadn't even fully woken up, and he already looked like a sin wrapped in a bedsheet.

I cleared my throat, desperate to pull my brain back on track. "He was making noise, so, you know, I thought I'd… calm him down."

Bob, the traitorous little bastard, quacked loudly, as if announcing to the entire world that I was lying through my teeth.

Beckett's eyebrow arched. "Right. And you calm ducks down by getting dressed at…" he looked at the clock on his side table, "two in the morning?"

"Maybe." I shrugged, trying to look casual. "I'm a woman of many talents."

His grin widened, lazy and knowing, and I hated—*hated*—how much it made my pulse jump.

"You were leaving." It wasn't a question.

I shifted uncomfortably, clutching my shoes tighter. "I wasn't *leaving* leaving. More like… temporarily relocating."

"Uh-huh." He pushed the sheet aside, standing in one smooth motion that had my stomach doing something it had no business doing.

"Beckett," I warned, backing up a step.

He stalked toward me anyway, naked as the day he was born, all calm, deliberate muscle and a look that warned me he was three seconds from doing something very, very reckless. "Frankie," he said, voice low, "where exactly were you planning to relocate to?"

"Home."

"You're already home."

The words landed heavier than they should have, his tone rough, almost soft under the teasing edge, and my heart tripped over itself.

I swallowed hard, glancing toward the door. "I don't want to complicate things."

His brow furrowed slightly, the grin slipping into something quieter. "Too late for that."

I opened my mouth to argue, but before I could get a word out, Bob let out another sharp quack, this one sounding way too much like laughter.

"Bob," Beckett said without looking away from me, "get out."

Bob ignored him, waddling closer, clearly delighted to watch me squirm.

"Out," Beckett repeated, his voice firmer this time.

The duck quacked again, but when Beckett took a step closer to me, Bob finally decided he'd done enough damage and waddled off, leaving me alone in the crosshairs of Beckett's gaze.

"You're not sneaking out, Frankie," he said finally, his tone brooking no argument.

I scowled, because of course he thought he could tell me what to do. "You can't stop me."

He gave me a look that said *Wanna bet?* right before he stepped forward, crowding me against the wall. My breath caught when he placed his palm on the wall beside my head, his body heat wrapping around me like a damn blanket.

"Try me," he said, voice low, almost a growl.

I hated that my pulse leapt. Hated it even more when my mouth betrayed me. "You're very full of yourself, you know that?"

"And you're terrible at lying." His lips quirked into the faintest smirk. "If you really wanted to leave, you wouldn't have kissed me like that a few hours ago."

I narrowed my eyes. "You think you're irresistible?"

He leaned in, close enough that his breath brushed my cheek. "No. I know what you taste like when you're trying not to fall apart in my arms. Pretty sure that means you don't actually want to run away."

My stomach flipped, traitorous and warm. "You're insufferable."

"And yet," he murmured, dipping his head so his mouth hovered just above mine, "you're still here."

I should have shoved him away. Should have at least pretended to argue. But then he kissed me—slow this time, coaxing instead of devouring—and my knees gave up the fight entirely. My shoes slipped from my hands and hit the floor with soft thuds as I melted against him, my hands sliding up his chest.

"Not fair," I muttered against his mouth.

He smiled against my lips, his hand sliding to my waist, pulling me flush against him. "Wasn't trying to play fair."

I kissed him back, because honestly? Screw fair.

He scooped me back into his arms and carried me toward the bed, my whole "sneak out before feelings get involved" plan officially dead.

He laid me back against the sheets, his weight settling over me. He stripped my clothes off me once more, tossing them haphazardly to the floor. This time the sex wasn't frantic or rushed. It was slower, deeper, almost reverent, like we both knew this wasn't just about heat anymore.

Every kiss lingered. Every touch burned, softer but more dangerous because of it.

When we finally collapsed together again, tangled in his sheets, his arms stayed wrapped around me, his face buried against my neck like he had no intention of letting me go this time.

"You're staying," he murmured, voice heavy with sleep but certain.

I should have argued. I should have said something sarcastic.

Instead, I sighed and curled closer, my hand resting against his chest. "For tonight," I whispered.

He made a low, satisfied sound, pressing a soft kiss to my temple. "Good enough for now."

And damn it, I didn't even try to fight him on it.

CHAPTER 26

KNOCK FIRST, IDIOT

BECKETT

I WOKE up to find I hadn't dreamed last night—and that Frankie was in fact in my bed.

Specifically, Frankie sprawled half on top of me like she'd been trying to stake a claim in her sleep. Her hair was a soft mess against my chest, her leg hooked over mine, her hand resting just below my ribs like she'd fallen asleep mid-grab. She smelled like sugar, vanilla, and my soap—that's how close she'd been to my skin, and every damn thing about her felt too good. Too right.

Mine.

The word lodged in my brain before I could shove it away, which was a problem. Because nothing about Frankie Bellamy was mine—not in any way that mattered.

Still, I didn't move. I let myself look at her—let my eyes trace the slope of her nose, the way her lips were parted just slightly, the faint pink flush that still lingered across her cheeks. Frankie didn't do soft for anyone, but here she was, curled into me like it was the most natural thing in the world.

I brushed a strand of hair back from her face, careful not to wake her. She murmured something that sounded suspiciously like *coffee* and burrowed closer, and yeah, I could've stayed like there all morning.

But my life didn't work like that.

The creak of my front door opening shattered the quiet, followed by heavy boots and the worst possible voice to hear when you've got a gorgeous, half-naked woman in your bed.

"Yo, Beckett!"

Nate.

I muttered a curse, glancing at the clock. Too early. Hell, any time of day was too early for Nate. Frankie stirred, mumbling something sleep-slurred again, and I snugged my arm around her automatically.

"Everything okay up there?" Nate called, his voice carrying as he climbed the stairs and came down the hall, and I could *hear* the grin.

"Don't you—" I started, but the bedroom door swung open before I could finish.

"Well, well, well." Nate leaned against the frame like he'd been invited, sipping from a to-go cup and grinning like an idiot. "Look who finally got laid."

Frankie shot upright, clutching the blanket to her chest, her hair tumbling around her shoulders as her cheeks flushed crimson.

I glared at Nate. I was already leaning out of the bed, hoping to find a shirt on the floor. "What the hell are you doing in my house?"

"Bringing you coffee." He lifted the to-go cup in his other hand, smirking. "Didn't realize I'd need to bring two."

Frankie groaned, dropping her face into one hand.

"Morning, Frankie," Nate added cheerfully. "Nice to see you again. No cupcakes today? Shame."

Her head popped up, her cheeks still pink but a small, embarrassed smile tugged at her lips. "Uh—hi, Nate."

I froze mid-motion, dragging my shirt over my head. "Really, Nate—could you get the fuck out?"

Nate smirked, clearly savoring this. "The cupcake that called you Daddy? Highlight of my month. Thanks for that, by the way. It's all we talk about at the firehouse."

Frankie bit her lip, and I didn't miss the way her shoulders shook like she was trying not to laugh.

"Out," I snapped.

"Relax, big bro. Just saying hi." Nate leaned casually against the doorframe, unfazed by my death glare. "For the record? She's way too good for you."

Frankie's muffled laugh into the blanket felt like actual betrayal.

"Nate." I slid from the bed, tugged on some discarded shorts and was across the room in three steps, grabbing his arm and steering him into the hallway and back downstairs.

"Boundaries," I growled. "You knock. You wait. You don't come in unless I say."

"Yeah, yeah," Nate said, handing me my coffee, grin still wide. "But seriously, proud of you, Beck. Didn't think you had it in you. You've been brooding so long, I was starting to think you were gonna die alone with the ducks."

"Fuck off, Nate."

He didn't budge. "Coffee first. And hey, tell Frankie I said sorry for interrupting. She's got a great smile, by the way. Keep her around."

I tightened my grip on his arm. "Get. Out."

Instead of listening, Nate twisted out of my hold and strode into the kitchen like he owned the place.

I followed, still glaring, as he leaned against the counter, sipping like he had nowhere else to be.

"She's gonna bolt, you know," Nate said casually. "Not because she doesn't like you. She does. But you've got that whole 'I'm constipated vibe going on, and that's terrifying to women who like fun."

I dragged my hand down my face. "Why are you still here?"

"Because I want to meet the woman who bought you porn cupcakes in person. She's basically a saint."

Before I could tell him to get the hell out again, soft footsteps came down the stairs.

Frankie appeared in the doorway, fully dressed, her hair pulled back in a messy knot. She looked un-put-together enough to suggest she'd gotten dressed in record time, and her wide-eyed glance toward Nate said it all—she was planning an escape.

"Hey," she said, her voice a little too bright. "I should probably get going."

"You don't have to—" I started, but she was already sliding her shoes on.

"No, it's fine." Her cheeks flushed again as she glanced at Nate. "I, um… I'll see you later, Beckett."

She gave me a small, soft smile—one that punched straight through me—then offered Nate a polite nod. "Nice to see you again, Nate."

"You too," Nate said, grinning like the devil himself. "Next time you buy cupcakes, bring some to the station. Beckett hogs."

Frankie laughed, biting her lip. "Noted."

The door clicked shut behind her, and I stood there for a second, staring after her.

"Smooth," Nate said finally, taking another sip of coffee.

I turned on him, scowling. "You need to leave. You've royally fucked up my morning, you dick. I'm three seconds away from punching your face."

"She likes you," he said, ignoring me entirely. "And you like her. Which is why you're standing there looking like someone just stole your favorite duck."

"Nate."

"Fine, fine. I'll leave. But for what it's worth?" He grinned as he headed for the door. "Don't screw this up. Women like that don't come around twice."

"I really hate you right now."

He saluted me with his coffee cup, smirking as he stepped onto the porch. "You're welcome for the wake-up call, by the way. Next time, lock the damn door."

The door shut behind him, and I stood there for a long moment, muttering under my breath, "I should've drowned him years ago."

CHAPTER 27
GLITTER AND CRACKS

FRANKIE

THE WALK back across the yard felt longer than it should have.

Morning sun glinted off Beckett's windows, the grass was still damp with dew under my shoes. The air smelled faintly of his pond—brackish, earthy, and somehow comforting—and, because of course, a sharp little quack drifted from somewhere behind me.

I didn't look back. Bob had probably stationed himself at Beckett's porch like some kind of overzealous HOA president, and I wasn't about to give him the satisfaction of eye contact.

Not after this morning.

My cheeks went hot just thinking about it. Even though no one was around, I looked at the ground as I walked, hiding my face in embarrassment. Waking up tangled in Beckett's sheets, my arm over his waist, his breathing slow against my hair —it had felt too good. Too natural. And then Nate had barged in, making jokes, grinning like he was watching a live soap opera. I'd prac-

245

tically sprinted out of there, muttering some lame excuse about needing to get going while Beckett looked at me like…

Like he didn't want me to leave.

I hated how much I liked that.

Shoving the thought aside, I climbed my porch steps, already picturing a hot shower and possibly hiding under a blanket until my brain stopped replaying the way Beckett had kissed me that last time.

But then I saw *her*.

Tess.

My best friend.

She was sitting on the top step, hunched slightly, hands wrapped around a to-go coffee cup like it was a lifeline. Her platinum pixie cut was mussed, her sharp eyeliner smudged under her eyes, and her stacked bracelets clinked softly as she shifted, the sound weirdly out of place in the heavy silence.

Tess didn't sit still. Tess didn't cry. Tess didn't look like *this*.

No, my bestie was the woman who'd once dumped a drink over a guy's head for saying something gross about me at a college party. The woman who killed it as a lead bartender in the city— fending off douchebags hitting on her and cutting off belligerent drunks without breaking a sweat. And the same woman who'd marched into court with me during my divorce, cracking jokes so I wouldn't cry. Tess was bite and brass, all glitter and bold jewelry and middle fingers to anyone who didn't like it.

But right now? She looked… cracked.

She glanced up when she heard me, and for a second, I barely recognized her.

"Bellamy." Her voice was soft, rough around the edges, and she tried for a smile that didn't even come close to reaching her eyes.

I crouched beside her. "Tess. What happened?"

Her jaw clenched, her fingers gripped the coffee cup so hard I was surprised she hadn't crushed it. "Don't." She shook her head. "Please don't ask me yet."

I sat down beside her, my shoulder brushing hers, and for once, I didn't push.

"Okay," I said quietly.

We sat in silence for a long moment, the sounds of leaves rustling and distant ducks filling the space. I stole a glance at her, cataloging every detail because I couldn't help it. Her jewelry—normally loud and perfectly curated—looked thrown on, mismatched. Her eyeliner smudges weren't intentional this time, and the faint red around her eyes said she'd been crying for a while.

I couldn't remember the last time Tess had cried. Hell, I wasn't sure I'd *ever* seen her cry.

"I just needed somewhere to go," she said finally, her voice low. "Somewhere not Atlanta. And you're the only person who won't ask me a million questions the second I show up."

My chest tightened. Tess had been my person for so long. My fierce, loyal, no-filter best friend. If she'd run here—left Atlanta without a word—it had to be bad. Her parents were divorced, her dad out of the picture, and she wasn't close to her mom. I was more like her sister than her best friend. Seeing her like this made my blood see-saw between ice cold and scorching with pure anger.

"Well, you're here now," I said, forcing lightness into my voice even though my stomach was a knot. "And lucky for you, my guest room is currently duck-free."

That earned me the tiniest flicker of a smile. "Still with the ducks?"

"Unfortunately." I bumped her shoulder gently. "Though I think Bob's organizing a coup."

Her mouth twitched, and for half a second, I saw the usual Tess peek through. "You mean Duck Daddy hasn't gotten his poultry army under control yet?"

I groaned, dropping my face into my hands. "Oh my God."

She actually grinned, though it was weak. "What? He seems so dominating, it fits."

I muttered something unintelligible because, yeah, Beckett was a hundred percent dominant… and the damn ducks just made the label even more comical.

Tess leaned back against the railing, taking a sip of her coffee. "So. I'm assuming, since you're walking across the yard at," she glanced at her watch, "nine in the morning—you two finally hooked up."

My head snapped toward her. "What? No—"

Her eyebrow arched, sharp even through her exhaustion. "Don't lie to me. You've got that post-good-sex glow. And considering how long it's been since you've gotten laid, I can put two and two together."

I opened my mouth to argue, but she cut me off with a pointed look.

"Frankie, please. You think I don't know you? The only other time you've looked this flustered was when we were twenty-two and that bartender with the tattoos taught you how to make an Old Fashioned with his mouth."

My face went hot, because of course she remembered that. Tess's grin softened a little, but her eyes still looked tired. "Good for you, though. You deserve someone who makes you look like that. And if it's Duck Daddy, then I'm happy."

The words sat heavy between us. Tess wasn't the type to get sappy, and hearing her say it like that—quiet, almost wistful—made my chest ache.

"You're deflecting," I said gently.

"Of course I'm deflecting," she said, rolling her eyes, but her voice cracked just slightly. She glanced away, her fingers tightening around the coffee cup again.

I reached over, covering her hand with mine. "You don't have to tell me yet. But when you're ready, I'm here."

She swallowed hard, and for a second, I thought she might actually say something. But then she took a long sip of coffee and forced a smirk. "Fine. But only if you tell me if Duck Daddy kisses as good as I think he does."

I groaned. "Tess—"

Her grin widened, though it was still fragile around the edges. "Come on, Frankie. Don't hold out on me. Details. Did he finally pull that stick out of his ass and give you his meat wand?"

I smacked her lightly on the arm, trying to glare, but she laughed, and I counted that as a win.

"Come on," I said, standing and holding out my hand. "Let's get you inside. I'll make fresh coffee, and you can keep on with the duck jokes while pretending you're not having a crisis."

Tess let me pull her up, brushing her hands over her jeans. "As if you aren't having your own existential crisis right now."

"Rude," I said, opening the door. "You had a three-hour ride. Want to use the bathroom while I start coffee?" She nodded.

"So," Tess said as she came into the kitchen and plopped herself down at the table, "was it good, or was it *good*?"

I shot her a look over my shoulder. "Really?"

"I need details. Consider it payment for emotional labor."

"You literally just got here."

"Exactly," she said. "And I'm in crisis. You owe me a story."

I rolled my eyes, pouring coffee into two mugs. "Fine. It was… good."

"Good?" Tess snorted. "That's all you're giving me? That man looks like he could bend steel with his bare hands. Don't you dare undersell this."

I set the mugs down on the table, narrowing my eyes. "You're impossible."

She grinned, taking her coffee. "And you're glowing. So… he's good with his hands, huh?"

I groaned, dropping into the chair across from her. But then, just as she opened her mouth to fire off another joke, her smile faltered. Her gaze dropped to her coffee.

"I just needed to get out of there," she said softly, almost to herself.

Before I could ask why, she straightened, plastering her smirk back on like armor.

"So," she said, wiggling her brows like she hadn't just looked like her world was falling apart, "did he make you breakfast, or is Duck Daddy still a broody hermit who thinks toast is a food group?"

I snorted into my coffee. "Breakfast? Please. I was too busy trying to sneak out before the walk of shame became a spectator sport."

Tess's grin sharpened. "Oh, do tell."

I sighed, because she wasn't going to let it go. "His brother walked in on us."

Her eyes went wide, sparkling like she'd just been handed front-row tickets to the best show in town. "The sheriff?"

"No, that's Hank. This was Nate."

"Wait. *He has two brothers?*"

I groaned. "Tess—"

She leaned forward, all fake seriousness. "No, no, don't you *Tess* me. You've been holding out on me. How many brothers are we talking about? And—" her grin turned wicked—"are they as hot as him?"

I dropped my forehead onto the table with a thunk. "Why are you like this?"

"Because you move to some small-town soap opera, start sleeping with your hot grumpy neighbor, and you didn't tell me there's a whole *brother buffet* involved? Bellamy, I'm offended."

I glared at her from under my arm. "They're not a buffet."

She ignored me, clearly lost in thought. "So… Nate. What's his deal? Hot book boyfriend energy or is he the responsible older brother type?"

"Nate's a firefighter," I muttered, because I knew she'd just keep asking until I answered.

Tess gasped like I'd confirmed the existence of Santa Claus. "Shut up. A hot firefighter brother? You've been holding out on me!"

"Sorry—I was dealing with other things," I said, exasperated.

"Okay, okay, focus," Tess said, practically bouncing in her chair. "So Nate walked in on you. Details. Was Beckett shirtless? Please tell me it was awkward."

I groaned again, covering my face. "Of course it was awkward. He was definitely shirtless, I was half-naked, and Nate decided to make jokes like it was open mic night."

Tess cackled, leaning back in her chair. "Oh my God, I love him already. Please tell me he called you out."

I muttered into my hands, "He said, *Look who finally got laid.*"

Tess laughed and slapped the table so hard her bracelets clinked. "I'm obsessed with him. Invite him over immediately."

"No," I said flatly.

"Fine, then give me the other brother's info."

I glared. "This is not Tinder, Tess."

She smirked, unfazed. "Frankie, I'm emotionally wounded. You owe me hot brother details as payment for my suffering."

"You're impossible."

"And you're glowing," she shot back with a smug little grin. "So whatever you and Duck Daddy are doing? Keep doing it."

I buried my face in my hands again, because of course she was never going to let this go.

But for the first time all morning, Tess looked more like herself —sharp, teasing, and alive behind her eyes. And if I had to endure endless Duck Daddy jokes to keep that spark there?

I'd survive it.

CHAPTER 28

BROTHERS, BOURBON AND BAD DECISIONS

BECKETT

THE BEER WAS COLD, the Rusty Tap smelled like fried food and bad decisions, and for once, I wished I'd stayed home to clean the damn pond. Again.

Because sitting here with my brothers? Pure hell.

Nate grinned across the table, spinning his bottle cap between his fingers like a kid who knew he was about to light a firework. "So. Still ghosted, huh?"

I took a long pull from my beer and didn't answer.

"She's avoiding you," Jamie added, smirking. His baseball cap was turned backward, his chair tipped back on two legs like he thought gravity didn't apply to him. "Classic."

"Shouldn't you be back at school?" I growled at him.

Hank didn't even bother looking up from his whiskey. "She's pissed at you."

I shot him a look. "You're supposed to be the reasonable one."

Hank shrugged, unbothered. "Reasonable doesn't mean blind. You slept with her, and now you're stomping around town like you don't know what to do with yourself. She's probably waiting for you to pull your head out of your ass and actually talk to her. Did you ever think that maybe she thinks you've chickened out or changed your mind—or worse, regret what happened?"

Nate snorted, leaning back in his chair, arms crossed. "To be fair, big bro, your head's been wedged up there for years."

"Thanks for the support," I muttered. But Hank wasn't wrong… maybe she thought I regretted our night together. Which was the furthest thing from the truth. That night had been all I'd thought about. The memory of that night with her consumed me.

Jamie grinned, all too happy to pile on. "Look, I'm just saying, if you're gonna sulk every time a woman doesn't text you after sex, maybe don't sleep with the one person you've been low-key obsessed with for months."

"I'm not sulking," I growled.

"Uh-huh." Nate lifted his beer in mock salute. "You've been sitting here staring at the door like a sad Labrador for twenty minutes."

I gave him my best death glare, which only made him grin wider.

"Have you even tried texting her?" Hank asked, finally meeting my eyes.

"Yes." I snapped.

It was apparently all the answer they needed because all three of them groaned in unison. "For the love of God," Jamie said, tipping his chair forward with a loud thud, "just go talk to her. You like her. She clearly likes you. Don't be an idiot."

I opened my mouth to argue, but Nate cut me off, his grin turning downright evil. "Or don't. I'm sure someone else will be more than happy to keep her company."

"What the hell is that supposed to mean?"

Nate shrugged innocently. "Just saying. Frankie's hot, funny, and single. If you're not going to step up, someone else will."

I slammed my bottle down hard enough to make Jamie snicker. "Not funny."

"Relax," Nate said, still grinning. "She's probably at home right now, curled up with a romance novel, pretending she doesn't want to text you back."

Hank raised an eyebrow. "Or she's out with friends. Which, by the way, she's allowed to do."

I grunted, ignoring them all and taking another drink.

Almost three days. Almost three days since she'd hurried out of my house after Nate barged in on us. Nothing since then. Just quick smiles when we crossed paths in town, a wave when I passed her shop. No calls. No porch talks. No boxes mysteriously appearing on my steps.

And yeah, maybe I was sulking.

I was still stewing when the bar door swung open, and laughter spilled in. Nate was mid-sentence, but I didn't hear a word because my eyes locked on her.

Frankie.

She walked in like she owned the place, her hair loose around her shoulders, a soft cream sweater slipping off one shoulder, jeans hugging every damn curve. Tess followed right behind her, platinum pixie cut shining under the bar lights, sharp eyeliner perfectly in place, looking like trouble in combat boots.

And then Oz.

My eyes narrowed the second I saw him. Oz was too close, too casual, laughing at something Frankie said like he belonged there, right beside her.

"Uh-oh," Nate muttered, clearly noticing the way my entire body had gone rigid.

Jamie let out a low whistle. "They look awful cozy."

Hank sighed, setting his drink down. "Don't do anything stupid, Beckett."

But it was too late. Because Frankie looked up then, and for a split second, her smile faltered when she met my eyes. She quickly looked away, laughing at something Oz said, and something hot and possessive snapped inside me.

I stood, the chair legs scraping across the wooden floorboards.

"Beckett," Hank warned.

I ignored him, crossing the room in long strides before I could talk myself out of it. Frankie's back was to me when I reached them, Tess smirking like she'd spotted me coming a mile away.

"Bellamy," I said, my voice low enough that she stiffened instantly.

She turned slowly, her wide eyes giving her away even though her mouth curved into something that tried very hard to be casual. "Beckett. Hi."

"Hi," I repeated, my gaze cutting briefly to Oz, who looked like he was trying to figure out if he should be worried. (Spoiler… he should.)

"Didn't know you were coming here tonight," I said, letting my tone drop just enough that Tess's smirk widened.

Frankie lifted her chin, that spark I loved flashing in her eyes. "I didn't realize I needed to run my social schedule by you."

Tess bit back a laugh, muttering under her breath, "Oh, shit."

I ignored her, stepping close enough that Frankie had to tilt her head back to keep eye contact. "You've been avoiding me," I said flatly.

Her cheeks flushed, and for a second, she looked like she might deny it. But Frankie Bellamy didn't lie—not well, at least, and we both knew it. "I've been busy," she said finally, lifting her chin higher. "Tess moved in with me and we've been getting her settled."

My eyes flicked to Tess who just smirked. "Too busy to answer my text?"

Her lips parted, a quick flash of guilt passing over her face before she crossed her arms, that spark in her eyes now a full fire. "What do you want me to say, Beckett?"

I took another step closer, close enough now that I could smell her perfume, warm and sweet. "Say you weren't avoiding me."

"Maybe I was," she shot back. "Maybe I didn't feel like dealing with… this." She gestured between us, her hand trembling just slightly.

"This?" I repeated. "You mean *us*."

Her lips pressed into a thin line, and for a second, we just stared at each other, heat crackling between us like it always did.

Tess let out a low whistle. "Okay, so this is definitely going to end in angry sex."

"Shut up, Tess," Frankie snapped without looking away from me.

Oz cleared his throat awkwardly. "Uh, I'm gonna... go get a drink."

"Good idea," I said, my eyes still locked on Frankie's.

"Beckett—" she started, but I cut her off, my voice low and unyielding.

"Don't."

Her pulse jumped in her throat, and for once, she didn't argue. I was about to tell her we were leaving, but Tess's voice cut in, bright and amused.

"So, these are the famous brothers I keep hearing about."

Frankie groaned softly, closing her eyes like she was praying for patience. Tess, of course, looked like she'd just walked into a candy store.

I looked back at the table. Nate, Jamie, and Hank were watching us with varying expressions—Nate grinning like an idiot, Hank looking unimpressed, and Jamie leaning back in his chair like this was better than television.

Frankie and I followed Tess as she sauntered over, arms crossed, her sharp grin aimed squarely at them. "Okay, let me guess. You're the sheriff—" she pointed at Hank, "—and you're the firefighter." Her finger swung to Nate.

Nate grinned, lifting his beer in acknowledgment. "Guilty."

"Right," Tess said, her smirk widening. "Frankie told me all about you two. Broody lawman, cocky firefighter. Very on brand."

Frankie muttered, "I did *not* tell you all about them," but Tess ignored her.

Then Tess's gaze landed on Jamie, and her eyes lit up. "And who," she said slowly, tilting her head, "is *this*?"

Jamie straightened, clearly amused. "Jamie. The sexy brother."

Tess blinked, then grinned like Christmas had just come early. "Frankie didn't mention you."

"She didn't?" Jamie asked, smirking.

"Nope," Tess said, her tone going teasingly sweet. "Which is a shame, because damn, Rookie, you're right… you are sexy."

Jamie laughed, leaning back in his chair just a little further. "Rookie, huh?"

"You look like a Rookie," Tess said. "Let me guess—baby of the family?"

"Yeah," Jamie said, still grinning. "Hank's the oldest, then there's that guy," he pointed at me. "Nate—Caleb, and then me. They saved the best for last."

"Oh, shit… there's four of you?" Tess said, drawing the word "four" out, her grin wicked now. "So that means you're the *fun* one. Unless Caleb is hiding somewhere and I can check to see if he's funnier."

"Caleb's in the Army. So, no. He isn't hiding somewhere. I'm all you got for fun, pretty girl."

Frankie groaned softly beside me. "Tess—"

But Tess had already stepped closer, leaning one hand on the back of Jamie's chair. "Wanna dance, Little Ford?"

Jamie raised an eyebrow, clearly entertained. "You asking me, or telling me?"

"Both," Tess said with a grin.

Oz—who'd returned with a drink and was hovering nearby like an unwanted houseplant—snorted. "Isn't he a little young for you, Tess?"

Without missing a beat, Tess flipped him off. "Shut up, Oz. I've dated older, I've dated younger, and I've dated smarter. Two out of three works for me."

Jamie nearly choked on his beer as he laughed, already getting to his feet. "I like her."

"Of course you do," Nate said, shaking his head.

Tess grabbed Jamie's hand, tugging him toward the dance floor. "Come on, Rookie. Let's see if you've got moves."

Jamie glanced over his shoulder at me as Tess pulled him away. "Don't wait up."

Hank just sighed into his whiskey. "This'll end well."

Nate grinned. "I'm betting she eats him alive."

Frankie groaned softly, dragging her hand down her face. "I hate all of you."

But I barely heard them. Because Frankie was still standing there, arms crossed, trying very hard not to look at me.

I stepped closer, lowering my voice so only she could hear. "Did you bring backup to avoid me?"

Her gaze snapped to mine, sparks in her eyes again. "You think this is about *you*?"

"Everything's about me," I said, because I couldn't help myself.

She narrowed her eyes, muttering something under her breath, but she didn't move, and that was all the invitation I needed.

The music from the dance floor thumped through the bar, Tess was spinning Jamie around like she owned him, Nate was laughing, and Hank sipped his whiskey like he was pretending he wasn't watching me.

But I didn't care, because all I could see was her.

Frankie Bellamy. Standing there like she hadn't been avoiding me for days, like she wasn't driving me half out of my mind just by existing. I stepped closer, close enough that the edge of her sweater brushed my chest. Her chin tilted up, defiant, even though her pulse jumped in her throat.

"I don't like that you've been avoiding me," I said, low so that no one else could hear.

Her eyes narrowed. "I told you—I've been busy."

"Yeah… I heard you. But that doesn't make it right."

She flinched just slightly, then straightened, fire flashing in her eyes. "I don't owe you updates on my schedule, Beckett."

That possessive heat I'd been holding back for days roared to life. "Maybe not. But the other night? You said you wouldn't pretend it didn't matter. We *both* agreed on that. So you don't get to pretend now that nothing happened."

Her lips parted, but before she could snap back, I glanced over at Oz, who was still hovering nearby, trying to look casual while keeping the drink he'd gotten close.

"Why is he here?" I growled.

Frankie's eyebrows shot up. "Oz? Because he's our friend, Beckett. Not that it's any of your business."

"Everything about you is my business," I said, my voice dropping.

Her breath caught, and for a second, I thought she might actually step back. But this was Frankie—she never backed down.

"You don't get to act like you own me," she said, her chin tilting higher.

I leaned in, my voice rough. "I don't *act* like anything. I'm telling you right now—I don't like seeing you with him."

Her eyes widened slightly, her cheeks flushing pink, and for a heartbeat, neither of us moved.

Behind us, Nate muttered something that sounded like, "Oh, this is gonna be good," but I ignored him.

"Beckett," she started, her voice quieter now, but I wasn't letting her walk away again.

"Come with me," I said, already taking her hand before she could argue.

"Beck—"

I cut her off. "Not here."

Her eyes darted to where Tess was still dancing with Jamie, laughing like she was having the time of her life. Tess caught Frankie's gaze, smirked, and gave her a thumbs-up as if to say she approved of me dragging her off.

Frankie sighed, muttering, "I'm going to kill her later," but she didn't pull away.

Good.

I guided her toward the far end of the bar, around the corner near the empty back hallway where the music dulled to a thrum.

When we stopped, I turned to face her, blocking her exit with one hand against the wall. "I don't like that you're avoiding me," I said again, softer now but no less certain.

She crossed her arms, but her voice wavered just slightly. "You're imagining things."

"Frankie." I stepped closer, crowding her against the wall, my free hand brushing her hip. "You all but ran out of my house like your ass was on fire, and then you avoided my text."

Her breath hitched, her fire dimming just enough that I saw something else, something softer behind her eyes. "I don't know what to do with this, Beckett," she admitted quietly, her chin trembling the tiniest bit. "You and me… this wasn't supposed to happen."

"Too late," I said, my thumb brushing the edge of her sweater. "It happened. And I'm not letting you pretend it didn't."

She let out a shaky breath, her hands gripping her biceps. "You make it sound so simple."

"It *is* simple," I said, leaning closer, my voice rough. "You want me. I want you. Stop fighting it."

Her eyes met mine, and for a second, she looked like she might argue again. But then her shoulders sagged, her lips parting on a quiet exhale.

"Damn it," she muttered, and then her hands fisted in my shirt, dragging me down into a kiss.

It wasn't soft. It wasn't careful.

It was everything.

CHAPTER 29
DUCK DADDY GETS BENCHED

FRANKIE

THE SECOND I grabbed his shirt and tugged him down, Beckett's mouth crashed into mine like we'd both been holding our breath for days.

Because maybe we had.

His kiss was hot and consuming. His hand slid to my waist, pulling me flush against him until the world tilted. My back hit the wall, the wood cool through my sweater, and his body was all heat and tension pressing into mine.

"Beckett—" I tried, but my protest came out breathless and pathetic, and he swallowed it with another kiss, his mouth teasing my lower lip just enough to make my pulse spike.

God help me, I kissed him back. My hands slid up his chest, clinging to his shoulders like I couldn't decide if I wanted to shove him away or drag him closer. News flash… I definitely wanted closer.

"You're driving me insane," he muttered against my mouth, his voice rough, wrecked.

"Good," I whispered back before I could stop myself.

He groaned low in his chest, pressing me harder against the wall, his thumb brushing under my sweater, skimming bare skin. I shivered, biting back a soft gasp that only made his grip tighten. Oh, this was bad. Very, very bad.

Because I wanted him more than I didn't.

And I'd been avoiding him precisely because of this—because I knew if I let him close again, I wouldn't be able to stop. But stopping wasn't happening now, not with Beckett Ford kissing me like I was the only damn thing in the world that mattered.

"Jesus Christ, can you two *not* do that in public?" We broke apart, breathless and flushed, both of us snapping our heads toward the voice. Hank stood a few feet away, arms crossed, his expression flat like he couldn't handle any snippet of happiness from someone else.

"Not now, Hank," Beckett growled, his hand still firmly on my waist.

"Yeah, now," Hank said, jerking his thumb toward the bar. "Because your night just got real interesting."

Something in his tone made my stomach twist. "What's going on?"

Hank's usual no-nonsense sheriff face slipped into something closer to *You're not going to like this* as he looked at me. "Your dickhead ex just rolled into the bar."

I froze, my heart dropping straight into my stomach. "Chris?" I asked, my voice quieter than I wanted it to be.

Hank nodded. "He's over by the entrance, talking to someone. Looks like he hasn't spotted you yet."

My fingers tightened in the hem of my sweater, a flood of unwelcome memories washing through me. Chris. Here. Of all places. Beckett went rigid beside me, his jaw clenched so hard I could see the muscle jump.

"He came here?" he said, his voice like gravel.

"Beckett—" I started, but he was already stepping closer, blocking me from view like some human wall. "Beckett, move," I said, trying to edge past him.

He didn't budge. "He's not coming near you."

My head snapped up, heat sparking through my chest. "You don't get to decide that."

"The hell I don't." His voice was almost threatening as his eyes burned into mine. "You're *mine*, Frankie. He doesn't get to come within ten feet of you—not after what he did."

My breath caught, my heart lurching because—God help me—I wanted to argue, but part of me didn't hate what he said. Despite that traitorous thought, I managed to keep my voice firm. "I am not yours."

He leaned in, his hand still warm on my waist. "Could've fooled me."

My cheeks heated, and for a second, I forgot how to breathe.

"Uh, Beckett?" Nate's voice carried across the bar as he moved toward us, clearly entertained. "You might want to hurry. Looks like her douche of an ex just spotted y'all."

I swore under my breath, but Beckett swore louder.

"I mean it, Frankie. He's not—"

"Don't." My voice snapped sharper than I intended, halting him mid-step. His eyes flicked to mine, surprised, but I didn't let him speak. "Don't you dare try to control this," I said, lowering my voice, though every word dripped fire. "I am not yours, Beckett. I'm not anyone's. And I'll be damned if I let you—or any man—fight my battles for me."

His jaw worked, his eyes dark, but he didn't argue. Not yet.

"I've spent too many years letting a man tell me what I could do, where I could go, who I could be," I continued, stepping in closer until we were practically nose to nose. "I left that life, Beckett. I will *never* go back to it. Not for Chris. Not for you. Not for anyone."

For a second, we just stood there, locked in a silent standoff. His breathing was slow and deep, his hands fisted at his sides like he was physically holding himself back. Then, finally, he gave me a short, rough nod.

"Fine," he said, his voice quiet. "But I'm not standing down if he touches you."

"Fair enough," I replied, my heart pounding, and then stepped past him before he could change his mind.

The bar grew louder as I moved through it, the music thumping, people laughing, most everyone oblivious to the fact that the worst part of my past had just walked through the door.

Chris Monroe was exactly as I had left him in Atlanta—expensive jacket, fake smile, and that practiced charm that had worked on everyone, including me for a while.

His eyes landed on me, and that fake smile widened. "There you are, Francesca."

I stopped a few feet away, crossing my arms. "It's Frankie. I've told you that over and over, Chris." He moved like he was going to come closer, but I held up a hand, halting him mid-step.

"Don't. Stay right there. I told you the last time you were here, not to come back."

His smile faltered. "Come on, *Francesca*," he spat my name like it was poison. "Don't be like that."

"Don't *call* me that," I snapped, my voice sharp enough to cut through the noise around us. Heads turned, but I didn't care.

Chris blinked, clearly not expecting this. "I just want to talk."

"You lost the right to talk to me the second the divorce papers were signed," I said, keeping my voice firm even though my pulse was hammering. "You don't get to keep showing up here, threatening me. I don't owe you shit."

"Francesca."

"No." My voice went steel, loud enough for him—and everyone else within ten feet—to hear. "I've built a life without you, and I'm not letting you ruin it. So, turn around, Chris. Leave. Now."

For a second, he just stood there, lips pursed, clearly not used to me telling him no.

Then Beckett's presence filled the space behind me, quiet but *there*, like a wall of heat and tension. He didn't say a word, didn't move, but the way his shadow loomed over us made Chris glance past me and think twice.

Chris swallowed hard, his fake charm slipping. "Fine," he muttered, adjusting his jacket. "Enjoy your little… small-town thing, Francesca. I'll get what I'm due one way or another."

I didn't blink. He stared at me for another beat, then finally turned, pushing through the bar crowd toward the door. The second he was gone, the tight coil in my chest unraveled, my shoulders sagging.

Beckett moved to stand in front of me and, for a few moments, just stared at me, something unreadable in his eyes. Then, voice intense but soft, he said, "Frankie, you're not anyone's. I get it. But for the record? You're still *mine*."

My stomach flipped, heat rushing up my neck, but not in a good way—not tonight.

I shook my head, stepping back. "No, Beckett. That's exactly what I'm talking about. You don't get to say things like that. Not after everything I left behind to make sure no man ever owned me again. I left a man who wanted to own me—control me once before. One who thought money bought them the right to whatever—whoever they wanted. I won't go back to that again."

His brows drew together as his eyes pierced me. "That's not what I meant."

"Doesn't matter," I said sharply, anger and adrenaline mixing in my chest until it burned. "You don't get to decide for me. Not now. Not ever."

Before he could answer, I pushed past him and headed for the door.

"Frankie!" Beckett's voice followed me, firm and commanding, but I didn't stop. Not this time.

Behind me, I heard Beckett call out my name again as he started after me. But before he could follow, another voice cut through the noise.

"Don't, Duck Daddy."

I glanced back just long enough to see Tess step right into his path, one hand pressed to his chest to physically stop him.

Beckett froze, looking down at her like she'd lost her damn mind, but Tess didn't budge.

"Move, Tess," he said, his voice low, warning. "Frankie, please just wait."

I paused, long enough to hear my best friend speak. "Not happening," she shot back, her platinum pixie cut shining under the bar lights, her sharp blue eyes narrowing. "She needs space. You go after her right now, all you're going to do is push harder—and she'll just run faster."

"I can fix this," he growled, his eyes locked on me.

Tess shook her head. "No, you can't. Not tonight. You care about her? Prove it by giving her time to get her head straight. I'll go with her."

Beckett stared at her for a long moment, his fists clenching and unclenching, like he was seconds away from ignoring her and coming after me anyway.

But Tess didn't flinch.

"Trust me, Ford," she said, her voice softer now but firm. "Let me handle her. You'll only make it worse."

For a long moment, he didn't move, his chest rising and falling hard, his eyes burning like a man fighting every instinct in his body not to chase me anyway. Then, finally, he exhaled sharply, stepping back. I saw Tess give him a quick nod, then I spun and pushed my way through the crowd. I could hear her boots clicking against the wooden floor as she hurried after me.

CHAPTER 30

DUCK, DUCK, YOU LOSE
BECKETT

I'D HAD ENOUGH.

Three days. Another three damn days of no contact. No calls. No texts. Not even one of Tess's obnoxious sticky notes that she'd been, for some unfathomable reason, posting on my front door, telling me to back off. Nothing since she'd stormed out of the bar.

I'd given her space—*too much space* as far as I was concerned. Tess had told me to let her breathe, and for some stupid reason, I'd listened. But today? Today, I was done waiting.

So I marched across the yard like a man with a mission.

The mid-morning sun was warm, the grass still damp with dew, but I didn't care. Bob quacked at me from somewhere by the pond, but I didn't even glance his way. My eyes were on one target—Frankie Bellamy's front door.

I stormed through the side gate connecting our yards. I stomped up her porch steps. I didn't bother knocking, just pushed the door open. And then stopped dead.

The room was full. I turned my head to look at the curb and, yup, there were cars parked outside. I'd been so consumed by my irritation that I'd completely missed them.

Frankie sat cross-legged in her armchair, glasses I'd never seen before perched on her nose, a book open in her lap. She looked… calm. Beautiful. Completely unbothered by the fact that I was practically vibrating with frustration.

Tess was sprawled on the couch, looking like she owned the place, grinning into her mug as if she'd been waiting for me to show up.

And scattered around the room were Ruth Simmons, Edna Grayson, and two other women I vaguely recognized from around town, each one perched in a chair with a book on her lap and a tea cup in her hand, like they were part of some sacred ritual.

Every single pair of eyes landed on me.

"Beckett." Frankie's voice was flat, her eyebrow arching over the rim of her glasses. "Can I help you?"

I crossed my arms, ignoring the heat creeping up the back of my neck. "We need to talk."

"Do we now?" she said, turning a page like I wasn't standing there about to lose my damn mind.

"Yes," I bit out. "Now."

She finally looked up, calm as ever. "I'm in the middle of something. You'll have to wait."

I blinked. "Wait?"

"Yes." She pushed her glasses up her nose, her gaze sharp. "Contrary to what you're used to, I don't drop everything just because someone barks orders at me. I'm my own goddamn person, Beckett. You'd do well to remember that."

That earned a hum of approval from Edna, who set her cup down with a clink. "Exactly, dear. Men need to learn patience. Always rushing around like they're God's gift."

Ruth smirked. "Especially this one. He's got that whole alpha male attitude. Thinks he can stomp in and claim what he wants. Reminds me of Captain Draven."

I frowned. "Who the hell is Captain Draven?"

"Oh, you'd *love* him," Tess said, her grin going positively evil. "He's the pirate in our book this week. Dominant. Broody. Bossy as hell. Total control freak."

Edna nodded seriously. "But he's got a tragic past, so it's *justified.*"

"Until he tried to tie the poor navy captain's daughter to his bunk for being *defiant,*" Ruth added, tapping her book.

Tess gasped dramatically. "Don't forget the spanking scene!"

Frankie's lips twitched like she was trying not to laugh, which only made me glare harder.

"Spanking scene?" I repeated, my voice flat.

"Oh yes," Tess said, leaning forward, clearly delighted by my discomfort. "She called him out for being overbearing, so he—" she held up her book, flipping through pages, "—threw her over his knee. Right here in chapter twelve. Gets me hot just thinking about it."

Ruth sipped her tea and nodded solemnly. "Very well written. Thorough descriptions of his—nether regions."

Edna added, "And to be fair, she seemed to enjoy it. His cock too."

I nearly choked at her words. I stared at them, wondering what in the hell was wrong with these women—alien porn and now… *pirates*. I tried to shake off my confusion. "What the hell does this have to do with me?"

Tess's grin turned wicked. "Oh, nothing. Except you barging in here right now, demanding Frankie talk to you, is *exactly* something Captain Draven would do."

"Dominant pirate energy," Ruth agreed, smiling smugly.

Edna tilted her head, eyeing me like she was sizing me up. "Plus, you've got a tragic past too. Maybe that's why you stomp around all scowls and big shoulders."

The other women murmured their agreement, Tess cackling outright.

"This is ridiculous," I muttered, dragging a hand down my face.

Frankie finally looked up at me, her eyes sparkling with amusement she didn't bother to hide this time. "No, Beckett. This is a book club. You're the one barging in here like some possessive ass."

"I'm not—" I cut myself off, exhaling hard. "Frankie. Please. Just come outside and talk to me."

"No," she said simply, turning back to her book.

My pulse spiked. "No?"

"You heard me. You can wait until I'm ready to deal with you. I don't ask *How high?* when a man says *Jump*. Not anymore."

The women all made approving noises, Tess practically doubling over with laughter.

"Good girl," Ruth said, nodding at Frankie.

"Teach him," Edna added. "Make him work for you, deary. It can't be all about good sex." She turned to look at me. "Sometimes you win, sometimes you lose, dear boy. Today you lose." She cackled at her own joke, sending my blood pressure even higher.

Tess winked at me. "Maybe he'll learn something if we read him chapter twelve."

My ears burned hot, and I was *this close* to throwing her smug ass into the pond. I stood there for another second, staring at Frankie, half tempted to just haul her outside whether she liked it or not. But one look at her face told me that would only make things worse.

"Fine," I said finally, my jaw so tight it hurt. "I'll wait."

Frankie didn't even look up. "Good."

I turned and stalked out, Tess's laughter following me all the way to the porch. By the time I got back across the lawn, I was steaming. I headed straight for my pond, hoping the quiet would calm me down.

The sun glinted off the water, the ducks lazily drifting. It should've been peaceful.

But then I spotted Bob.

Bob was climbing onto Willow's back, his little wings flapping like he was trying to impress her. Willow floated serenely, tilting her head toward him like she was… encouraging it. What the fuck was happening right now? My goddamn ducks were… getting more action than me.

"Jesus, Bob," I muttered, rubbing a hand down my face. "Really?"

He quacked, entirely unapologetic.

"Unbelievable," I muttered. "You've got better game than I do. At least *you're* getting somewhere."

My phone buzzed in my pocket, interrupting my duck-induced humiliation. I pulled it out, frowning at the name on the screen— my attorney.

"Yeah?" I answered.

"Beckett," he said, his voice clipped. "We need to talk. Daniel Maddox showed his hand. He filed a motion this morning claiming you're hiding company secrets. I'm afraid you're going to have to come to New York again as soon as possible."

I closed my eyes, the peaceful pond suddenly feeling like the calm before the storm.

"Of course he did," I muttered.

Because apparently, my life wasn't complicated enough already. When the call ended, I stood there for a long moment, staring at the pond like it might offer some kind of answer. It didn't.

Finally, I pulled my phone back out, scrolling to Hank's number and hitting call.

He answered on the second ring. "How's it going, Duck Daddy?" Hank chuckled at his own joke. "You and that sexy bookshop owner get things worked out?"

"No," I said flatly. "I—."

There was a pause, then Hank's voice, steady and wary. "Beckett, what's going on?"

I exhaled, staring at the water where Bob was still happily climbing all over Willow. "Maddox just filed something. I have to go to New York. And if this goes bad, it's going to be worse than anything I dealt with before."

Hank swore under his breath. "What the hell did he pull now?"

"It doesn't matter. I'll handle it, but I need you to watch after the ducks," I said, my fingers tensed around the phone.

The silence on the other end stretched before Hank finally said, "No, Beckett, you don't get to do this again. You think you're supposed to carry the weight of the world on your shoulders but you're not. Tell me everything, Beckett, and let us, your brothers, help you with whatever this prick is trying to pull."

I hesitated for a moment but then glanced toward Frankie's house. I was tired of running from the things that were good for me. But to have any kind of future, I had to let someone in. And for the first time in years, I did—I told my brother everything that had happened. Everything about why I left New York.

CHAPTER 31

WHAT THE DUCK?

FRANKIE

TESS DROPPED the last empty box onto the counter with a dramatic sigh.

"I'm starting to think you ordered these new releases just to torture me," she said, brushing a strand of platinum hair out of her face.

I slid a hardcover onto the romantic fantasy shelf, trying not to smile. "You offered to help, remember?"

Tess shot me a look. "I offered to drink coffee and make fun of your customers. This"—she waved a hand at the towers of new books we'd been unpacking all morning—"is manual labor. I'm too pretty for this."

"You're fine," I said, handing her another stack to shelve. "Besides, you're distracting me, so technically you're still doing your job."

She smirked. "Distracting you from what?"

I hesitated, biting my lip as I turned to face her fully. "From everything that's not bookstore related. I'm still avoiding Beckett and dealing with my ex. Plus, you haven't told me yet what happened in Atlanta."

Her grin faltered for half a second before she plastered it back on, busying herself with shoving the books onto a shelf. "We're not doing that today, Bellamy."

"Yes, we are," I said firmly. "You showed up on my porch looking like you'd been hit by a truck, and you've been dodging me ever since. Don't get me wrong, I'm over the moon you've decided to move here, but seriously Tess… What happened?"

"Nothing I want to talk about," she said lightly, not meeting my eyes.

I crossed my arms, planting myself in her path. "Tess."

She sighed, glaring at me for all of two seconds before her gaze slid toward the window. And then her face lit up like a damn Christmas tree.

"Oh my God," she whispered, abandoning the books completely.

I frowned, glancing toward the window. "What—"

"Oh. My. *God.*" Tess pressed her face to the glass like a kid in a candy store. "Frankie, why the hell is his *hot brother* next door and in the pond?"

I blinked. "What?"

"Out there. In the backyard." Tess pointed dramatically. "In the gray T-shirt. Playing with ducks. Sweet merciful—look at his arms."

I moved to the window, following her gaze, and sure enough, Jamie Ford was standing knee-deep at the edge of Beckett's pond, tossing food to the ducks, his T-shirt clinging to muscles he clearly didn't earn by accident.

I groaned. "Oh, no."

"Oh *yes*," Tess said, already heading for the door.

"Tess—"

"Don't *Tess* me, Frankie," she said over her shoulder, her grin positively feral. "I'm going over there to get me some seconds."

I grabbed the nearest book and set it down with a thud. "Seconds?" I palmed my face. I knew she'd gone back to the bar after she'd walked me home that awful night and that she hadn't come back until late, but *seconds*? "Tess! Wait!"

But she was already gone, the bell jingling cheerfully as she shoved the door open. I muttered a curse and jogged after her, nearly tripping over a box in my haste. By the time I caught up, Tess was halfway across the yard, her hips swaying like she was auditioning for a damn music video.

"Hi there!" she called, her voice bright and unapologetic.

Jamie looked up, blinking in surprise before his mouth curved into a slow grin. "Hey, beautiful."

Tess slowed her pace just enough to look coy. "Whatcha doing here, Rookie?"

He tilted his head, amused. "Feeding ducks."

I finally caught up, crossing my arms. "Tess."

"Frankie," she said sweetly, not looking at me.

I sighed, stepping closer to the pond. "Jamie, where's Beckett?"

Jamie glanced at me, still looking entirely too amused. "He's not here. Left early this morning."

My stomach dropped. "Left? For where?"

"New York," Jamie said, his tone casual even though the words made my pulse spike.

"New York?" I repeated, my voice higher than I wanted.

"Yeah." Jamie tossed another handful of feed to the ducks. "Something came up."

"By *something* you mean something bad? Right… why else would he go to New York."

Jamie studied me for a moment, "You know about New York?"

"Um." I shifted on my feet. "He told me a little about it, plus what I learned when I Googled him."

Jamie shook his head, his smirk growing bigger. "Well… someone tipped off his slimy ex-partner, Maddox, that Beckett had trade secrets or some crap. All lies, but now Maddox is suing him—again."

My chest tightened. "Beckett didn't say anything to me."

Jamie raised an eyebrow. "Maybe because you've been avoiding him?"

I winced, heat crawling up my neck. "I wasn't avoiding him, I was just—"

Tess snorted. "You were *absolutely* avoiding him."

I shot her a glare, but before I could defend myself further, my phone buzzed in my pocket, pulling my attention away. I pulled it out, expecting maybe a text from Beckett. But the name on the screen made my stomach lurch.

And the message? Even worse.

Chris: I told you I'd ruin your life.

The words blurred as I stared at them, my fingers clutching the phone.

"Frankie?" Tess's voice softened, her teasing tone gone in an instant. "What is it?"

I swallowed hard, my breathing shallow, every ounce of irritation I'd felt earlier evaporating, replaced by something cold and sharp. Chris was pulling some kind of bullshit. Maddox was suing Beckett. And somehow, I had the sinking feeling those two things weren't just coincidental.

"Frankie?" Tess's voice had lost all its teasing edge, concern replacing her usual sass.

I forced my lungs to take a deep breath, but my fingers were still clenched around the phone like it might fly away. "Chris, um, he, uh—" I swallowed the bile burning in my throat.

Tess stepped closer, her voice low. "What did he say?"

I held the phone out for her to see. She read the message, her mouth pressing into a hard line. "Son of a—"

"What's going on?" Jamie asked as he climbed out of the pond and moved toward us, his tone sharper now, the easy grin gone.

"Chris," Tess said before I could answer. She planted her hands on her hips. "That slimy piece of trash is threatening her again."

Jamie frowned, stepping closer. "You mean your ex-husband? That weasel from the bar?"

"Yeah," I said, my voice thready. "He's been… quiet. But I should have known he wouldn't just go away."

"Quiet's just his way of setting traps," Tess muttered darkly. She looked like she was ready to throw hands on my behalf.

Jamie glanced between us, his expression serious. "We should call Hank, he can—"

"No," I cut in, shoving the phone back into my pocket.

Jamie blinked. "Frankie—"

"I said no," I repeated, meeting his eyes. "I'm not running to the sheriff every time Chris sends some cryptic message. I'm done playing by his rules. Done letting him pull strings just to make me dance."

Tess tilted her head, studying me carefully. "So, what's the plan, bestie? Because you're right—Hank can't fix Chris. But sitting here letting him continue to poke at you isn't an option either."

My hands curled into fists at my sides, anger and something colder twisting in my gut. "I'm going back."

Tess's brows shot up. "To Atlanta?"

I firmed my chin and nodded once. "Yes. I should've done this months ago. He's not going to stop unless I face him—and my family—head-on. If I keep letting him throw punches from the shadows, he wins."

Tess blinked at me for a moment, then her expression filled with something that almost looked like fear, making me question her motives for leaving the city again. "You want to go back to Atlanta," she whispered, her voice losing some of its earlier edge.

Jamie looked less convinced. "Are you sure that's a good idea? It could make things worse for you."

"I don't care," I interrupted, shaking my head. "I left my whole life behind to get away from him, and I'm done running. I'm going to Atlanta, and I'm going to make sure Chris Monroe never has a reason to threaten me again. I venture to say he's behind this shit with Beckett too."

At Beckett's name, my chest squeezed, but I shoved the feeling down. I couldn't think about him right now.

Tess glanced at Jamie, then back at me. "Then I guess we're going to Atlanta. I'll call his office to be sure he's in town."

I looked at her, startled. "We?"

"Puh-leeze," Tess said, rolling her eyes as she scrolled through her contacts. "Like I'm letting you march into that snake pit alone. You're stuck with me."

I stared at her for a second before finally nodding, a lump forming in my throat. "You don't have to, Tess. I know something happened there, and if going back is going to send you off the rails, I can do this alone."

"I'll be fine." Tess smirked, her tone softening. "Someone's gotta keep you from punching him in the throat in front of your family."

"I make no promises," I muttered, my phone burning in my pocket with Chris's message.

Tess walked away a few feet and I could hear her speaking softly into her phone. Jamie looked between us, shaking his head. "You're both insane. And since I know my brother would kick my ass if I didn't, I'll go with you."

"I can't ask you to do that." I closed my eyes and took a deep breath.

"You didn't ask, Frankie. And someone needs to make sure neither of you gets arrested."

I managed a weak smile. "Thank you, Jamie."

Tess came back with an evil grin on her face. "It's a go. I'll update you on the drive."

Jamie clapped his hands. "Hell yeah. I'll call Hank and fill him in so he can check on the ducks. Meet you two ladies back here in an hour?"

"Yeah. That works." I turned back toward the house, my resolve hardening. "You sure you'll be okay, Tess? Maybe you should tell me what happened in Atlanta."

"No. Not until this is all done, Frankie. You need to keep your focus on setting Chris straight. When everything is over, I'll tell you, okay?" She cocked her head at me, watching my reaction.

"Fine. But I'm not going to let you avoid it."

"Deal. Now… let's go kick that shithead ex of yours' ass."

"This is it," I said firmly. "No more running. No more letting my weasel of an ex terrorize me. And when I'm done with him? He'll regret ever—"

SPLASH.

I froze, turning toward the pond.

"What the fuck?" Tess whispered, her hand flying to her mouth before she burst out laughing.

Jamie choked on a laugh too, shaking his head. "Jesus, Bob."

Sure enough, Bob was *on top of Willow again*, his little wings flapping furiously while Willow floated placidly like this was her Tuesday routine.

"Are they—?" Tess started, then laughed harder. "Oh yeah. Oh, they are. That's… wow. That's enthusiastic."

Willow let out a contented quack, and Bob—the smug little bastard—looked over at us, puffing out his chest like he knew exactly what we were talking about.

I pressed a hand over my face. "Really? Right now? *This* is what I get as a sendoff before I go confront my nightmare of an ex-husband?"

Tess wiped at her eyes, still laughing. "Hey, at least someone's getting lucky."

"Unbelievable," I muttered, glaring at Bob, who quacked again like he agreed.

Jamie tossed the rest of the feed into the water, grinning. "He's got better timing than Beckett."

I shot him a look. "Not funny."

"Little funny," Tess snorted, elbowing me.

I turned back toward the house, determined to ignore the feathered porn happening in the pond. This was it. No more running. No more cowering before my past.

And when I was done with my ex?

He'd regret ever fucking with my life.

CHAPTER 32
PODUNK AND PROUD

BECKETT

THE CONFERENCE ROOM smelled like overpriced cologne, leather briefcases, and bullshit.

I sat at the long glass table, forearms resting on its edge, fingers drumming against the polished surface before I forced myself to stop. Every twitch, every movement mattered in rooms like this. Daniel Maddox thrived on reading people—he'd taught me that years ago when I was young and stupid enough to think he'd been worth learning from.

The floor-to-ceiling windows behind Maddox offered a sweeping view of Manhattan's skyline, glittering like it was in on the joke. It reminded me of Maddox himself—shiny on the surface, rotten in places underneath.

He hadn't changed a damn bit. His slicked-back hair gleamed under the recessed lights, his tailored three-piece suit screamed *money for show, not substance,* and his smirk—the same one he'd worn back when I worked under him—made me want to drive my fist into his teeth.

His attorney sat beside him, a young guy with expensive cuff-links and that neutral, I'm-just-here-for-the-retainer expression law schools probably trained into them. But Maddox? He was enjoying this far too much, leaning back in his chair like this was a casual lunch instead of a meeting about the lawsuit he'd blind-sided me with.

"This entire situation could've been avoided, Beckett," Maddox said finally, leaning back and steepling his fingers like some goddamn motivational speaker. "You should've just agreed to work with me when I offered. But no, you had to run home, to your podunk little town. Where you're playing with… ducks."

I didn't flinch, didn't give him the satisfaction of a reaction. "That 'podunk little town' has more integrity in one square mile than you've had in your entire life."

His smirk widened, shark-like. "Integrity doesn't make money." He gestured lazily toward the glittering city behind him. "This does. And instead of sitting here as my partner, you're about to sit as the defendant in a very public case. Public perception matters, Beckett. People will think you're a man who stole trade secrets from a multimillion-dollar cyberse-curity firm."

I resisted the urge to grind my molars, knowing that seeing the motion would please him. Voice even, I refuted his claim. "You and I both know that's not true. And if you had anything solid, you wouldn't need to sit here trying to spook me."

Beside me, Elijah—one of the only lawyers I trusted—adjusted his glasses, his tone clipped. "Mr. Maddox, unless you have documented evidence to support these claims, this case will be dismissed before it ever hits trial."

Daniel didn't even glance at him. His eyes stayed on me, smug and unblinking.

"Where'd you get this bullshit information, Maddox?" I asked, leaning forward slightly.

He shrugged, too casual, then lifted his hands in an *I don't know* motion. His cufflinks caught the light. "Does it matter?"

"Yeah," I said, my voice dropping to that low, cold tone that used to make junior execs practically sweat in meetings. "It does if you're dragging my name through the mud all because you can't run this corporation on your own merit. So I'll ask again— where'd you get it?"

For a long moment, he just looked at me, his grin widening like a shark circling its prey. He liked this—liked knowing he had my attention, liked that I was angry.

Finally, he tilted his head, his tone deliberately casual. "You should be careful who you piss off, Beckett. Fucking around with a powerful man's ex tends to lead to… unfortunate consequences."

The words landed like a punch, sharp and deliberate. And just like that, the pieces snapped together. *Chris Monroe.* Frankie's piece of shit ex-husband.

Heat crawled up my spine, my fingers curled against the table. "You're basing a lawsuit on gossip from a bitter ex-husband." My voice was low, cold. It wasn't a question.

He didn't deny it. He didn't need to. The smug twist of his mouth said everything.

"Chris Monroe has friends in high places," Maddox said, leaning back like he had all the time in the world. "If he says something looks suspicious, people listen."

I stood abruptly, my palms flat on the table, rolling my chair back hard enough to make Elijah shoot me a warning glance.

"You've got to be kidding me," I said, my voice rising despite trying to keep myself outwardly calm. "You're throwing away your own damn credibility because you fell for the lies of a man hellbent on hurting his ex-wife? You don't even *like* men like Monroe—you just want leverage, and you're too desperate to care where it comes from."

That grin finally slipped, just a little, the smallest crack in his mask.

"You've got no real proof," I continued, my voice rising, no longer bothering to keep it level, "and you're willing to ruin not just my life, but hers. Frankie didn't ask for any of this, but that doesn't matter to you, does it? As long as you get to feel like you've won."

"Beckett—" Elijah started, his voice a warning, but I shook my head sharply.

"Do yourself a favor," I said, my voice husky with the anger overtaking me. "Drop this before you look like a bigger fool than you already do. Because when this goes to court, and it will, I'll make sure every single person sees exactly what this is—slander built on the word of a bitter man, a man with a grudge and no actual knowledge of how to run a multi-billion-dollar company."

Maddox's attorney shifted uncomfortably, clearly not wanting to be in the middle of this, but Maddox only sat there, that thin smirk crawling back into place like a cockroach returning to crumbs.

"Done?" Maddox asked smoothly. "Because I will get what I want, Beckett. Either you agree to help me, or I let this out to the world. The choice is yours. How important is your new life, Beckett? Are you willing to risk it? Go on back to your little town and your stupid ducks. Because when I'm done with you, you'll be lucky to have anything left."

I glared at him for one long, steady beat. "Screw you Maddox."

I grabbed my jacket from the back of my chair, ignoring his quiet laugh as I turned toward the door. My hands were fisted so hard my knuckles ached, every muscle in my body was strung tight enough to snap.

I was halfway out the door when my phone buzzed in my pocket. I relaxed a hand enough to pull it out, glanced at the screen—and froze. The message was short. Five words.

Hank: Frankie needs you in Atlanta.

My breathing stalled, the conference room fading into nothing but white noise. Maddox's quiet, self-satisfied chuckle behind me only made the contrast sharper. I stared at the message, my jaw locking, my decision made before the thought had even fully formed.

"Beckett?" Elijah's voice cut through the haze, cautious now.

I turned just enough to meet his eyes. "Push the court date. Do whatever you have to. I'll deal with this when I get back."

Elijah frowned. "Back from where?"

"Atlanta."

Maddox's laugh followed me to the elevator, smooth and cutting. "Run along to your little country girl, Beckett. But when you get back, you'll find out the world doesn't care about your ducks or your morals."

I didn't bother answering him.

The elevator doors slid shut behind me, silencing him.

If Chris Monroe thought he could screw with me and threaten

Frankie in the same breath, he was about to find out exactly how wrong he was.

CHAPTER 33

CHAMPAGNE, LIES, AND DADDY ISSUES

FRANKIE

JAMIE LET out a low whistle as I parked Tess's Lincoln Aviator beside the Cadillacs, Rolls, and BMWs already positioned in ruler-straight lines, exactly three feet apart by the valet staff. It had been the right choice to take her car instead of my rusty pickup.

When Tess had called his office to try to find out where he'd be, she learned from his assistant, far too easily, I might add, that he was hosting a soirée this evening. The poor girl would probably get chewed out by Chris for that, but I'd worry about that later. *Maybe I'll send her some cupcakes as an apology.*

"Well," he said, leaning forward between the seats for a better view of the house, "that's… subtle."

I rolled my eyes, staring at the white-columned monstrosity where I'd lived with Chris. It looked like it should be on a plantation tour brochure instead of in the middle of an Atlanta suburb, but he knew my parents loved the whole *Southern aristocracy aesthetic*, and he'd wanted to impress my dad. He had certainly succeeded with this horrible place he called a house.

"Subtle isn't really Chris's thing," I muttered.

Jamie tilted his head, a grin tugging at his mouth. "This is the kind of house that smells like polished wood and generational trauma."

"Accurate," Tess said dryly from the passenger seat, adjusting her sunglasses as she looked at the house. "This place screams *We own three country clubs and at least one yacht.*"

"It's worse inside," I said, unbuckling my seatbelt.

Before I could get out, Oz chipped in from the backseat. "I always thought this house explained a lot about Chris. And I was right, because only a guy with a house like this would have the ego to text you *I told you I'd ruin your life.*"

"Please don't make me regret bringing you," I muttered, shoving the car door open.

Oz followed me out, stretching like this was just another casual day. "What? I told you before—guys like him always have one of those rooms full of creaking leather chairs and shelves of books they've never read."

"Truth," I said flatly, stepping onto the perfectly manicured lawn.

Jamie chuckled behind me. "Oh, this is gonna be fun."

"It's not supposed to be fun," I shot back, my pulse already picking up.

But Jamie just grinned wider, falling into step beside Tess as we headed for the side of the house. "Yeah, but I'm about to watch you verbally castrate your ex-husband in front of rich people. That's my idea of entertainment."

Oz snorted, nodding. "I second that."

I sighed, but the truth was, a tiny part of me agreed. Chris deserved to be humiliated. And if this went sideways, at least I wouldn't be alone. As we rounded the side of the house, the sound of voices and laughter floated through the warm late-afternoon air.

Chris was holding court on the back terrace, of course. A small crowd had gathered around him—men in tailored suits, women in expensive summer dresses, their champagne glasses glinting in the sun.

His *investment firm people,* no doubt. And front and center, sitting stiffly at a patio table like they were auditioning for a commercial about old money perfection, were my parents.

My stomach plummeted the second I saw them. Harold and Margaret Bellamy, both wearing their usual public faces—polished, composed. And, if the subject of me came up, ready to pretend their daughter didn't exist since she had made them look bad.

Chris caught sight of me first. His smile froze for a split second before morphing into something more practiced. "Well, well," he drawled, setting his glass down. "Look who decided to visit. I would've rolled out a red carpet if you'd told me you were coming."

"Don't bother," I said, walking straight toward him, my shoes crunching on the gravel path, its edges perfectly straight, not a weed in sight. "I'm not staying long."

"Shame," Chris said, his eyes flicking briefly to Tess and Oz behind me, then widening slightly when he noticed Jamie. His smirk sharpened. "Though I see you brought... friends, Francesca. How quaint."

Jamie snorted under his breath, but I didn't look back.

I stopped a few feet from him, crossing my arms. "Cut the crap, Chris. Why are you doing this?"

His brows lifted innocently. "Doing what?"

"You know *exactly* what," I snapped. "Beckett. You fed his old partner Maddox some lies, and for what? To hurt me? Congratulations, it's working."

A few murmurs rippled through the crowd, people exchanging looks like they'd just gotten front-row seats to a scandal. Chris chuckled, shaking his head. "Oh, Francesca. Always so dramatic. I didn't do anything except point out a few… questionable business moves to the right people."

"Bullshit," I said flatly.

My father stood then, clearing his throat like this was some polite dinner argument he could referee. "Francesca, maybe we should discuss this somewhere private—"

"No," I cut him off, my voice sharp. "Stay out of it, Harold."

He blinked, looking genuinely startled, but I didn't back down.

Chris's smirk widened, his tone dripping condescension. "You should listen to your father. You've always had trouble handling things like an adult."

I balled my fists, forcing myself to keep my voice steady. "You're hellbent on ruining my life because I left you. Because I wouldn't keep living like some trophy you could parade around in public, but *beat* in private?" A small gasp from my mother sounded off to the side. "That's all this is, isn't it?"

Chris tilted his head, his grin turning cruel. "You always did think too highly of yourself. You weren't special, Frankie. Just convenient. And now? Now you're just a sad little girl playing house with a bunch of nobodies."

I blinked in shock at his vitriol, but then forced a dry laugh, letting the sarcasm drip. "Nobodies, huh? Funny, because at least the 'nobodies' I spend time with aren't trying to take something from someone just to feed their egos."

Tess stepped closer, her voice cool but sharp. "Frankie… maybe we should just go."

"Listen to your friend, Francesca. You're way out of your depth here, and you're embarrassing yourself." Chris smirked.

Jamie shoved his hands in his pockets, his grin gone, his voice low. "You keep talking like that, and I might forget I'm supposed to behave."

Chris ignored him, his attention back on me. "You think these… little friends of yours make you better than me? Newsflash, Francesca—you're still the same immature girl who ran away because she couldn't handle real life."

I felt the words hit, sharp and mean, but I didn't let it show. Instead, I smiled. "Funny you call this 'real life,' Chris. I call it pathetic. Standing here, throwing parties for people who'd sell you out the second you stop making them money? *That* is what's really sad."

Out of the corner of my eye, I noticed a few of his colleagues glancing at each other. Chris must have noticed, too, because his chin went up a notch. I stepped closer, my voice dropping.

"You want to ruin me? Fine. But don't you dare drag Beckett into this just because you can't stand the fact that someone actually likes me for who I am."

That hit him, I could see it in his eyes, but before he could answer—

The air shifted.

A low murmur rippled through the crowd as heads turned toward the gate.

I turned too—and my heart stopped.

Beckett stood there, framed by the afternoon sunlight, looking every bit the billionaire tech CEO. Dark suit, sharp lines, and that hard, unreadable expression that I bet had once made entire boardrooms go silent.

Chris's smug smile faltered for the first time.

And me?

I finally exhaled, tension uncoiling in my chest.

Because Beckett was here.

And something told me Chris's little show was about to blow up in his face.

CHAPTER 34
BLESS HIS HEART, BUT I HOPE HE CHOKES ON IT
BECKETT

THE MONROE BACKYARD looked exactly how I imagined hell might—polished, expensive, and full of people who smiled while sharpening knives behind their teeth.

Chris Monroe stood in the center of it all like a damn ringmaster, drink in hand, surrounded by men in tailored suits and women who looked like they'd never bought their own groceries.

I recognized Harold and Margaret Bellamy from my initial Google search on Frankie. They sat at a patio table, stiff, their faces set in polite masks, no doubt watching everything with thinly veiled judgment.

And Frankie…

Frankie stood a few feet from Chris, chin high, fire in her eyes, looking like she'd rather be anywhere else but refusing to back down. Tess stood off to the side, arms crossed, looking ready to leap across the lawn and strangle someone. Jamie and Oz hovered behind them, both looking far too casual, but I could see Jamie's jaw twitch every time Chris opened his mouth.

Chris caught sight of me as I stepped into the yard, as did everyone else, apparently. The ripple that went through the crowd was obvious as people straightened, murmuring to each other. Good. Let them wonder who I am.

Chris's smirk spread, smug as hell. "Well, well, well. If it isn't Beckett Ford." He turned to his guests. "You've all heard about Beckett Ford, I'm sure. The disgraced tech billionaire?" He turned back to me. "Corporate espionage, I believe. Surprised you had time to stop by, what with all the new lawsuits I've been hearing about."

A few of the investment guys chuckled nervously, trying to stay on Chris's good side. I didn't answer. Not yet. I just kept walking, every step deliberate.

Chris gestured to me like he was introducing me to a crowd. "Everyone, let's give a round of applause for the man who once had the world at his feet… until he decided ducks and dusty bookstores were a better investment."

I stopped a few feet from him, hands in my pockets, voice calm. "Are you finished?"

That earned me a few quiet snickers from the crowd, but Chris just smiled wider, like this was his stage. "Not quite," he said. "Though I've got to hand it to you, Ford. You've got a hell of a PR spin going. This whole small-town act? Very convincing. But let's be honest—you're only here because of my wife."

He gestured lazily toward Frankie, who stiffened, but I didn't look at her. Not yet.

Chris's grin turned cruel. "You think she's worth it? Because I'll tell you what I told Maddox—you're just her rebound. She's always been good at running to the next shiny thing when she's bored."

Frankie inhaled sharply, her hands curling into fists, but before she could speak, I stepped forward.

"Are. You. Finished." I repeated, more sternly this time but my voice still low.

Chris chuckled, clearly enjoying himself. "Not even close. But by all means, go ahead. Say something noble for my friends and associates."

I tilted my head slightly, meeting his smug expression with a calm I didn't feel. "You're a disgrace."

That wiped the grin off his face, just a fraction, but I didn't stop.

"You're standing here, surrounded by people who wouldn't piss on you if you were on fire, throwing parties to prove you're still important. And you think ruining your *ex*-wife's life makes you powerful? That's not power, Chris. That's desperation."

A few gasps rippled through the crowd. Tess's grin widened like Christmas had come early.

Chris straightened, his jaw jutting forward. "Careful, Ford—"

"No," I cut him off sharply. "You don't get to talk. Not after what you've done. Feeding Maddox lies because you can't stand that Frankie left you? That's not just low. That's cowardly."

"You don't know what you're talking about," Chris snapped, his voice rising now, the mask cracking.

"Oh, I know exactly what I'm talking about," I said, stepping closer, my voice quiet but lethal. "You don't care about Maddox. You don't care about trade secrets. You care about control. Frankie walked away from your pretentious ass, and you hate that you can't pull her strings anymore. That's why you'll lose. Because real men? Real men don't need to destroy women just to feel relevant."

The entire backyard had gone silent. Even Harold Bellamy looked like he wasn't sure if he should intervene. Chris's face flushed, his hand tightening around his glass. "You think you're better than me, Ford?"

"I don't think," I said, my tone flat. "I know."

His mouth opened like he was about to say something else, but he stopped when I took one more step forward.

I didn't touch him—I didn't need to. The way he flinched was enough.

"Leave her alone and stop trying to take away her dreams," I said finally, my voice quietly lethal, my words meant only for him but loud enough for everyone to hear. "Because if you don't, I promise you, I will make sure every person in this city knows exactly what kind of pissant you are."

Chris swallowed hard, but he didn't say anything. Not this time.

I finally turned my head toward Frankie, my anger ebbing the moment I looked at her. She was staring at me, wide-eyed, her lips parted like she wanted to speak but couldn't find the words.

"You okay?" I asked softly.

She nodded slowly, though her throat bobbed like she wasn't sure what to say.

Chris muttered something under his breath and stalked toward the house, his colleagues whispering as he passed.

Tess let out a low whistle. "Well, damn. That was better than Netflix."

Jamie grinned, clapping me once on the shoulder. "Ten out of ten, man."

Oz, for once, was quiet, just giving Chris the kind of look that promised *he'd* be happy to finish this fight later. I ignored them all, my eyes still on Frankie.

She blinked, finally finding her voice. "Why are you here?"

I took a step closer, my voice soft but firm. "Because you needed me. And when I told you that you were mine, I meant it."

The backyard stayed silent, all eyes on us.

And just when I thought the moment was over, Harold Bellamy stood, clearing his throat. "Francesca, I think you've said enough for one day. Maybe if you'd just handled things properly—"

Frankie turned to face him so fast it made him pause. Her voice was sharp, clear, and cutting. "No. You don't get to lecture me. Not now, not ever. You want to know something, Harold? When you cut me off, you did me a favor. You thought you were punishing me, but you freed me. Because for the first time in my life, I don't have to play by *your* rules—or his. You never really loved me unless I fit into your perfect little box. Well fuck you and fuck your box." Harold's mouth opened, but Frankie's glare stopped him cold. "And my name is Frankie."

She turned back to me, her chin lifting. "I'm ready to go."

Tess grinned, clearly holding back a cheer, and Jamie gave a satisfied nod.

Frankie walked past her father without a glance. I followed her without hesitation, Tess, Oz and Jamie falling in behind us. I grabbed my duffle as we rounded the building.

When we reached the car, Frankie raised an eyebrow at me. "You ride-sharing this show, or what?"

I huffed a quiet laugh, shaking my head. "Uber dropped me off."

I snagged the keys from her and smirked at the others. "You three are in the back seat"

I glanced at Frankie, who had slid into the passenger seat without a word, her hands clasped in her lap. "You okay?"

She glanced at me, her eyes filled with emotion as she gave me a simple nod.

"Let's get this show on the road." Oz tapped the back of my seat. "Being crammed back here with these two is going to be torture."

I glanced in the rearview mirror, noticing how Jamie played with Tess's hair. "Jamie." He glanced my way. "Thank you."

"You got it bro. I'd do anything for you—Hank and Nate too. And I'm pretty sure if Caleb had been here, he would have throttled that mother fucker."

As I pulled away from the Monroe mansion, the silence in the car felt heavy but not uncomfortable—more like the calm after a storm. Frankie sat beside me, staring out the window, her reflection soft in the glass. For the first time since I'd met her, she looked… unburdened. No fire, no forced composure—just Frankie.

She caught me watching her and arched a brow. "What?"

I shook my head, lips curving despite myself. "Nothing. Just trying to decide if I'm more impressed by the way you told off your father… or by how damn good you looked doing it."

Her lips twitched, the corner of her mouth lifting. "Careful, Ford. You're starting to sound like you actually like me."

I grinned as the car rolled onto the main road. "Oh, sweetheart… I'm way past *like*."

CHAPTER 35
WALL SEX AND WATERFOWL

FRANKIE

BY THE TIME we pulled into my driveway, it was going on nine and my nerves were strung tight enough to snap. The entire ride back from Atlanta had been one very long exercise in trying not to explode. The whole day had just been so much.

Both bad and good. Chris. My parents. The way Beckett had stood up for me in front of everyone. The way he'd looked at me when he said, *Because you needed me.*

And now he was sitting in the driver's seat, dimly illuminated by the street light between our houses. He'd removed his tie, opened the top two buttons of his dress shirt and rolled back his shirt sleeves on our first pee break.

I watched him swallow, saw the flex of his forearms as he gripped the steering wheel, staring out the windshield with that unreadable expression he wore when he was barely keeping himself in check. Desperate to get out and breathe for five minutes, I reached for the handle and opened my door.

But Beckett's voice stopped me. "Come to my house."

I turned to look at him, thrown off by the demand. "What?"

His gaze locked on mine, steady and unyielding. "We need to talk. Just… come over. Please."

I opened my mouth, ready to argue, but Jamie cut me off. "Go, Frankie. Seriously."

I glanced at him in the back seat. The dome lights had come on when I opened my door, and I could see him grinning like this was the best entertainment he'd had in weeks. "I've got to head out, anyway. School's starting back up, and Coach'll murder me if I miss another practice."

"You're leaving already?" Tess asked him, arching a brow.

"Yeah." Jamie wove his fingers together and stretched his bent arms as far up as he could, looking infuriatingly relaxed for someone who'd ridden three hours each way to watch me go nuclear on my ex-husband in front of half of Atlanta. "But don't worry, I'll be back soon to check on you. Someone's gotta keep Duck Daddy humble."

Beckett groaned under his breath, and Tess smirked at his use of her pet name for Beckett. Oz, who'd been silent most of the ride, finally leaned forward. "Go with him, Frankie. Tess and I will hang out here. Maybe crack open a bottle of wine and talk about why she's here and flirting with Beckett's younger brother."

Tess gave a very pointed nod. "*Hot* younger brother."

Jamie just grinned, completely unbothered, as he opened his door and hopped out of the car, dragging Tess after him.

I sighed. "Fine. But I'm not promising to stay long."

Beckett didn't answer, just opened his own door and got out. He retrieved his suit coat, stuffed his tie in a pocket, and folded the coat over his forearm before raising an eyebrow at me and tipping his head toward his house.

The walk felt longer than usual, the warm evening air clinging to my skin. My heart thumped harder with every step, and no matter how much I told myself I was just going over to *talk*, my body wasn't buying it.

When we reached his porch, the door swung open before Beckett even touched it. Nate stood there, arms crossed, looking somewhere between annoyed and traumatized.

"Finally," he said, running a hand through his hair. "You need to get your ducks under control, man."

Beckett frowned. "What?"

"They're horny little fuckers," Nate said flatly. "I'm not kidding —I had to hose them off. I can't handle that again. I'm never duck-sitting for you. Ever."

I choked on a laugh, my hand flying to my mouth, but Nate kept going. "Bob was… *stuck* to Willow. Do you know how disturbing it is to have to pry ducks apart with a broom handle?"

That did it. The laughter burst out of me, uncontrollable, my sides aching almost instantly. I bent at the waist, tears stinging my eyes. "You… you pried them apart?"

Nate's expression was dead serious. "They were *making eye contact with me the whole time,* Frankie."

I couldn't breathe, laughing so hard I had to grab the porch railing to stay upright. "Get out, Nate," Beckett muttered, dragging a hand down his face.

"Gladly." Nate grabbed his keys, shaking his head. "Seriously, Frankie. Don't let him rope you into duck-sitting. It's not worth the therapy bills."He stomped through the doorway and down the porch steps to his truck. As he drove away, Beckett pulled me into the house and slammed the door shut. I was still doubled over, gasping between fits of laughter. "Oh my God—stuck together? Beckett, *what are you feeding them?*"

"Enough," Beckett said, dropping his suit coat onto the floor and stepping toward me, but I couldn't stop.

I leaned back against the wall, still laughing, wiping at the tears on my cheeks. "After today, I needed that laugh. But you own a bunch of perverted ducks. You know that, right? *Perverted ducks!*"

Beckett's hand came up, cupping my jaw, tilting my face to his. The laughter caught in my throat instantly, my pulse spiking at the sudden intensity in his eyes.

"Enough," he said again, softer this time, and then his mouth was on mine.

The kiss hit like a lightning strike, stealing the breath from my lungs. His lips were hot, insistent, his fingers sliding to the back of my neck as he pressed me against the wall.

My hands fisted in his shirt almost instinctively, pulling him closer, and he responded immediately, his body slotting against mine, all heat and coiled strength. I let out a soft gasp, and he deepened the kiss, his tongue sliding against mine with a possessive hunger that had me dizzy.

"Beckett—"

"Not letting you run this time," he murmured against my lips, his breath ragged. "Not tonight, not ever again."

And God help me, I didn't *want* to run.

His hands slid down, gripping my hips, pulling me flush against him, and I felt every inch of just how much he wanted me. Heat pooled low in my belly, my laugh long gone, replaced by something far more dangerous.

"Beckett," I said again, but it came out more like a plea than a warning.

He groaned, the sound deep and rough, and his mouth left mine just long enough to trail hot kisses along my jaw, down to my neck. His teeth grazed my skin, making me gasp again, my nails digging lightly into his shoulders through his dress shirt.

His hands slid under my summer-weight sweater, rough palms dragging across my stomach, leaving heat in their wake. My breath hitched, my back arching instinctively as his thumbs brushed the underside of my bra.

"God, Frankie," he muttered, his lips returning to mine in another desperate kiss.

I kissed him back with the same urgency, my hands sliding up to tangle in his hair. He lifted me suddenly, his grip firm on my thighs, and I wrapped my legs around his waist, a startled sound escaping me as he pressed me harder into the wall.

I could feel him, hot and hard against me, and it sent another rush of heat straight through me. "This what you wanted?" he asked, his mouth brushing my ear.

"Please," I breathed.

Our kisses turned deeper, hungrier, his hips pressing into mine as his hands gripped my ass, pulling me tighter against him. A soft moan slipped from my throat, and his answering growl vibrated against my chest.

"Hold on to me." When I'd wrapped my arms around his shoulders, he slid his hands under my sweater, pushing it up before he braced me against the wall again. He broke the kiss just long enough to say, "Lift your arms," and then yank my sweater over my head. "Much better," he murmured, his gaze darkening as it swept over me.

I flushed under his stare, but before I could say anything, his mouth was back on my neck, trailing lower this time, down to the edge of my bra. His teeth grazed the swell of my breast, and I gasped, returning my arms to his shoulders and arching into him.

"Beckett," I said again, my voice breathless, and his hands moved behind me, unhooking my bra with practiced ease.

The fabric slipped away, and his mouth was there instantly, his tongue circling a sensitive peak before sucking gently. I moaned, my fingers threaded into his hair, tugging as his other hand kneaded the other breast roughly.

"Perfect," he muttered against my skin, and I felt the words like a spark straight through me.

He eased me back to my feet, and then his kisses moved lower, down my stomach. And before I could blink, he was sinking to his knees, tugging at the button of my jeans.

"Beckett—"

"Shh," he said, glancing up at me with a dark, hungry look. "Let me have a taste." My breath caught as he pushed my jeans and panties down in one smooth motion. "Lift your foot." I did, and he slid off my shoe and freed one leg from my clothes. We repeated it for the other leg, and I was naked before him. "Beautiful."

His hands firm on my thighs, he pressed a kiss to the inside of one, his teeth grazing lightly, making me shiver. "Beckett, I—oh God—"

His mouth moved higher, his tongue sliding against me in a slow, deliberate stroke that made my knees buckle. His hands gripped my hips, holding me steady as he worked me with a focus that made it hard to think, let alone breathe.

"Oh my God," I gasped, my hands tangling in his hair as heat built low in my belly.

"Let go for me darlin'," he murmured against me, his voice vibrating through every nerve in my body.

I cried out softly as the tension finally snapped, pleasure washing through me in a wave so strong I couldn't stop shaking. Beckett held me through it, his grip firm, his mouth relentless until I finally sagged against the wall, breathless.

When he stood, his lips glistening, his expression dark and possessive, I barely had time to catch my breath before he kissed me again, letting me taste myself on his lips. My hands were already fumbling with his belt, fingers tugging at the leather strap like my life depended on it.

His hand slid between us, unbuttoning and then unzipping his suit pants in one smooth motion, and I could feel how hard he was through the fabric of his boxers. My body ached for him, every nerve sparking under his touch.

"God, you drive me insane," he muttered, pressing his erection against me as his lips moved down my neck, nipping just hard enough to make me gasp.

I shot back, breathless, tugging at his pants until they slipped over his hips. "You deserve it."

He chuckled darkly, a sound that sent a shiver straight down my spine. "Mouthy as ever."

"Would you like me quiet?" I teased, lifting a brow even as my pulse hammered.

"No," he said, his voice dropping, dangerous and full of heat. "I like you exactly as you are."

And then his hands gripped my thighs, hoisting me up effortlessly once again. My legs wrapped around his waist, my back was pressed into the wall as he ground against me. I bit back a moan, my head tilting back, hitting the wall as his hips rolled into mine.

"Beckett—"

"Feel that?" he asked, his mouth brushing my ear, his voice low and commanding. "That's what you do to me, Frankie."

"Then stop teasing," I breathed, my nails digging into his shoulders.

His smirk brushed my neck before his teeth did, biting lightly as he adjusted me higher against the wall. "Say please."

I scoffed, even as heat pooled low in my belly again. "Not a chance."

He growled, the sound vibrating against my skin, his hips grinding harder, making me gasp. "You're going to kill me, you know that?"

With one hand braced against the wall, he let the other slide between us, his fingers brushing against my slick heat. I bit back a moan, my hips jerking at the contact. "Always so wet for me," he murmured, his voice almost reverent. "Even when you're trying to stay mad."

"Shut up and—oh, God—"

His fingers slid into me, curling perfectly, and my words dissolved into a moan as he worked me expertly, his thumb circling my clit in slow, deliberate movements.

"Beckett," I gasped, my nails raking lightly over his shoulders.

"Look at me," he demanded, his tone sharp but full of heat.

I forced my eyes open, meeting his dark, focused gaze.

"Good girl," he murmured, his pace quickening. "That's it. Let me see you fall apart again before I slide my cock inside of you, Frankie."

My body trembled, tension building fast as his fingers worked me, precise and relentless. The pleasure tightened, sharp and overwhelming, and I couldn't stop the soft cry that escaped me as I came, clenching around his fingers, shaking against him.

He watched me the whole time, his expression hungry, possessive, like he'd just claimed something only he had a right to. When the waves finally eased, I sagged against the wall, gasping for breath. But he didn't give me long to recover.

How had I orgasmed twice already, when he hadn't even been inside me yet?

"Now we can move to the bedroom," he said roughly, his mouth crushing mine again before lowering me, tugging up his pants, and pulling me toward the stairs.

I clung to him, still dizzy, as he kicked the bedroom door open and set me on the bed. My clothes were already gone, and he took a moment to look at me sprawled out in front of him, his chest rising and falling hard.

"You're beautiful," he said simply, his voice quiet but firm, like it was a fact, not a compliment.

I flushed, trying to regain some control. "Are you just going to stand there staring, or—"

"Smart mouth," he interrupted, unbuttoning his dress shirt and shrugging it off. His undershirt came off next, revealing the broad, tanned shoulders and chest that had been tormenting me for weeks. "You'll pay for that."

"Promise?" I teased, biting my lip.

His eyes darkened further, and before I could blink, he was on me, pressing me back into the mattress, his mouth claiming mine again. I pushed at his pants, shoving them down while he toed off his shoes.

And then all he had on were black boxer briefs that did absolutely nothing to hide how hard he was. I watched as he palmed himself and gave his dick a squeeze through the fabric.

I swallowed, my eyes flicking down, and his smirk widened. "Like what you see?"

"Shut up and lose the underwear," I shot back, my voice breathless.

"Yes, ma'am," he said mockingly, sliding them off.

And holy hell, I'd forgotten just how big he was. His cock was truly a masterpiece, and I was about to claim it as mine. My breath caught, and he grinned like he knew exactly what I was thinking.

"Frankie." His voice pulled my gaze back to his. "We can stop."

Instead of answering, I tugged him down to me, kissing him hard. "Does that feel like I want you to stop, Beckett?"

"I need a condom." He started to move, but I grabbed him.

"I have an IUD… and I trust you, Beckett."

His eyes held mine for a beat before he gave me a slight nod. He growled low in his chest as he positioned himself between my thighs. His hand braced on the mattress beside my head and in one smooth thrust he was filling me so completely I gasped, my nails digging into his back.

"Beckett—"

"Fuck, Frankie," he groaned, his forehead resting briefly against mine as he gave me a moment to adjust. "I've never… You feel —God, you feel incredible."

His hips moved with strong, deliberate thrusts, each one hitting deeper, harder, sending sparks of pleasure shooting through me. I met his rhythm eagerly, our bodies moving together like we'd done this a hundred times before, like we'd been made for it.

The sound of skin meeting skin filled the room, mixed with gasps and soft moans that neither of us tried to hold back.

"Faster," I gasped, arching into him.

"Bossy," he said, smirking even as his pace quickened, his thrusts growing even harder, deeper.

One of his hands slid between us, his thumb circling my clit with just the right pressure, and I cried out, my hips jerking against him. "That's it," he murmured, his voice low. "Come for me again, Frankie. I want to feel you shatter around my cock."

The pleasure built fast, and with one more thrust, I detonated around him, crying out his name as I came, trembling under him. He groaned, his own pace faltering as he followed me over the edge, spilling into me with a deep, shuddering moan.

For a long moment, we stayed tangled together, breathing hard, his forehead resting against mine. "Holy shit," I whispered finally, still trying to catch my breath.

"Yeah," he agreed, kissing me softly this time, his usual restraint creeping back into his voice. "Holy shit."

I laughed, still breathless, and he kissed me again, slower, like he wasn't ready to let go just yet.

And honestly?

Neither was I.

CHAPTER 36
DUCKS DON'T NEGOTIATE, NEITHER DO I
BECKETT

THE FIRST THING I noticed when I woke up was Frankie soft and tangled against me, her arm draped lazily across my chest, her face tucked into my neck like she belonged there.

The second thing was pounding.

Not the good kind.

A loud, insistent banging rattled the front door, followed by Nate's voice. "Open up, Beckett!"

Frankie groaned, shifting against me, her hand rubbing my stomach. "Tell him to go away," she mumbled, her voice muffled against my skin. "He better not barge in here again."

"I *would* tell him, if he ever listened," I muttered, brushing a stray lock of hair from her face.

The pounding came again, louder, more urgent—and this time on the bedroom door. Then Hank's voice followed, calm but firm. "Beckett, I'm serious. You need to get your ass into the living room. Now."

Frankie groaned again, dragging the blanket over her head. "Go out there before they both get a wild hair and storm in here. One brother seeing me naked in your bed is enough."

I kissed the top of her head, forcing myself to move. "Yeah, I don't want to have to kill either of them. Stay here. I'll deal with it."

She peeked out from under the blanket, her hair a crazy halo, eyes heavy with sleep but already narrowing in irritation. She made a small noise of agreement and flopped back onto the pillow, muttering something that sounded suspiciously like, "If he wakes me up again, I'm killing him."

I dragged on a pair of sweatpants I found on the floor, running a hand through my hair as I opened the bedroom door.

Nate stood on the other side, arms crossed, his usual grin absent. "Finally. Took you long enough."

"You ever heard of patience?" I asked, voice still rough from sleep.

"Not when the world's on fire," he shot back, already turning toward the stairs.

When we got to the living room, Hank was standing there, his sheriff's stance on full display, arms folded, expression grim. The TV was on, the low murmur of a reporter's voice filling the room.

I frowned, following their gazes to the screen. "What's going on?"

"Just watch," Hank said, nodding to the TV as he turned up the volume.

My eyes went first to the chyron at the bottom of the news feed.

"CYBERCORP CEO UNDER INVESTIGATION: FRAUD, WITNESS TAMPERING ALLEGED."

The camera cut to B-roll footage of Daniel Maddox being hounded by reporters, his once-perfectly composed image slipping. His face looked stiff, almost panicked.

The reporter's voice-over cut through the room.

"Daniel Maddox, CEO of CyberCorp, is under investigation for multiple charges, including alleged violations of the Computer Fraud and Abuse Act. Sources close to the investigation have confirmed that several employees anonymously submitted evidence suggesting Maddox forged company documents and fabricated data to implicate his former business partner, Beckett Ford, in corporate espionage."

Nate let out a low whistle, crossing his arms. "Well, damn."

I didn't answer, my emotions in overdrive as I stared at the screen.

The reporter continued.

"Additional allegations claim that Maddox manipulated internal audits and destroyed records to cover up his misconduct. He is also under investigation for the suspicious death of a long-time employee last year. Initially ruled a suicide, the case has been reopened after multiple employees came forward, alleging the company pressured the victim and withheld evidence that could indicate negligence or even foul play."

The footage cut back to Maddox, his hair mussed, his expensive suit wrinkled as reporters shouted questions at him:

"Mr. Maddox, did you forge the documents used against Beckett Ford?"

"Do you deny the allegations of witness tampering?"

"What about the reopened suicide case?"

Maddox shoved past them, refusing to answer.

Nate glanced at me, grinning despite the tension. "I'd pay money to watch him squirm in court."

Hank gave me a look, steady and serious. "This clears you, Beckett. Maddox is fucked."

I exhaled slowly, rubbing a hand over my jaw. Relief hit, sure, but it wasn't as strong as I would have expected. My primary emotion was anger—at Maddox, at Chris, at the fact that Frankie had been dragged into all of this. Because I knew that the fight for our happiness wasn't over.

The sound of soft footsteps behind me made me turn.

Frankie stood in the doorway, wrapped in the dress shirt I'd worn yesterday, her hair a mess, her legs bare.

She blinked sleepily at us, then at the TV. "What's going on?"

Nate grinned immediately. "Morning, Sunshine. Nice shirt."

Frankie shot him a look sharp enough to cut steel, then turned back to me. "Beckett?"

I ran a hand down my face. "Maddox is done. It's over. He's under investigation for fraud, witness tampering, and... other things."

"Other things?" Her brows knit.

"Employee death," Hank said quietly. "Looks like a lot of people finally decided to talk."

Frankie's gaze returned to the TV, her expression unreadable. "So it's over, and you can go back to your life," she said quietly.

"This *is* my life," I said, watching her carefully. "I'm not going anywhere."

Nate clapped his hands together. "Good. Now maybe you can stop brooding and actually keep the girl this time." Frankie turned her head sharply toward him, and Nate just held his hands up, grinning. "Podunk life suits you, Beckett," he added, smirking.

I ignored him, still focused on Frankie. "You okay?"

She blinked, then nodded, though the stiffness in her shoulders said otherwise. "Yeah. Just… a lot to process."

"Now we need to get your ex to leave you alone and then maybe you two could have a real go at a life together." Hank plopped down onto the couch. "Because, let's be honest, your ex-husband's a dick, and none of us are thrilled about him lurking around like some wannabe Bond villain."

Frankie snorted, "What's your idea? Because if I know Chris, he isn't going to just give up. And since he's so far up my parents' asses, he thinks he has all the power."

Hank and Nate turned to me. I glanced at Frankie, who was still watching me like she was trying to figure out if I was about to suggest something reasonable or completely insane. "I could pay him," I said finally, leaning against the back of the couch.

Frankie's brows shot up. "Excuse me?"

"Money's what he wants," I said with a shrug. "If throwing some at him keeps him away from you, it's worth it."

Frankie's mouth fell open slightly, then snapped shut, her eyes narrowing. "Oh, absolutely not. No way in hell are you paying off Chris like he's some stray dog sniffing around for scraps. There has to be another way, Beckett."

"Frankie—"

"No," she said firmly, coming closer to me, fire sparking in her eyes. "You don't get to fix this with your checkbook. Chris wants control and giving him money gives him exactly what he wants. I am done letting him control me, Beckett. And I sure as hell won't let you do it for me, even if your heart's in the right place."

Nate winced, muttering, "Yikes. She's right, though."

"Thanks, Nate," Frankie said, still glaring at me.

I scrubbed a hand over my face. "You'd rather what? Wait around for him to try something else?"

Her chin lifted. "No. I'm going to handle him when it's time. But right now? I need to check on Tess. She owes me an explanation as to why she left Atlanta behind. Then I'll deal with dickface."

"Chris is a higher priority," I said, my voice low, controlled.

Frankie's gaze sharpened. "Tess is my friend. She. Comes. First. I can handle Chris when I need to. This is my life, Beckett. My fight."

The silence stretched for a beat before Nate let out a quiet, "She's terrifying when she's mad. Kind of love it."

"Shut up, Nate," Hank said without looking at him.

Frankie crossed her arms, still staring me down. "So unless you plan to tackle me to keep me here, I'll be back later."

I stared at her for a long moment, the protective part of me screaming at me to argue. But looking at her now—strong, defiant, completely in control—I couldn't help but respect the hell out of her for it.

Still didn't mean I was letting her walk out that door without conditions.

I stepped closer, ignoring Nate's muttered, "Uh-oh, here we go," and pulled Frankie to me. Her eyes widened slightly as I cupped her jaw, tilting her face to mine.

"I'm not letting you run," I said, my voice low enough so only she could hear. "If you're not back in an hour, I'm coming for you."

Her breath hitched, her eyes searching mine. "You're impossible."

"Yep."

Before she could retort, I kissed her—right there in front of my brothers, hard enough that she let out a soft, startled sound against my lips.

Nate made a strangled noise. "Well, damn. Guess subtlety's dead."

"Subtlety was never alive," Hank said dryly.

Frankie finally pulled back, her cheeks flushed, her eyes still bright with fire. "One hour," she said, pointing a finger at me. "Don't you dare come over before that."

I smirked. "Clock's ticking."

She rolled her eyes, muttering something under her breath as she turned for the front hallway. I heard rustling and assumed she was gathering the clothes we'd peeled off of her last night.

The second we heard the door shut, Nate let out a low whistle. "You've got it bad, big bro."

"Shut up, Nate," I said, already watching the clock in my head.

CHAPTER 31

DUCKS, DIVORCE, AND BLACKMAIL

FRANKIE

THE BELL over the door jingled as I stepped into the bookstore, the familiar scents of paper and coffee wrapping around me like a comfort blanket. The quiet was almost too perfect, as if the universe was trying to make up for the circus that had been the Monroe house yesterday.

But then Tess's voice broke the calm. "Well, look who decided to show up."

I pulled my panties from the pile of clothes in my arms, then dropped the rest to the floor. Giving a shudder, I turned them inside out and then slipped them on. Ew. But I was not having this conversation with Tess bare-assed.

I turned toward the corner reading nook and found her curled up in one of the oversized armchairs, legs draped over the arm like she owned the place. Her platinum pixie cut was as sharp as ever, eyeliner on point despite the fact that it was barely nine. She had a coffee in one hand, and her grin was way too smug.

"You look… comfortable," I said, narrowing my eyes at her.

Tess's grin widened. "Well, when your best friend finally stops being a stubborn idiot and gets laid by the broody duck king next door, it tends to prove that real love does exist. I like your outfit, by the way."

I groaned and crossed my arms over Beckett's shirt. "Oh my God, Tess—"

She smirked, leaning back in the chair. "What? I'm just saying, you and Beckett are basically like Bob and Willow. He's grumpy, you're sassy, and apparently the sex is great."

I buried my face in my hands. "I hate you."

"No, you love me," Tess said cheerfully, taking a sip of her coffee. "So, are you gonna give me deets or am I supposed to just assume there was dirty hot sex involved?"

I groaned louder, grabbing a book from the display just to have something to throw at her if necessary. "Not happening. This is not why I came here instead of staying in his bed." I cocked a brow at her, daring her to try and avoid this conversation.

"Fine," Tess said, though her grin said she wasn't letting this go forever. She shifted, tucking her legs under her. "So why are you here, then?"

I hesitated, biting my lip. "Because you owe me the truth."

Tess's smirk faded slightly, her expression softening. "About?"

"About why you left Atlanta," I said quietly. "You've been dodging me for weeks, Tess. And I get it, you don't want to talk about it—but I need to know. You're my best friend. If something happened to you, I need to know."

Tess stared at me for a long moment, her fingers flexing slightly on her coffee cup.

Finally, she sighed, setting the cup down on the table beside her. "You're not gonna let this go, are you?"

"Nope," I said, sliding into the chair across from her.

She gave a dry laugh, shaking her head. "Stubborn as ever. Fine. You want to know the truth? It's ugly."

"I can handle ugly," I said gently. "I mean, you know my parents and my ex."

Tess stared at me, then nodded once, exhaling hard. "Okay. You remember that guy I told you about a few months ago? The one I was seeing?"

I nodded slowly. "The marketing guy? You said he was nice."

"Yeah," Tess said bitterly. "He was nice. He was also married. I didn't know—he sure as hell didn't tell me. But his wife? Oh, she figured it out. She showed up at the bar one night, and screamed at me in front of half the staff. Grabbed the drink I was fixing and threw it in my face. Told me I was trash for trying to steal her husband."

My chest tightened. "Tess…"

"I swear to God, Frankie, I didn't know," Tess said quickly, her voice sharp now, defensive. "If I had, I would've ended it the second I found out. But by then, it didn't matter. Word spread. The bar owner didn't want the drama, so guess who got fired?"

I clenched my hands in my lap, anger bubbling in my chest. "That's bullshit. You didn't do anything wrong."

Tess let out a humorless laugh. "Doesn't matter, does it? Perception is everything. The married guy gets to keep his fancy job. The bartender? She's just disposable."

I reached across the table, grabbing her hand. "You are not disposable, Tess. And anyone who thinks otherwise doesn't deserve to have you in their life."

Her lips twitched, like she wanted to smile but couldn't quite manage it. "You always were better at pep talks than me."

"I'm serious," I said firmly. "You're strong, you're smart, and you're one of the best people I know. So screw him, and screw anyone who thinks you're anything less than incredible."

Tess gave me a small smile, finally squeezing my hand back. "God, you're such a sap sometimes."

"Shut up," I said, grinning despite the lump in my throat.

Tess leaned back in her chair, shaking her head. "You know, I came here to get away from all of that, but I think I just needed to say it out loud. So thanks for forcing me to talk, Bellamy. Now… what are we going to do about douchenozzle?"

"Ugh, I don't know. You know, Beckett—" I was cut off by a loud knock on the door. "What the hell?"

Tess raised an eyebrow. "Expecting anyone?"

"No," I said, frowning as I stood. "Beckett promised he'd give me an hour."

Another knock, followed by Beckett's voice. "Frankie, open the door."

Tess smirked instantly. "Ooooh, sounds like Duck Daddy couldn't wait, or just can't tell time."

I shot her a look before pulling the door open—and freezing.

Beckett stood there, looking as annoyingly hot as ever in a black T-shirt, his hair slightly mussed like he'd run a hand through it a thousand times.

But it wasn't just Beckett.

Standing beside him, looking entirely out of place on my little porch, was my mother. Margaret Bellamy, perfectly put together in a pastel blouse, her hair neat, her expression carefully neutral.

Before I could speak, a loud quack broke the tension.

I looked down just in time to see Bob waddling in through the open door, Willow close behind him, both heading straight toward the pirate romance display like they owned the place.

"Oh my God," I groaned. "Beckett—"

"Don't look at me," he said, shrugging. "They followed me."

Tess snorted, clearly enjoying every second. "Well, at least they're well-read ducks."

Bob quacked again, jumping up against the bottom shelf, knocking a paperback to the floor. Willow immediately started nudging it with her beak, like she was trying to read the damn thing.

Margaret Bellamy blinked, her perfectly arched brow lifting. "Are… You allow ducks in here?"

"Yes," I said flatly. "There are ducks in here."

Beckett gave me an unapologetic half-smile. "I found your mom standing in the driveway."

"Margaret," I said finally, crossing my arms. "Why are you here?"

She glanced up at me, her face composed, but her eyes… her eyes were softer than I ever remembered seeing them. "May I come in, Frankie?"

"Why are you here?" I repeated, sharper this time.

For the first time, her perfect posture faltered. She clasped her hands in front of her, exhaling softly. "Because I'm tired, Frankie. Tired of your father keeping me away from you. Tired of pretending I agree with everything he does."

I blinked, thrown off by the words. "What?"

She took another step closer. "I called my lawyer this morning. I'm filing for divorce."

The room went quiet except for Bob, who let out a loud, approving quack, as if punctuating her statement.

"You… You're filing for divorce?" I repeated, my voice a little too high.

"Yes," she said firmly. "I should have done it years ago, but I didn't. I let Harold dictate everything—how I spoke, how I acted, how I raised you. But this? What he's doing to you now? Using Chris to manipulate your life? I realized yesterday that I can't stand by and allow it anymore."

I stared at her, trying to process her words. "Wait—what do you mean 'using Chris'?"

Margaret's lips thinned. "Chris is Harold's puppet. He always has been. Harold encouraged him to pursue you in the first place, Frankie, because it was convenient for him. And now he's encouraging him to harass you because it punishes you for leaving."

Anger boiled in my chest. "Of course he is."

Margaret stepped closer, lowering her voice. "I told Harold yesterday, as soon as you left, that if he doesn't put an end to this, if he doesn't get his little crony Chris to leave you alone immediately, I will release photos he's desperate to keep hidden."

And this morning's news suddenly made sense. My brows shot up as I registered her last words. "What photos?"

Margaret's expression hardened. "The ones of Harold and several of his friends, including Chris, with girls he should never have been with. He swears they were eighteen, but from what I can tell, they weren't. He's been paying people off for years to keep it quiet."

I sat down hard in the nearest chair, my head spinning. I wanted to vomit. How was this man my father? "You—you threatened him with that?"

"Yes," she said without hesitation. "I may have been silent for too long, Frankie, but I'm not anymore. I won't let him hurt you anymore."

Bob quacked again, waddling toward Margaret and pecking lightly at her shoe as if in agreement. Willow followed, settling by her feet like she'd declared allegiance to my mother.

"See?" Tess said, smirking. "Even the ducks approve."

I ran a hand through my hair, trying to catch up with everything. My mother, my mother—standing here in my bookstore, filing for divorce, threatening Harold Bellamy with blackmail for my sake?

"This is… a lot," I admitted finally.

Margaret's expression softened, her voice quieter now. "I know I haven't been the mother you needed me to be. I can't undo the years I let Harold control everything, but I can protect you now."

My throat tightened, trapped my words while my emotions fluctuated between anger and gratitude. Beckett stepped closer then, his warm hand brushing my arm briefly. His presence grounded me instantly.

Margaret gave me a small nod. "I'll leave you to think about it, but Frankie—please believe me when I say I'm on your side now."

She turned toward the door, her heels clicking against the hardwood floor as she left. Bob tried to follow her, but Beckett stepped neatly in front of him.

When the door closed, silence settled over the room.

Tess broke it first, leaning back in her chair. "So… your mom's kind of a badass. Divorce and blackmail? Respect."

I exhaled hard, my head dropping into my hands.

Beckett moved in front of me and crouched, meeting my eyes. "You're free from him now, Frankie," he said softly but firmly. "From Chris, from all of it. And that means we can finally have a real shot at forever."

My heart stuttered, and for the first time, I really believed him.

CHAPTER 38
QUACK OFF, CHRIS

BECKETT

THE DUCKS WERE loud that morning, raising hell at the pond like they were in the middle of some board meeting. Normally, it was just background noise, something steady to keep my mind quiet. But not today.

Today, I couldn't shake the edge in my chest.

It had been three days since Margaret Bellamy walked into Frankie's bookstore and shattered the Bellamy-family-perfect-image glass house with one sentence, *"I'm filing for divorce"*. Three days since Frankie sat on my porch after her mother's visit, her hand in mine, eyes too guarded as she said she needed time to process.

I'd agreed to give her that time, as much as it killed me. Because if there's one thing I'd learned about Frankie Bellamy, it's that you can't push her. She'll dig her heels in just to spite you.

But patience had never been my strong suit, and the longer I waited, the more I wanted to take matters into my own hands and fix them, to protect her the only way I knew how.

The crunch of tires on gravel cut through my thoughts. I turned from the pond, narrowing my eyes as a familiar sleek black sedan rolled up near the fence line.

Chris Monroe.

Of course. He stepped out of the car like he was stepping onto a red carpet, and even from here I could see his smug grin firmly in place, his expensive suit too perfect for someone who was supposed to be licking his wounds after Maddox's public downfall. He started toward Frankie's house, as if he had a right to be there.

Heat crawled up my spine, and I quickly beelined toward him. "You've got five seconds to get back in that car before I make you regret stepping foot out of it."

Chris didn't flinch. He smirked, brushing a speck of lint from his jacket. "Now, now, let's not get violent. I just came to talk."

"She's not interested."

"Come on," Chris said, changing course and walking closer to me, completely ignoring my warning. "Let's be reasonable. You've got everything you wanted now. Your name's cleared, Maddox is finished. So why don't you let me and Frankie sort our personal business without you interfering?"

"She's not your business," I snapped. "That woman is more than you or I deserve, but I plan to show her what forever looks like with a real man."

Chris's grin sharpened. "Oh, she'll always be my business. She's still a Bellamy, Ford. You think she's going to stick around here forever? You're temporary. She'll get bored eventually. She always does. She got bored with me, didn't she?"

I clenched my fists, fighting the urge to knock that smug expression right off his face.

And then a voice cut through the tension, sharp as glass. "Funny you say that, Chris. Because I didn't get bored with you—I got disgusted."

Chris's head jerked around as Frankie strode toward us, her hair loose around her shoulders, her expression deadly calm. She looked furious, sure, but there was something else in her eyes too, strength.

Chris recovered quickly, pasting his charming smile back in place. "Frankie. There you are. I was just having a civil conversation with—"

"Save it," she snapped, stepping between us before I could say anything. "You don't get to waltz in here like you have a damn right to be on my property or his. What are you even doing here?"

Chris straightened his jacket, his voice softening like he thought he could smooth-talk his way out of this. "I wanted to talk to you. Privately."

"Not happening," Frankie said, folding her arms. "Say what you need to say, Chris. Everyone here knows what a piece of shit you are. They got to see that firsthand at your soirée." She rolled her eyes in derision. "So say what you came to say, then get the hell out."

Chris's fake charm cracked just a little. "You've changed."

"No, Chris," Frankie said, her tone razor sharp. "I finally woke up."

Chris's smile slipped further. "You think this little country fantasy is going to last? You think you're really happy here? This isn't you, Frankie. You belong in Atlanta. With people like us."

"People like us?" Frankie laughed, the sound sharp and humorless. "You mean with people who smile at you while they stick a knife in your back? With a family that only cares about me when I'm doing what they want? Or a father that likes younger—*too* young, women? No thanks. I'd rather spend my life with ducks that can't keep it in their pants than with you."

Bob, as if on cue, waddled up beside her, quacking loudly like he was agreeing with her assessment. Willow followed, tilting her head at Chris like she was deciding whether or not to bite him.

Chris looked down at the ducks, then back up at Frankie, his face twisting. "This is ridiculous."

"You're ridiculous," Frankie shot back. "Showing up here, trying to throw around the same old insults like they mean anything to me anymore. Newsflash, Chris, you don't have any power over me. Not now, not ever again."

"Frankie—"

"No," she interrupted, stepping closer, her chin lifting. "You listen to me. You lost me the second you treated me like I was something to control instead of someone to love. You lost me when you chose my father's approval over my happiness. You lost me when you thought I would be willing to be your punching bag at home while you were out doing god knows what with your tiny pecker. And you sure as hell lost me for good when you decided to try to ruin Beckett's life just to get to me."

Chris's jaw clenched, his smug façade gone. "You don't get to talk to me like that—"

"I'll talk to you however the hell I want," Frankie snapped, her voice rising. "Because you don't matter anymore. You're done,

Chris. You can run back to Harold and tell him *his* little game is over too. My mother already made sure of that."

Chris's eyes narrowed. "What does that mean?"

"It means if either of you so much as breathe in my direction again, those pictures she's got of Harold and you with underage girls are going to hit every news outlet in Georgia."

That landed like a punch. Chris's face went red, his mouth opening and closing like he couldn't decide what to say.

Frankie stepped even closer, her finger jabbing at his chest. "You leave me alone. You leave Beckett alone. You leave my life alone. Or I swear, Chris, I will make sure everyone sees exactly what kind of men you and Harold Bellamy really are."

The silence that followed would have been deafening except that Bob quacked, just once, almost approvingly.

Chris finally straightened his jacket, his face stony. "You think you've won, Frankie. But you'll regret this."

Frankie didn't flinch. "No, Chris. I regret ever giving you the time of day. Now fuck right off, before I let Bob bite you."

As if he understood, Bob waddled closer, snapping his beak. Chris muttered something under his breath, spun on his heel, and stalked back to his car. Gravel sprayed as he tore out of the driveway.

Frankie stood there, chest rising and falling fast, her hands balled into fists at her sides.

I stepped up behind her, sliding my arms around her waist, pulling her back against my chest. "You handled that better than I would've."

She let out a shaky breath, leaning back into me. "I meant every word."

"I know you did," I said softly, pressing a kiss to her temple.

She tilted her head, looking up at me, her eyes softening for the first time in days. "Forever, huh?"

"Yeah," I said, brushing my thumb along her jaw. "Forever."

And for the first time since I'd met Frankie Bellamy, she didn't argue.

CHAPTER 39
ALIEN PORN AND DUCKLINGS

FRANKIE

IF YOU HAD TOLD me six months ago that I'd be standing in my own bookstore, hosting a book signing for an author who writes alien porn, I would've laughed in your face. But here I was, standing behind a table covered in sparkly purple bookmarks that said *Take Me to Your Leader (and His... Tentacles)*, smiling as a line of giggling readers wrapped halfway around the store.

The place was packed with readers decked out in neon-green antenna headbands. One woman had actually brought a stuffed alien plushie to be signed, and someone else had painted little green glitter dots on their face like "alien freckles."

Tess, my best friend and co-chaos creator in human form, was behind the cash register, winking at customers every time someone bought the "Special Collector's Edition" with its glow-in-the-dark sprayed edges.

The author, a bubbly woman with blue streaks in her hair and a T-shirt that said *Tentacle Daddy Loves You,* was laughing with readers, happily posing for selfies and signing books with a flourish that screamed she was having the time of her life.

Hank and Nate were here too, although I was sure it was more to check out Tess and the other women than because they loved to read alien porn.

And then there was Beckett. My six-foot-four, broad-shouldered, broody man was standing near an alien romance display like a bodyguard at the gates of hell, arms crossed, looking about as comfortable as a grizzly bear in a tutu.

His blue eyes scanned the crowd like he was expecting an alien abduction to break out any second, but every time his gaze found mine, it softened, that stubborn loyalty written all over his face.

I slid from behind the signing table when there was a short break in the line and wove my way through the crowd until I was standing in front of him. Tilting my head, I said. "You look miserable."

"I'm fine." His voice was flat, expression unreadable, but his eyes stayed locked on mine, warm and steady.

"You're standing two feet from a cardboard cutout of a shirtless alien with six arms and a strategically placed blaster," I pointed out, suppressing a grin. "That's not *fine*, Beckett. That's torture for you."

"Maybe," he admitted, his lips twitching slightly like he didn't want to give me the satisfaction of seeing him smile. "But I'm not leaving."

"You could," I said, crossing my arms. "Nobody's going to think less of you for escaping this level of weird. You don't even read alien porn."

"Not leaving," he repeated, his tone final.

"Why?" I asked, half amused, half curious.

His eyes softened again, his voice dropping low so only I could hear. "Because you're my woman, and I'm not missing a damn thing you do. Not ever."

My chest squeezed, my smart-ass comeback dying on my tongue. "You're ridiculously sweet, you know that?"

"Sweet, huh?" His lips curved just a little, his expression shifting to something that made my pulse jump. "You think it's sweet when I say I'm going to marry you one day?"

I blinked, heat rushing to my cheeks. "Excuse me?"

"Not asking," he said simply, no hesitation, no teasing. "I'm telling you. One day, Frankie Bellamy, you're going to marry me. And we're going to have a lot of babies running around this place."

I opened my mouth, trying to form words, but a loud laugh cut through the store.

"Well, hate to break it to you, big bro," Nate said, strolling over with his usual cocky grin, "but you already have babies."

Beckett frowned. "What the hell are you talking about?"

"Look," Nate said, pointing toward the front door.

I turned, and my jaw dropped.

Bob and Willow waddled into the store like they owned the place, followed by four tiny, fuzzy ducklings trailing behind them in a perfectly chaotic line.

"Oh. My. God." I crouched instantly as they waddled toward me, my heart melting. "Are those… ducklings?"

"They're yours alright," Nate said, grinning like this was the best thing he'd ever witnessed. "Congratulations. You're officially parents."

The readers in line squealed, several pulling out their phones to record videos as Bob puffed up proudly and Willow nudged the smallest duckling forward like she was showing it off.

Beckett groaned under his breath. "They're ducks."

"Don't listen to Daddy," I whispered to the ducklings, scooping one into my hands. It squeaked, nuzzling into my palm, and my chest squeezed. "He's just shy about being a parent."

Tess leaned over the counter, laughing so hard she nearly knocked over her coffee. "Oh, this is priceless. Can we name them after the aliens in this author's books? Like, I call dibs on Tentacle Tony."

Beckett shot her a look that would've sent lesser mortals running for their lives, but Tess only grinned wider.

Hank, who had been leaning quietly near the register, finally spoke, his voice perfectly calm. "Guess all that wall-banging finally paid off."

My head snapped up, my face going crimson instantly. "HANK!"

The entire store went silent for a second—then burst into laughter.

Tess gasped for breath, nearly collapsing behind the counter. Nate slapped his knee, wheezing, "Oh, my God, Sheriff, that was savage. Ten out of ten." The alien porn author herself stopped mid-autograph to grin at me like she'd just gotten inspiration for her next book.

I covered my face with one hand, wishing for a meteor strike, but Beckett? Beckett didn't even flinch. He crouched beside me, his arm brushing mine as he looked down at me, his smirk softening into something that made my chest ache. "See?" he said, his voice low enough for only me. "Told you. We're already halfway to forever."

My heart thudded hard, and for a second time, I didn't argue.

The rest of the signing blurred into organized chaos. Readers gushed over alien princes—and ducklings, Tess pitched merch like she was born to hustle, and Nate took pictures of the ducklings like a proud uncle.

Beckett stayed the whole time, and I even caught him pretending that he wasn't actually reading the back of one of the more graphic books, his ears pink. Every time our eyes met, he'd give me that small, steady smile, the one that still made my stomach flip.

Hours later, when the store had emptied and Tess was counting cash at the register, Beckett was still there, leaning against the wall talking to Nate. Hank had left hours ago because he had to be at work early in the morning.

I dumped glittery stickers out of a basket next to the register and carried it over to the ducklings' little makeshift corner. I crouched and began trying to catch the surprisingly fast little fluffballs to move them back to Beckett's pond. Well, our pond. I'd moved in with him a few weeks ago, leaving Tess to *woman* the house alone.

"You're staring," I said without looking up.

"I like watching you," Beckett replied simply, his voice soft but sure.

I glanced up, meeting his gaze. "You mean you enjoy watching me wrangle ducklings after hosting alien porn hour?"

"That too," he said, pushing off the wall to come closer. "But mostly I like watching you happy."

I smiled despite myself, and as he crouched beside me, his hand brushed mine as I passed him the basket.

"Beckett," I said after a moment, biting my lip, my voice softer than I had meant it to be. "Were you serious? About what you said earlier?"

His eyes met mine instantly, unwavering, like the answer had already been carved into stone. "About marrying you? About forever? Frankie, I've never been more serious about anything in my life."

My throat tightened, my heart doing that squeeze it always did with him, and I looked down at the duckling in my hand, trying to hide the stupid smile tugging at my mouth.

Beckett leaned in closer, his lips brushing my ear, his voice low and certain. "Get used to the idea, Frankie. One day soon, you're going to be Mrs. Ford. And if I have it my way, we're going to have a house full of kids and, apparently, more ducks than I ever signed up for."

I laughed softly, shaking my head as I glanced at him. "You're insane," I told him as I gently set the last duckling in the basket.

"Probably," he said, kissing me right there among the ducklings, soft but sure, sealing the promise he'd just made.

And damn it, I loved him.

"Alright, you two lovebirds," Nate's voice broke the moment, and I looked up to see him strolling over with his trademark grin. "I'm out. I've got a shift tomorrow."

He tugged me up and into a hug before I could stop him, which earned him a low growl from Beckett. "Calm down, big brother," Nate teased, pulling back just enough to smirk at Beckett. "I can hug my future sister-in-law."

"Get off her," Beckett said, tugging me right back against his chest with one strong arm. The ducklings seemed to echo his demand as they gave tiny quacks from the basket in his other hand. "Get your own woman."

"Fine, fine." Nate held his hands up in mock surrender, still grinning. "Call me later. And take care of my nieces and nephews." He nodded toward the ducklings, his smirk only growing when Beckett scowled. "They're adorable. Don't screw it up, Duck Daddy."

"Out," Beckett barked, but Nate just laughed, scooting out the door before Beckett could grab him.

I rolled my eyes, trying not to laugh. "Let's get these babies and their parents back to the pond. I'm beat."

Beckett leaned in, his breath brushing my ear. "I hope you're not too beat." His hand slid down to give my backside a firm smack, making me gasp and shoot him a look.

"Behave," I warned, my cheeks heating.

"Not a chance," he murmured with a grin as we headed toward the door.

"Later, Tess," Beckett called over his shoulder as we stepped outside.

"Later!" Tess yelled from behind the counter, her laugh following us out. "And don't do anything I wouldn't do!"

"She's a menace," Beckett muttered, shaking his head as we

stepped into the evening air, the ducklings chirping softly from the basket.

"I pity the man who falls for her," I said, leaning into his side as we walked toward the pond.

"Me too," Beckett said, his arm tightening around my waist.

A grin curved across my lips as I looked up at him. "But when she falls for him in return, it's gonna be fun watching her be brought to her knees."

Beckett chuckled, leaning down to press a kiss to the side of my head. "Yeah, but let's be honest—she's probably going to drag the poor bastard straight to hell first."

I laughed, the sound carrying out into the quiet evening, and for the first time in a long time, the future didn't feel scary or uncertain. It felt like exactly where I was meant to be, right here, with him.

Forever didn't sound so impossible anymore.

BOOK TWO

NUTTIN' BUT TROUBLE

NATE

I'D NEVER BEEN a fan of libraries or bookstores. Too quiet, too full of paper cuts waiting to happen. But Frankie's bookstore? *Shelf Love* had grown on me—because it sure wasn't like any other bookstore I'd ever been in. Yeah, it was still full of potential paper cuts, but it wasn't quiet.

And I liked it there for other reasons, too. The smell of coffee. Those damn ducks that had claimed it as a second home. The books that made my eyes pop—I'm no prude, but I was never going to get those alien porn book covers out of my head.

The main reason, though, was because Shelf Love was where my brother's new forever thing—Frankie, was most days, and family sticks together. Even when that family includes a giant, broody billionaire who falls for a bookstore-owning smartass.

Plus it did my protective firefighter's heart good to see Beckett finally stop scowling twenty-four seven. To see him settled in the way only Beckett Ford could manage. Hell, he even smiled now without looking like it physically hurt.

And as much as I teased him, I wanted that.

Maybe not the bookstore. Definitely not the alien porn.

But… the real thing. For the first time in a long time, I wondered what it would feel like to have someone look at me the way Frankie looked at Beckett.

That thought stayed with me after I'd left the bookstore, buzzing through my head as I drove down the two-lane highway toward home. It was early evening, and the sun was beginning to throw gold streaks through the trees. I had just started to tell myself I was being ridiculous for the level of envy I was feeling, when something up ahead caught my eye.

A car sat pulled off to the side of the road, hazard lights blinking.

And standing beside its open hood was a woman.

Not just any woman.

Piper Jameson.

I hit the brakes before my brain caught up, my truck rolling to a stop behind her car. She straightened, her eyes locking on mine through my windshield, widening in instant recognition as I threw the door open and stepped out.

"Nate—um hi," she said as I slammed the door to my truck, her voice carrying just enough disbelief to sting and soothe all at once.

"Piper," I managed. "Long time."

She crossed her arms, her expression somewhere between wary and annoyed, though the corner of her mouth twitched like she was fighting a smile. Her fiery red hair was exactly how I remembered it— the curls were wild just like they had been years ago. "Five years."

Five years.

Five damn years since she'd left this town—and me—without so much as a goodbye. And still, she had the power to knock the wind out of me just by standing there. Before I could think of something halfway charming to say, a muffled noise came from under her car's hood—something frantic and alive.

Piper spun toward it, muttering under her breath, "Oh, for the love of—stay put!"

I raised an eyebrow. "You talking to me or…?"

"Not you," she said, blowing a strand of hair out of her face, crouching slightly to peer under the hood again.

"Well, that's comforting," I said, walking closer. "Looks like you need a professional."

She gave me a look over her shoulder. "You're a firefighter, not a mechanic."

"Yeah, but I'm good at rescuing things," I said, grinning despite myself. "Cars, cats… whatever you've got going on under there."

Her brows shot up. "Cocky as ever."

"Confident," I corrected. "And you don't look like you're in a position to argue."

Standing on the side of the road, the setting sun catching in her hair, Piper Jameson had me all over again. Five years gone, and she still had the power to knock me on my ass without even trying.

"Alright," I said, stepping closer, "let's see what the hell kind of trouble you've gotten yourself into."

Her lips parted like she wanted to argue, but she stepped back as I reached the car.

The second I leaned in, something shifted inside—fast. A rustle, a frantic scrabble of claws against metal.

I froze. "What the—"

Piper winced, blowing a strand of hair out of her face. "Okay, so… I *might* have hit something."

My head snapped toward her. "*Might?*"

She gave me a guilty smile, her cheeks flushing. "And then… well…" She waved a hand helplessly toward the engine. "It's complicated."

"Complicated," I repeated, raising a brow as the noise under the hood got louder. "Jameson, if this thing bites me, you're paying for my rabies shots."

Her mouth twitched, like she was fighting a laugh. "You're not going to get rabies."

"Not reassuring," I muttered, leaning closer as the rustling grew louder.

She crossed her arms, watching me with the stubborn tilt to her chin that I remembered all too well. "You're a firefighter, right? Big hero guy? This should be easy for you."

I shot her a look. "You know, most women just ask for a tow, not a wildlife rescue."

Piper smiled—soft, amused, and infuriatingly familiar.

And just like that, I knew two things for certain.

One—Piper Jameson was still trouble.

And two—whatever was under that hood? Yeah… unlike her, I wasn't walking away.

357

ACKNOWLEDGMENTS

To my husband—thanks for not asking too many questions when I typed "creative ways to pin someone against a wall" into Google at 2 a.m. You married this madness, and now you're stuck with it.

To LeeAnn—your chaos energy is unmatched, and somehow, it made me believe I could wrangle my own. Your friendship is more than that… it's a sisterhood. Also, thanks for reminding me that caffeine counts as self-care.

To Jess—thanks for talking me off the ledge every other Tuesday (and sometimes Thursdays). You're the reason I didn't throw my laptop into traffic. Plus, you do more than you should without expecting anything in return but friendship.

To Gabbie—the ducks are your fault.

Speaking of ducks… you're welcome, Mr. Owens.

And to Diana—aka Momma D—TikTok queen, hype woman, and absolute force of nature. You've been instrumental in every bit of success I've had as an indie and as a bookstore owner. Thank you for shouting louder than I ever could and making sure people listened.

And to Giulia—your books ruined me (in the best way), your friendship was a happy fangirl moment turned into more. Not to mention your "you can do this" pep talk made me believe I could not only *do this*, but do it *good*.

And to Becky—finding you was like finding a diamond in the rough. Only shinier. And way better at commas.

Basically, if this book makes you laugh, swoon, or need to fan yourself—it's their fault.

ABOUT LC

"Tattoos, whiskey, and bullets—where passion meets protection."

An International and USA Today Bestselling author, LC's an unapologetic down-home southern gal—with a bit of a dirty mouth who bleeds red, white, and blue. LC's never met a brooding hero she didn't love. She writes her men cut, tattooed, and tender for their down but not out ladies who need a little love from the right man. Her alpha heroes are less shades of gray and more shades of blue.

When she's not writing her hunky heroes, creating swoon-worthy love connections—you'll find LC curled up on the couch with a glass of peach crown and her very own sexy tattooed cop watching true crime on the television.

www.AuthorLCTaylor.com

www.ShelfLoveAtlanta.com

www.ingramcontent.com/pod-product-compliance
Lightning Source LLC
Chambersburg PA
CBHW070656010826
48975CB00014B/1676